A MOONLIT WALTZ

The devil within Duncan drove him. "Do you take dresses as well as jewelry?" he demanded.

Willie looked at him apprehensively. "I swear, Lady Katherine gave me this dress. 'Twas too short for her. I wanted to hear the music better, and I . . . I was pretending to dance. I saw no harm in it."

"Hah, I saw you with Teagardner. You had no business leading him on—"

"Mr. Teagardner said he didn't know how to dance and I offered to teach him a step or two. Is that a crime?"

Lord, he wanted to believe her. She sounded so convincing that once more guilt threaded through him. He smiled ruefully. "No crime, Willie, but I fear I owe you an apology."

"Why, whatever do you mean, my lord?"

"I caused Mr. Teagardner to run off, and now you have no partner," he explained. "Will you allow me the pleasure of this dance?" Not waiting for an answer, Duncan placed his hand lightly upon Willie's waist and with the other took her hand. He felt her body quiver when they touched. Although he feigned indifference, he was keenly aware of her responses.

It was not difficult to tell that this was the first time she'd danced intimately with a man.

ZEBRA REGENCIES
ARE
THE TALK OF THE TON!

A REFORMED RAKE   (4499, $3.99)
by Jeanne Savery

After governess Harriet Cole helped her young charge flee to France—and the designs of a despicable suitor, more trouble soon arrived in the person of a London rake. Sir Frederick Carrington insisted on providing safe escort back to England. Harriet deemed Carrington more dangerous than any band of brigands, but secretly relished matching wits with him. But after being taken in his arms for a tender kiss, she found herself wondering—*could* a lady find love with an irresistible rogue?

A SCANDALOUS PROPOSAL   (4504, $4.99)
by Teresa DesJardien

After only two weeks into the London season, Lady Pamela Premington has already received her first offer of marriage. If only it hadn't come from the *ton's* most notorious rake, Lord Marchmont. Pamela had already set her sights on the distinguished Lieutenant Penford, who had the heroism and honor that made him the ideal match. Now she had to keep from falling under the spell of the seductive Lord so she could pursue the man more worthy of her love. Or was he?

A LADY'S CHAMPION   (4535, $3.99)
by Janice Bennett

Miss Daphne, art mistress of the Selwood Academy for Young Ladies, greeted the notion of ghosts haunting the academy with skepticism. However, to avoid rumors frightening off students, she found herself turning to Mr. Adrian Carstairs, sent by her uncle to be her "protector" against the "ghosts." Although, Daphne would accept no interference in her life, she *would* accept aid in exposing any spectral spirits. What she never expected was for Adrian to expose the secret wishes of her hidden heart . . .

CHARITY'S GAMBIT   (4537, $3.99)
by Marcy Stewart

Charity Abercrombie reluctantly embarks on a London season in hopes of making a suitable match. However she cannot forget the mysterious Dominic Castille—and the kiss they shared—when he fell from a tree as she strolled through the woods. Charity does not know that the dark and dashing captain harbors a dangerous secret that will ensnare them both in its web—leaving Charity to risk certain ruin and losing the man she so passionately loves . . .

Available wherever paperbacks are sold, or order direct from the Publisher. Send cover price plus 50¢ per copy for mailing and handling to Penguin USA, P.O. Box 999, c/o Dept. 17109, Bergenfield, NJ 07621. Residents of New York and Tennessee must include sales tax. DO NOT SEND CASH.

Lord Wakeford's Gold Watch
Paula Tanner Girard

ZEBRA BOOKS
KENSINGTON PUBLISHING CORP.

ZEBRA BOOKS are published by

Kensington Publishing Corp.
850 Third Avenue
New York, NY 10022

First Printing: June, 1995

Printed in the United States of America

Chapter One

Three women, one a tall, willowy blonde, one an older but robust lady, and the last, a tiny, dark-haired nymph, passed through the portals of the ancient Scottish fortress and descended the broad stone steps.

Beneath a cap of black hair, the older girl's violet eyes widened as she beheld the elegant carriage awaiting them. Willie, as she was affectionately called, could still not believe that after fourteen years of preparing for this event, they were finally embarking on the journey to England. In just a few more days, Lady Katherine, Baroness of Gilfallen, would make her bow to London society. She did so at the behest of her English father, the Duke of Hammerfield.

"Watch yir step ye don't tumble noo," Broonie clucked. The old family nurse shooed the girls toward an attendant, clad in the duke's distinctive blue and gold livery, who waited to assist them into the carriage.

Willie, as if she were inhaling the rarest of perfumes, took a deep breath of the crisp spring air. The highlands were at their most magnificent. Nature had painted the hills purple with heather and the massive stone walls of the medieval fortress overlooking Loch

Tay created a dark contrast to the intense silver-gray backdrop of the sky.

Feeling delighted with the world, Willie ran her hands over her new black cape, confident that her appearance was quite unexceptionable. And Katy, in her elegant carriage dress, was the picture of a proper young noblewoman, and lovely enough to bring tears to one's eyes.

Willie studied her friend's perfect features and thick, flaxen hair that shimmered when the sun peeked through the clouds. For a second she envied the baroness' tall figure, but the feeling quickly passed. She thanked the good Lord every day for the home she'd been given. Katy had her own problems to solve and would need all the help Willie and Broonie could offer.

She watched her beloved Katy proceed across the rough-hewn flagstone with a skip instead of a graceful glide. Willie knew it was the excitement of the adventure ahead, not any lack of training, which caused the young baroness' lapse in deportment.

With the Dalison family coat of arms emblazoned on its door, the duke's coach stood in the driveway, ready to whisk them to England.

"Will ye look at that," Broonie's voice boomed. "Hain't it a grand one. Fit fir a princess."

A marvel it was to Willie's eyes, too, with its six prancing black horses, impressive coachman, a uniformed groom and two out-riders.

"Oh, Broonie," Willie whispered, just before they entered. "I do pray we shall be able to find Katy a suitable husband, before she steals the crown jewels."

With her folded umbrella, the formidable Scotswoman swatted away the hand of the young man trying to hand her up. Turning to Willie, she said, "Don't ye be worryin yirself about our darlin'. One look at that angel's face and every lad in England will be on his knees a'beggin' her to marry him."

Willie climbed up and settled herself against the comfortable squabs. She hoped the dear old soul was right. Katy, for all her sweet ways, did have one flaw. Generous to a fault, she thought nothing of removing her fine woolen shawl to wrap around the shoulders of a freezing child. But she also thought nothing of taking things which did not belong to her.

The village folk of Killin had grown to accept it as just one of their beloved mistress' eccentric ways. When the baroness brought back some article to the castle, a pair of shears or a too large sweater, the cottager's wife or the shepherd missing his belongings appeared the next day and the item was returned with a penny recompense for the inconvenience. Willie was not so certain the British had as charitable dispositions as did the Scots, and she and Broonie had exacted a promise from Katy to behave herself while in London. But Katy, alas, had promised before to no avail. Sometimes temptation was just too strong for her to resist.

After Katy and Willy waved farewell to the servants lining the parapets of the old fortress, the coachman lost no time in springing the team. Off they went, the younger girls laughing and bouncing, bouncing and laughing.

"Oh Willie," Katy cried. "Look! There is our herd of deer upon the hill. They have come to say good-bye, too. How can anyone harm such gentle creatures?" She turned her large, soulful eyes to her companion. "Do you think a shooting party will come while we are gone?"

Willie disliked it as much as Katy when the hunters trespassed into their hills. "Don't you fret," Willie said. "Filbert will chase anyone off."

She glanced out the window, but her attention and affection were focused upon her mistress, sweet, gentle Katy . . . Lady Katherine, she amended silently. Although they had grown to be more like sisters instead of mistress and servant, she must remember to call her friend by her proper title from now on.

Willie didn't know for certain when she herself was born. Broonie said she couldn't have been more than a year older than the baroness, brought as she was from a foundling home to Gilfallen Castle by the Duke of Hammerfield to serve his motherless three-year-old daughter. Until then, Katy had never had another child to play with.

Broonie liked to tell Willie the story about how she got her name. Soon after she arrived, the little baroness began to learn her nursery rhymes. "My Katy were so taken at seeing yirsel, such a darkhaired, cheery, little wain, runnin' up and doon the stairs, she called yir Wee Willie Winkie." And the name had stuck like sticky candy to a child's fingers.

The little girls never saw the Duke of Hammerfield after that day. So when the elderly nurse explained, "The duke has many hooses to be runnin' noo, an' dun't ye be fergettin it," the two little girls did not think it out of the ordinary to have no parents about because they knew of no other family who lived in a castle with whom to compare themselves.

They went about their days running free in the huge fortress, thriving under the unbroken attention of a large devoted staff and the acceptance of the peaceable folk in the tiny village of Killin.

"Me wee whippets," Broonie called them. "One with the sunshine oon her head, an t'other darkhaired as a storm in spring."

They ran with the red deer through the primeval Caledonian pine forests which covered the Highlands, fished in the River Lochay, splashed in the falls of Dochart, and gathered wild flowers. It did not weigh heavily upon Willie's mind that in all those years neither of them had ventured farther than ten miles from Gilfallen Castle.

But their lives were not all idleness. Soon after the duke departed Scotland, a steady stream of strangers from the Lowlands appeared. Stern governesses, tutors, dance instructors, musicians and seamstresses, even an elocutionist who had been hired to make certain the baroness showed no trace of country dialect.

A taciturn, straight-nosed Frenchwoman came to teach Lady Katherine French and Latin. She was instructed in watercolor, the pianoforte, and voice lessons, though the last was the only subject in which she took any interest. It was not that the baroness was a slow-wit, for she knew the names and habits of every animal of the forest and every plant in its season. But she paid little attention to geography or mathematics, and if not for Willie's persistent drilling, Lady Katherine would not have been able to add up the simplest of sums. Willie feared she was learning far more than Katy.

It was from one of these fairy tales that Katy conceived the idea of adopting Willie, and nothing would persuade her to set aside her notion.

"I don't think you can do that," Willie said.

"Why not?" Katy asked stubbornly. "I am not a queen, but I am a baroness and I can have anything I want."

"But in the story the queen has a husband," reasoned Willie.

"Then as soon as I marry, I will adopt you," she had declared.

As they grew older, the girls spent hours in the cool shade of the trees beside a stream reading poetry to each other, and the romantics from Katy's late mother's innumerable collection of novels. The latter the girls found most fascinating as they grew older, for their acquaintance with the opposite sex evolved around elderly servants, staid tutors, and the simple fustians of Killin.

They began to despair that the only men of substance and beauty were in the imagination of the authors of the novels they read.

"Do you believe there are such men, Willie?" Katy asked one afternoon when they'd finished one of Mrs. Radcliffe's exciting gothics.

"The books say there are."

"Then they must be hiding, for I have never seen such as those in the stories hereabouts in Scotland."

"I am certain your father is collecting them in London, waiting for you to grow up. The women of England must be very educated, so you shall have to work hard to outshine them. That is surely why he is having you tutored. Now concentrate on your lessons to please him."

When she spoke of the duke, Willie's childhood memory filled with the image of the handsome, fair-haired young man who had appeared at the orphanage many years ago to rescue her from who-knows-what kind of life of drudgery.

Willie could not recall how she had come to be in that big damp house with all those other children, but she remembered well the magical night her prince came. She, the shortest, had been lined up with four other girls.

The platter-faced matron had called him "Your Grace" and Willie thought that was his name. The stern set of his jaw and the lordliness of his voice made her quickly look down at her rag-swatched feet. He was the most awesome personage she had ever encountered and surely the most beautiful man in the world.

Why he chose her, Willie did not know, but it was probably because she was about the same age as his daughter. The next morning she set out with him on a long journey which brought her to Gilfallen Castle.

Pleasing her benefactor became the most important thing in Willie's mind, and she decided she must be very stern with Katy about learning her lessons. "You are the Duke of Hammerfield's beloved daughter, and whatever his lordship wants is surely in your best interest."

Broonie, not to be left out of the instruction of her darling, was strict also. "I brought yir mither up from the time she was a wee mite, and I'll not be having ye bring shame upon the name of MacNab." So they acted out every imaginable situation they felt Lady Katherine would encounter in society. On and on each day, they drilled their precious Katy to be the most gracious lady in the land.

After the dancing and tea serving lessons were over, Katy would sit back, fold her hands in her lap, and listen dutifully as Willie went over her sums.

As Willie grew older, she found her own relaxation in far different diversions. She discovered that the vast library at the castle was filled with more fascinating volumes than Katy's romantic books. She read about people and lands she could barely imagine. India, Africa and beautiful islands where it never got cold. Were there really such places? She absorbed books about mythology, law, animal husbandry, and even the stars with a hunger that was never satisfied.

Now, after all the years of educating Katy, they were setting out on an unbelievable four-hundred-mile journey south to the big city of London. She would actually be able to see some of the places she'd read of

and the notion filled her with unbearable excitement.
They were to stay at Katy's Aunt Jacomena Dalison's
townhouse.

"I did not know I had an aunt," Katy exclaimed,
when a letter came from her father telling her that his
sister had agreed to sponsor her for the Season. Her
curiosity did not go farther, and it was Willie, who
having no family of her own, wondered if there were
more Dalison connections of which they were not
aware.

They traveled through Killin, situated at the eastern
end of the mountain-encircled Glen Lochay. From
there, they headed east to catch the post road at Edin-
burgh. The grand old mountain, Ben Lawers, loomed
off in the distance, the highest for many miles around.
A small island near Dochart Bridge, adjacent to the
falls, was the traditional burial grounds of the Clan
MacNab. "There," Katy told her, "my mother and
little brother, Adrian, lie sleeping."

Excitement and wonder filled their first two days.
From the coach, Willie watched the panorama sweep
by like pictures in a storybook. They shared the country lanes with cherry-cheeked maidens, drovers herd-
ing their flocks, and overloaded wagons drawn by
hairy-heeled horses.

The slow pace pleased her. It gave her time to reflect
on their goal to find a husband for their lovely Katy.
She knew that from his years of careful planning, the
duke had to be a father *nonpareil*. Anticipation sent
shivers down Willie's spine. She would soon meet the
man whose image remained imprinted on her mind as
the ideal being.

For herself, Willie had little hope she could attract
a worthy husband as the pretty Cinderella did in the
tale which the French tutor had related to them. No,
she must stick to their plan to help her beloved Katy

find her prince. Then, Willie was sure, they would all live happily ever after.

When they reached the high road going south, the rough vehicles were joined by brightly uniformed, mounted soldiers, gentry in their splendid carriages, and mail coaches. At the end of each day, the coachman stopped at little wayside inns for meals and to rest the horses overnight. The duke had made arrangements for a change of cattle to be awaiting them at the posting house in York and an inn in Huntingdon.

On the third day of their trip, they made an unexpected stop at a small market town. While their driver tended to one of the horses which had lost a shoe, the women enjoyed a walk through the labyrinth of colorful stalls filled with farmers hawking their fruits and vegetables, crofter's wives exhibiting their stitchery, a tinker repairing kitchenware, and most entertaining, an actor with a puppet show.

It wasn't until they were once again rolling along the highway that an apple fell out of Katy's pocket. She looked up apprehensively as the golden fruit plopped onto the floor of the carriage.

Two accusing pairs of eyes turned to Katy.

"If ye wanted the apple, we would've bought it," Broonie scolded. "We're not at Gilfallen. We canna go back and pay the vendor."

"Katy, you promised," Willie added with a mournful sigh.

"Oh," Katy said, looking at the telltale evidence of her guilt, then back up at her companions. "I'm sorry." Tears filled her eyes. "I did not think."

"I know, dear," Willie said, placing her hand over Katy's trembling one. "But from now on, you must think."

Her lips drawn in a straight line, Broonie nodded her agreement.

"I will," Katy said, looking from one to the other. "I promise."

The next day passed without mishap, and Willie began to feel that Katy had in fact learned her lesson. Toward evening, the weather turned cold, wet and windy. Willie was relieved when they pulled into the spacious courtyard of the Landed Gull Inn outside Huntingdon. Several other travelers had arrived ahead of them, all trying to get out of the rain, and some time passed before the Dalison groom could clear a path for them to the door.

That same rainy afternoon, Duncan Fairchild, the Earl of Wakeford, was one of the first wave of travelers to enter the Landed Gull. There he was immediately accosted—there was no better word for it—by Lady Thurston, the wife of a friend of his late father. The corpulent matron, dressed in every conceivable shade of blue, topped her finery with a sweeping cape secured with several gittering pins, and an awe-inspiring hat of feathers dyed a deep indigo.

The earl was tired, soaked to the skin from the downpour, and out of humor. The mingled odour of damp clothing, smoldering hearth fires and kitchen aromas caused a dizzying effect. Consequently, he was not the least interested in hearing the latest gossip. Knowing better than to ask how she fared, he bowed over the lady's hand and said, "How well you are looking, Lady Thurston." Before she could refute it, he added, "It must be your good health that puts the glow in your face."

His ploy did not work. Lady Thurston chattered, complaining of the ills she'd suffered on her journey. The earl listened with one ear, thankful that he'd sent his valet ahead to Wakeford. Charles, though polite and loyal, hated chattering females even more than the earl did. He also hated to get wet, and the present downpour would have set him scolding.

Between his valet and his mother, who would certainly add her lectures about over-working, Duncan was almost glad he'd been delayed by the weather. After his hectic schedule in London, he needed a few quiet hours before he was confronted with his mother's helter-skelter system of allowing life to make its own schedule. A peaceful night at the inn would give him the opportunity to work on his arguments for reform of the criminal law system. Or it would if he could rid himself of Lady Thurston.

She was still chattering on, her voice grating on his ears. Duncan cast about for a tactful way to excuse himself, but Lady Thurston suddenly focused her attention elsewhere. Thankful for whatever had caught the woman's attention, he pulled out his gold watch. It was a splendid piece, the one thing he most admired and doubly cherished because it had been his father's. He depended heavily upon it at Wakeford to keep him on schedule. Punctuality ruled his life—a trait not shared by his mother. Indeed, no two clocks in her house struck the hour at precisely the same moment. How the staff got anything accomplished was beyond his imagination.

Silence overtook the room. Duncan looked up and let his gaze follow the crowd's. In his tired state, he ordinarily would not have taken note of the three women entering the inn, but the blonde goddess in their midst was of such exceptional beauty she overshadowed every person in the room.

An elderly, heavyset woman preceded the beauty, hacking her way through the throng with a large umbrella. He watched, entranced, and it was several moments before he noticed the third member of the trio.

She led the way but was so tiny she was barely visible through the crowd. Then he heard her clear, strong voice.

"Are you the proprietor, sir?"

"Aye! Pennywhistle's the name."

"Lady Katherine requires accommodations with a nice view."

She appeared to Duncan a spirited little blackbird, her nose no higher than the innkeeper's chest.

Mr. Pennywhistle, whose bushy head and large frame towered over the others, stared downward at the impertinent sprite before him. The huge man's glowering look soon cleared a wide path around them.

Duncan nearly choked with laughter at the bold audacity of the tiny minion. At least the chit afforded some amusement on so miserable a day. A room with a view? Surely, she was jesting. As crowded as it was tonight, he knew there would be many a disgruntled traveler sleeping on the floor of the common room. The women would fare well to have a room.

The bewhiskered Pennywhistle, thick as an old Spanish galleon, ran a tight ship. Few men had the courage to challenge the former seaman's authority over his establishment. His wife's good food and clean accommodations were always in demand. Duncan stayed there often on his way to Wakeford when he did not want to push on the last few miles to his family seat. Now he waited to see what the elfin creature would do next.

Meanwhile, across the room, Willie continued to stare at Mr. Pennywhistle, hoping she appeared more knowledgable than she felt. With only the three former nights to gain experience, she wasn't quite certain what to expect at inns, but she was not going to let on to that deficiency. Katy and Broonie depended upon her.

The other hostelries had been able to fill her requests, so it did not seem unreasonable to her to expect the same from this much larger establishment. Their needs were simple. After the cavernous rooms in the castle, she and Katy felt confined in small spaces. Also, Broonie snored, so they required separate rooms, side by side, as they had the first three nights.

As was her habit, Willie stood on her toes to appear taller, and faced the large man in front of her. His long sideburns bristled and his cheeks puffed out in his florid face until she thought he looked like a fish gasping for air. He appeared a frightening apparition, but she refused to allow him to intimidate her. She had noticed during the last few days that any mention of Katy's rank seemed to have a salutary effect. Stretching as tall as possible, she said, "The Baroness of Gilfallen will, as I said, require two rooms."

The hefty man's gaze darted quickly to the wide-eyed beauty standing with the old broody hen behind her, and immediately became most solicitous.

Willie decided if that were the way things blew down here in England, adding a little more wind to his sails would not hurt. "I am certain," she added, with a little sniff and a tilt of her nose, "that the Duke of Hammerfield will be most appreciative of anyone showing his daughter the proper hospitality."

Well, that really got results, Willie was glad to see. Deflating like a hot air balloon landing in a briarpatch, Mr. Pennywhistle exploded a blast of wine-soaked breath that nearly knocked her over. But Willie held onto her cap and withstood the gale.

"The duke of Hammerfield, you say?"

"Yes, indeed, and as soon as we are settled please have a light repast sent up. Nothing too heavy. We ate quite heartily this afternoon."

Across the room, Duncan watched the drama unfold with fascination. The little maid gave her orders as though she were royalty, and everybody jumped.

Mr. Pennywhistle turned into a whirling dervish. He ordered a servant to fetch the baroness' baggage.

"Where is the missus?" he bellowed. "Missus Pennywhistle!" A singularly rotund figure, as big around as her husband was tall, came waddling in, wiping her hands on her apron. She received some urgent message from her husband which sent her scurrying back to the kitchen.

Bemused, Duncan watched the by-play. He'd never seen Pennywhistle so obsequious. He was unacquainted with the duke of Hammerfield, but the name sounded familiar. He recalled the tale of a recluse who hadn't been seen for years. He glanced at the tall noblewoman. Was it possible that this young beauty's father could be one and the same? The elf referred to her as baroness, but he knew that did not necessarily mean she was already married. A Scottish woman could inherit her title from the female side of the family. The beauty might still be single and a newcomer to the marriage mart, which would prove most interesting.

Although he had not yet met all of this season's young debutantes, the earl was familiar with all those presented during the last few years, thanks to his mother's constant reports. He wondered if she knew the baroness of Gilfallen. Since his father's death, Lady Wakeford seldom ventured into Town, and it amazed Duncan how she obtained so much information isolated on their country place outside St. Ives. Could it be he was to get the march on his mother about one of this year's contenders? That would be a first for him and the thought brought him a satisfying feeling of triumph.

As the older woman helped her mistress remove her

damp outer garments, the young lady seemed sub-limely unaware of the sensation she caused. She was taller than most females he knew. Fashionably so, and impeccably dressed in the latest of styles. If the gown Lady Katherine wore was an example, her wardrobe must have cost a king's ransom. Yet as sophisticated as she appeared, Duncan noticed that her curious gaze skipped about the room like that of a young child. Here, he thought, was innocence personified.

His gaze shifted to the sprite in servant's attire, tiny in stature, mighty in her demands. Her mob cap, wet from the rain, clung precariously to one side of her dark curls. As she continued to list the foods her mistress liked, strong emotions animated the little heart-shaped face. Definitely no innocence there, he determined.

But, Willie, had he known it, was confused, and was finding herself quite at odds as to how she should behave. She pondered her predicament. Why hadn't the duke had the insight to send someone to teach her how to be a proper lady's maid? He'd sent dozens of tutors to instruct Katy on how to be a lady. It was an oversight, Willie decided, which she would have to overcome with her own imagination. Now was not the time to be faint of heart.

It wasn't until she turned around that Willie realized a great many eyes were watching her. Curiosity or disapproval? She could not tell, but indeed, if she were doing something wrong, at least she was getting re-sults. How strange these British were. It appeared they could not do anything unless told.

Boldly she took a look about the room, until her gaze came to an abrupt halt upon a most unusual-looking gentleman consulting his watch. It was not that he stood out in the crowd because of the tall beaver hat sitting upon his head, for others were similarly attired. But his dark brown hair and strong, square face set off inquisitive ebony eyes which swept over the crowd as sharply as a hawk assessing a field. Her mouth agape, she acknowledged that her past experience with the male sex had been sorely limited, but he was quite possibly the most handsome male she had ever seen, except, of course, for her memory of the Duke of Hammerfield.

Willie was abruptly recalled to her sense of duty as she noticed a huge cloud of blue descend upon Katy . . . Lady Katherine, she reminded herself.

"Baroness Gilfallen!" The woman's head bobbed down and up again like a plumed ostrich. "Forgive me for being so bold, my dear, but I am Lady Thurston, and I knew your mother and father many years ago."

Katy's questioning gaze darted to Willie, who moved quickly to her side. Giving her mistress a reassuring shove forward until she nearly touched the plumed bluebird, Willie prayed Katy would remember her training.

The baroness smiled bravely. "How nice to meet you, Lady Thurston."

At the sound of Lady Katherine's melodious voice, Duncan heard a collective sigh from every male in the room. He, too, found the young noblewoman a pleasurable sight, but had he observed correctly? Had he actually seen the diminutive abigail push her mistress?

The maid glanced his way, and he forgot all else. Their eyes met and his heart turned in him. Violets! Like the millions of blossoms which covered the forest floor in the springtime, her eyes sparkled from beneath thick dark lashes. Then, just as quickly, she looked away.

Duncan shook his head and pocketed his watch. He must be more weary than he thought to have his head turned by the sight of a common servant. Surely he could excuse such thoughts with the reasoning that he had not permitted himself to engage in any frivolous pursuits these last few months.

As healthy as any other young blade, Duncan had had his share of the muslin crowd and had kept a mistress or two. But he held exceptionally high standards. The women who now captured his attention possessed more than beauty and were intelligent enough to converse on a number of topics. The current bag of Cyprians in London held little appeal for him.

Perhaps his mother was right and it was time he wed. But what exactly were the qualities he most desired in a wife? He would have to give it serious thought. Unfortunately, he'd yet to meet the lady who would not bore him to tears within a few months.

Chapter Two

"How did I do?" Katy asked, as soon as they were alone in their room.

"Just fine, dear," Willie replied.

"There weren't a mon's hart in the inn that didn't go flippity-flop for ye," Broonie assured. "Every lad in London will wont tae be yer husband."

"Oh, we are going to have so much fun! I just know we are." Katy grabbed Willie and swung her around the room. As she wheeled, a glittering pin slipped from her grasp and clattered on the floor.

They each stared down at a lovely, jeweled brooch, its blue stones twinkling up at them.

"Katy!" Willie and Broonie cried in unison, "How could you?"

Eyes wide, Katy looked down at the incriminating evidence, then up at her two companions.

"You promised you wouldn't," Willie said, picking up the trinket.

"I tried. Really I did," Katy cried. "I couldn't help it. It was so pretty."

Broonie wrung her hands. "Oh, we're in the pot, noo."

Katy began to cry.

"There, there." Broonie put her arms around the

girl's shaking shoulders. "Doon ye be cryin' an ruin yir pretty eyes."

Willie doubted anything could spoil Katy's looks. Tears only made her eyes more luminous and added a becoming tinge of pink to her porcelain complexion.

She sniffed and turned to Willie. "You can take care of it, can't you? You always do."

The sight of Katy crying was sufficient to soften the hardest of hearts, and for Willie and Broonie, who loved her, it was unbearable. Willie took out her hand-kerchief and dried Katy's tears. "Yes, dear. I'll take care of it," she said, with more assurance than she felt, but what could she do? A valuable piece of jewelry was a far cry from an apple or a pair of scissors. She could not offer Lady Thurston a penny for her inconvenience.

Hiding her fears, she reassured Katy, "Don't worry. I'll make everything right somehow." Looking about for a diversion, she opened the door to the connecting room. "See, they gave us two nice rooms."

"You won't leave me alone, tonight, will you Willie? You know I have never slept alone."

"And you will not tonight, silly. Broonie is the eldest and gets a room all to herself."

When Willie heard the sounds of snoring from the next room, she rose and slipped into her dress. It was dark, but she dared not light a candle for fear of waking Katy. She picked up the brooch, and conceal-ing it in the folds of her skirt, quietly slipped out into the dark hallway. Willie sighed. She would have to gather her wits to get them out of this pickle.

She could simply go down and ask Mr. Pennywhis-tle which room was occupied by Lady Thurston's party, then deliver the brooch and tell her she had found it lying on the floor, or she could tiptoe up and down the hallway and listen at each room to ascertain if the occupants were still up. It wouldn't be difficult to distinguish Lady Thurston's throaty voice, if she heard her speaking.

The first idea seemed the most practical. Willie started down the stairs and had but gone halfway when she became aware that only male voices could be heard below, and to her way of thinking, very happy ones at that. She smiled. The English were fun-loving. She liked that.

Willie almost made it to the last step when two young gentlemen bounded up and bumped into her. The first, thin, rumpled and very loud, grabbed her by the arm to keep them both from tumbling, and broke into a toothy grin.

"Here, here! If it ain't the pretty little maid from Scotland. Would you not agree, Mr. Duddle?"

Willie smiled and waited for them to step aside for her to pass—for weren't gentlemen to give way to ladies? That is what one of the governesses had told Katy. Instead, they continued to block her way.

"I do believe you are right, Mr. Wickett," said the second man, a jolly sort with a thatch of red hair. He peered over the shoulder of his companion. "Now that her mistress is out of the way, the chit's looking for some fun."

Were these the same men she'd seen upon their arrival, who bowed and tipped their hats when they'd entered the inn? Willie did not have time to figure out what sort of game they played before she found herself grabbed about her waist by Mr. Wickett, who turned and thrust her into the arms of Mr. Duddle. That gentleman seemed intent on crushing her, face first, against his hot, odiferous body. Her fist which held the brooch was the only thing which kept her separated from him.

A howl escaped from the wide-eyed Mr. Duddle's throat. "The drab stabbed me!" he shouted, pushing her away.

The pin! The clasp had come undone. Willie held her fist firmly in the folds of her skirt. She did not dare have the brooch found now.

"Not man enough for her?" Wickett roared.

Willie felt a hand grab her from behind in a most intimate part of her anatomy. Yes, definitely a hand. She turned and glared. Laughter filtered up to her from those who watched the highjinks from below.

Wildly, she jabbed backwards. Her elbow embedded itself in a soft spot in Mr. Wickett's stomach, judging by the *wooshing* sound which came from his lips. When he loosened his grip, she wriggled free.

Bending over to nurse his injury, the man cursed her, "Demmed feisty little chit."

Willie turned on her heels and stomped back up the stairs. Pondering this puzzling display of male behavior, she decided that her plan was not going to work. What a strange lot men were turning out to be. Not at all what she and Katy had expected. What should they do if they all proved to be so disappointing a species? Poor Katy. Willie only hoped that London had a better selection than they had seen thus far.

Now that she had gained the landing once more, she wondered how she was going to distinguish which room was Lady Thurston's. Her only hope was to listen at each door.

Willie tried six rooms before she reached the last one at the turn of the corridor. Nothing but silence greeted her. Only her determination to set matters right for Katy kept her from giving up and going to bed. Turning the corner she pressed her ear against the solid oak paneling. Suddenly the door opened and she sailed into the room, coming to rest in a tumbled heap on the floor. Strong hands lifted her as if it were no effort at all and turned her around. Only a breath separated her from the handsome gentleman with the watch.

"I say now! What have I caught in my net?" he said. "Can it possibly be the testy little magpie who put old Pennywhistle in such a quake?"

She blurted out the first thing that came to mind. "I couldn't find my room." Willie thought she saw the corner of his mouth twitch, but the narrowing of his eyes dissuaded her to think he was amused. "I meant no disrespect, sir, I assure you. It is only . . ."

This wouldn't be the first serving girl who had followed him to his chambers. "Yes?" he asked huskily.

Willie looked up into the face above hers, quite overcome by the mesmeric effect he had upon her. She couldn't say a word.

Duncan frowned and he nearly let the girl go. But that same strange feeling he had experienced when he first looked into her eyes, came over him again. Without another moment's hesitation, he kissed her.

This unexpected turn of events sent Willie's senses reeling. How firm his body felt! Much harder than Mr. Wickett's, nor did he smell of stale food and ale like Mr. Duddle. Never before held by a man, now, within a few minutes, she had been in the arms of three. Hugged, pinched, and kissed. Of the three, she decided, the latter was the most pleasant. As he gently increased the pressure of his lips against her tender mouth, Willie forgot everything else. Exquisite sensations shot through her slender body. Involuntarily, her hands stretched up to caress his shoulders, and she dropped the brooch. It clattered to the floor, breaking the spell between them.

He reached down and picked it up.

"Why, you little thief! You were going to break into my room." His fingers captured her wrist. "This is Lady Thurston's. So you lost your way, did you? I'd say you lost your way long ago." He lifted Willie up until she was nose to nose with him. "Does the baroness know of your nightly activities?"

"No!" Willie gasped. "That is—oh, please, sir, don't say anything to Ka—Lady Katherine. I mean, I found it. I was trying to return it."

"Likely story." Duncan's mind whirled. He did not consider himself to be so privileged as to be beyond caring for those of lesser station.

The wily minx was a pickpocket, but if he called the Huntingdon authorities, there would be a long investigation. Thieves were not treated kindly by the law, as he well knew, and though she was clearly a thief, it went against the grain to think of this gamin in the hands of the authorities.

"I shall see that it is returned to Lady Thurston and tell her I found it after she had retired to her room." To show her how serious a matter he thought it, Duncan gave her a little shake. "I should do worse, but I shan't if you promise never to steal again. Do you have any idea what would happen to you if you are found guilty of theft?"

Anxiety gripped Willie. What did they do with criminals in England? In the old dungeons of Castle Gilfallen, she and Katy played and imagined all sorts of sordid things, but did the British have such places?

In the meantime, this odd man gave her another shake. He looked so angry she would have promised anything at that moment for she had the feeling her head was about to bob off her neck.

"Yes!" she managed to croak.

Duncan dropped his hands. "Well and good. See that it doesn't happen again," he said, quickly escorting her out the door. *What had come over him? Never before had he touched a woman in anger.* She looked back over her shoulder as if to say something, but before she could speak, he cut her off. "Good evening, madam," he said, shutting the door in her face.

Willie stood in the hallway, staring at the closed door. *What a strange man,* she thought, heading back to her room. *Well, at least the jewelry will be returned, and no one the wiser about Katy's part in the caper.*

The next morning, Duncan planned to make an early start. Thanks to the little pickpocket, he was no more rested than he had been when he came in the night before. Fortunately, on his way down the stairs, he'd encountered Lady Thurston's maid carrying a pot of hot chocolate to her mistress, and had given her the brooch, inventing a tarradiddle about finding the jewelry on the floor.

Now, coming out of the dining room, he stopped to check his timepiece at the very moment the three women from Scotland made their way into the common room.

He bowed, trying to project his interest toward the lovely Lady Katherine, but curiosity forced his gaze to go to the dark-haired chit behind her. Certainly that little maid would be contrite and nervous after their encounter of the night before. Duncan tried to give her a sign of encouragement to remain on the straight and narrow path, by fastening her with an imposing look. But instead of a humble demeanor, he found a pair of deep violet eyes staring boldly at his mouth, setting it afire as if she had walked right up and kissed him.

A trickle of moisture ran down Duncan's brow, but he quickly collected himself and nodded coolly. Then he changed his stern look to one more pleasant. "Lady

Katherine," he said, allowing them to brush past him
to enter into the courtyard.

"Good morning," the baroness said, returning his
greeting with a smile.

The elderly woman beside her looked at him suspiciously and prodded the baroness with her umbrella.
"Never speak to a mon ye ain't been introduced to. Ye
doon't know how dangerous he might be."

Duncan was hard put not to grin at the prospect of
himself being a dangerous *mon*.

The three women had no sooner entered their coach
when Mrs. Pennywhistle herself hurried past him and
handed them up a large covered basket.

"Here are the victuals you requested, my lady," she
said. "I hope they be pleasing you."

"Oh, thank you, Mrs. Pennywhistle," Katy chirped,
taking the basket before either of the other two women
could. "I am certain we will enjoy whatever you fixed
for us." She then shifted her gaze to her abigail. "You
are so thoughtful, Willie. Did you go down early to
order a repast?"

"Yes, dear," Willie said, watching with amusement,
as Broonie took the hamper and tucked it up on the
seat next to her where Katy could not get to it. "I went
down earlier to settle our account."

After their groom closed the door and climbed into
his seat in the rear, the coach set off. The man who
kissed her had nodded, which Willie took as an indica-
tion that he had returned the brooch. What did his
strange behavior mean? Did all young men kiss any-
body they pleased? She had to admit it was quite pleasurable. She wondered who he was.

Willie had ample time to ponder the mysterious
gentleman's behavior during the long drive to Lon-

don. Katy soon grew bored watching the scenery passing and napped. Broonie's snores had long since filled the carriage and seemed to fall rhythmically with the rolling throb of the wheels. But Willie remained wide awake, her pansy eyes drinking in the strange sights and sounds with a thirst that could not be slaked.

As they neared London and Lady Jacomena's, her excitement increased. As though sensing her tension, Katy woke with a yawn and Broonie heaved herself erect with a sigh.

"We're almost there. I saw a sign," Willie told them. "Just think, Katy, soon you will meet your aunt."

"Do you think she will like me?" Katy asked.

"How could anyone not like my Katy?" Broonie bristled, as though the notion was absurd.

"Do you not think it strange my father never mentioned he had a sister? Perhaps there is something wrong with her."

"Now why would you think that?" Willie asked.

Katy shrugged, but then grinned impishly. "You don't think she may have two noses or no hair?"

Willie laughed. "I am sure she looks just fine." But she, too, had a great many questions.

"All in the same, I want to look my best," Katy said nervously, digging in her reticule. "Will you comb the curls around my face?"

"If you wish, but you look lovely just as you are."

In her haste, Katy could not find her comb.

"Here," Willie said, and taking the bag from Katy's hands, turned it upside down. "The excitement has put you in such a dither you cannot find anything. Let me sort things out for you."

Katy grabbed for her bag, but too late. The contents lay scattered across Willie's lap. Six hair pins, a tiny mirror, a lace handkerchief, several personal articles, and staring up at Willie from the midst, shone a gold watch.

A particular gold watch which Willie recognized immediately.

"Oh, Katy!"

At that moment, the carriage came to a stop, and the coachman called down. "Baroness Gilfallen, we have arrived at Dalison Hall."

That same afternoon, Duncan sat in one of the small sitting rooms at Wakeford Hall, pleasantly passing the time of day with his mother. She had an uncanny way of gleaning the smallest of details from everyone, even from her son who preferred to keep his personal life to himself. He had just told her of encountering Lady Thurston at the inn and mentioned the young woman who had attracted quite a lot of attention.

"A Lady Katherine, Baroness of Gilfallen," he said nonchalantly, waiting to see his mother thwarted for once in knowing every eligible young debutante in England.

It took no more than a second of concentration before Lady Wakeford tapped her forehead with her finger and said, "Why, I believe she must be the daughter of a young woman I knew years ago. Did you hear her father mentioned?"

"I understand he is the Duke of Hammerfield."

"Ah, I thought so. His wife and son died in a tragic coach accident—only a year after the terrible scandal."

Duncan waited hopefully for his mother to clarify her statement, but to no avail. She could be frustratingly vague, although he knew he would hear the tale eventually.

"I believe it was more than the dear man could bear. His daughter must have been an infant at the time, and the rumor has it that he hardly ever saw her after the tragedy. Left her in a castle in Scotland she inherited from her mother, while he went into seclusion at one of his estates in Derbyshire. I thought perhaps something was wrong with her. Pretty, did you say?"

Duncan shook his head. He should have known not to try to outfox his mother. "Very! Very pretty, indeed. I would even go so far as to say she's a rare diamond of the first water."

"That is high praise, coming from you," Lady Wakefield commented, her eyes lighting up. "Did she have the good taste to admire my handsome son?"

"Not that I noticed." Lord, he hoped not. Duncan thought back to the amusing trio. His idea of a wife was not a china doll.

"She may be like her mother," Lady Wakefield mused.

"I beg your pardon?"

"I said, that perhaps she is like her mother and will fall in love at first sight. That was the way it was with Katherine McNab, the Baroness of Gilfallen, when she set eyes on young Harcourt Dalison."

"The marquis?"

"No, no. The marquis was Harcourt's older brother, Adrian. They had one sister, Jacomena. She and I attended Madame LaFarge's Academy at the same time, so I often saw her family. She was a bit older than I and quite serious about her studies, but for some reason she took a liking to me. Perhaps because I enjoyed reading the classics and attempted to write poetry. Lady Jacomena never married. A bluestocking, I hear. She still lives in London in the old section near Covent Gardens. The marquis was a highflyer," she continued, "thoroughly spoiled, wealthy, and too handsome for his own good. When Adrian came of age, he took his younger brother, Harcourt, with him everywhere, and, it was rumored, introduced him to every vice known to mankind."

"Aren't you being a little hard on him, Mother? If I'm not mistaken, your accusation would apply to over half the men in England."

"True, dear boy," she said, giving him a tap on the arm. "From a woman's point of view, that might extend to nearly ninety-eight percent of the male population. But needless to say, the two brothers were charming rogues. Turned every woman's head wherever they passed. Blonde hair the color of cornsilk. Eyes so blue . . . " her voice trailed off.

Duncan found himself hard pressed to keep a straight face. "Mother, you were saying?"

Lady Wakefield jumped. "Oh, my, where was I? I fear my mind wandered off for a minute. Well, all that wild oats thing ended for Harcourt when the Baroness of Gilfallen came down from Scotland to visit relatives in London. Who can blame him? The late Lady Katherine was a lovely, fresh breath of air blowing in from the Highlands, with hair the color of an autumn sunset. Quite tall, as I remember, but that is fashionable now with our Royal Princess Charlotte so stately, is it not? I ran into the Scottish baroness at several of the social functions, but did not get to know her well. Lord Harcourt took up all of her time—after he had warned off most of the competition. He was besotted with her, as were half the bucks in London, but Harcourt won out. It seemed the attraction went both ways, and after a very short courtship, they were married." She paused a moment, her eyes took on a pained look.

"Is something the matter, Mother?"

"No, no. I was just thinking of the tragedy that set off the scandal soon after that."

Now Duncan thought he would hear the end of the story.

"Live by the sword. Die by the sword. The marquis was killed in a duel and Harcourt succeeded to his brother's titles and subsequently became the Duke of Hammerfield. He and Lady Katherine had a daughter and a year later a son was born. I believe they named him Adrian after his dead brother. The duke's future seemed assured, but returning to Scotland, his wife and son were killed in a coach accident and Harcourt injured."

"What about their daughter?"

"She apparently was unhurt. But they say that the poor man nearly went insane, what with all that coming so soon after the murder and suicide. As soon as he healed, he left his daughter in the Highlands and went into seclusion. No one has seen him for years."

Duncan was thoroughly confused now. He was about to ask her to explain the murder-suicide when she wiped away a tear and turned to smile at him.

"But that is neither here nor there, is it? Now, you say his daughter is coming to London to make her debut? It does not seem possible that so many years have gone by. You must call on Lady Jacomena when you return to London, Duncan. Tell her I would like to renew our relationship."

Duncan was not fooled by his mother's ploy. Thoughts of a pending romance had chased the story of the marquis out of her mind.

"Of course, if she is as lovely as you describe her, you will not be unhappy to extend your acquaintance with the baroness. Surely she will be staying with her aunt?"

Strangely, Duncan's thoughts were not on Lady

Katherine, but on the dark-haired maid with eyes the color of violets. "Yes, you are probably right."

"And you will call on my old schoolmate on my behalf?"

Duncan wondered if the waif's hair was as curly as the wisps he'd seen peeking from beneath her cap. "Yes, Mother."

At that moment the old mantel clock chimed thirteen times and they had to wait for it to stop. When it finally finished, they both laughed.

"Oh, dear, what time is it? We must have been talking for hours," Lady Wakefield exclaimed cheerfully.

Duncan shook his head in exasperation and reached for his watch. "That old clock still can't tell time, can it?" Abruptly, his smile disappeared. The gold chain dangled from his pocket, its clasp broken. He swore under his breath.

"What is it, dear?"

"Nothing, Mother." Duncan rose from his chair. "Pray excuse me. I'll see you at dinner."

He left the room and, taking the stairs two at a time, hurried to his room where he searched the pockets of his various garments. *Is it possible that she stole my timepiece right from under my nose?* Finally, Duncan gave up his search. *Wait until I get my hands on you, you ungrateful little pickpocket.*

Chapter Three

Lady Jacomena's house sat back from the street in a row of similar, three-story structures, their old brick fronts clothed with many years' growth of ivy. Although no longer thought fashionable, they were the sort of residences whose ancient facades spoke of wealth and tradition. Only Dalison Hall's painted door, a faded cobalt blue, distinguished it from the others.

As soon as all three women were helped out of the coach, a groom assisted them up the front steps. While his hand was still on the knocker, the door was opened with such a flurry that the young man nearly tumbled into the foyer.

They were greeted by a round, vivacious woman of middle years. Wisps of gray hair escaped from under her mob cap and stuck out in all directions. "Welcome, welcome, Lady Katherine," she said, bobbing up and down like a wind up toy. "Do come in. Do come in." Her smile extended to all, then she laughed, the sound bouncing off the walls of the large entry hall. "Bless my soul. Can't come in if I clutter up the doorway, can you?" With that, she stepped aside to make way for the party, then turned and called toward the back of the house. "Daisy, I see you hiding. Come take the ladies' cloaks."

A serving girl, blushing to the roots of her hair, emerged from behind a potted plant, dropped a curtsy to Katy, then shyly did as she was told.

The older woman beamed her approval, then announced, "I am Mrs. Butterworth, the housekeeper. My, oh, my! What excitement we have had since her ladyship announced we was to have the pleasure of helping with your come-out, Lady Katherine. Would you like to freshen up first before you see Lady Jacomena?"

"I . . . I think I should like to meet my aunt first." Katy looked quickly at her companions, and smiled when Willie and Broonie nodded their agreement.

Surely, Willie thought, if Mrs. Butterworth and Daisy were representative of the household, their visit would be most pleasant. But she did wonder why they had not been greeted by the butler.

After giving the groom instructions, Mrs. Butterworth led them to the back of the entry hall, which was lined on both sides by feathery-leafed plants, new to Willie, and statues representing various characters of mythology. Oil paintings, dark with age, hung on the walls, but it was so dimly lit, she could not make out their subjects. They passed several rooms before stopping at a lovely carved archway, its great wooden doors flanked by marble busts, set upon pedestals of Greek origin. Plato and Aristotle. Willie recognized them from the books on Greece she'd read in Gilfallen's library.

The housekeeper knocked loudly. "Y'er ladyship. Y'er niece has arrived."

"Quit yelling, Butterworth, and come in." The voice, deep, formidable and in direct contrast to the housekeeper's cheery and amiable greeting, shot through the thick door as if it were a mere piece of paper. Willie noticed that even Broonie, who wasn't afraid of anything or anyone, raised her eyebrows.

Mrs. Butterworth opened the door and stepped aside, but it took both the large Scotswoman and Willie to push Katy ahead. The door closed behind them.

"Are you all glued together? Step up here, young woman, and let me have a look at you," the voice commanded from across the room. "Lord, I hope you are not missish."

As Willie's vision became better adjusted to the shadows, she saw a woman all starched elegance, sitting like a queen on an ornately carved, highbacked chair. No, more than a chair, a throne.

Katy stood frozen. Lady Jacomena did not rise. Instead, like magic, the throne began to move toward them. Willie noted two wheels at either side, a smaller one in front, which had been hidden by the woman's full skirt. A stick with a handle guided the wheel.

"What's the matter, girl? Never seen a Bath chair before? They are quite fashionable and I reckon what is good enough in that watering spot is good enough for London. Had one made for myself to get around in. Knees aren't what they used to be." Then, as if speaking to a spirit, she said, "Forward!" The chair moved.

Willie believed she was witnessing a miracle until a serving girl looked out from behind the chair. At first Willie thought it was Daisy. No, it could not be the little maid, for she had remained in the hall when they entered the room. The mystery was soon cleared up. "Come, Pansy, did you run out of energy?"

Twins.

Her ladyship was remarkably handsome. The finely chiseled features, the blue eyes seemed strangely familiar. A little knot formed in Willie's chest as the memory of a beautiful young man sprang into her mind. Of course, this was the Duke of Hammerfield's sister.

Katy, too, stood entranced, and Willie could see she wasn't going to go anywhere without assistance, so she gave her a nudge. She winced when she saw the sharp look Lady Jacomena directed her way when she touched Katy.

"How old are you, Katherine?"

Katy curtsied, prettily. "Seventeen." Mindful of her manners, she added, "I am pleased to meet you at last, Aunt Jacomena, and thank you very much for inviting me to visit you."

"It wasn't my idea, gel, and I should have known better than to agree to such foolishness. At my age, I don't have the patience to deal with a silly young chit making her come-out."

Broonie's challenge boomed over their heads, "Lady Katherine is a fine young woman and I'll be takin care of her. Don't you be worryin' aboot that."

Lady Jacomena's rigid mask did not change. "That is exactly why I wrote Harcourt that if he wished me to sponsor his daughter, she was to bring her own chaperone."

Willie's eyes went back and forth between the two. They talked as if Katy wasn't even present.

"Step up here, old woman."

Arms crossed over her ample chest, Broonie marched forward and faced Lady Jacomena. "Me name be Miss Abbot. We been servin' the McNabs faithful for generations. Me grandfather, Sir Phineas, were a true Scotsman, ye understand, but King Charles did see fit to beknight him fir savin' his majesty's life. It were from those fanatic followers of Cameron back afore the slaughter o' Bothwell Bridge."

"So said your poet Robbie Burns," barked Lady Jacomena.

Willie noticed that Broonie didn't curtsy, merely nodded, and wondered if that meant the Abbots were as important as the Dalisons. It seemed the legends of the fierce warrior Phineas Abbot, defender of the king, had even reached her ladyship's ears. With a nod, Lady Jacomena said, "You'll do, Miss Abbot," then turned her critical gaze on Willie.

Fascinated, Willie could not turn her eyes away.

"This is my friend, Willie," Katy said, taking her hand.

Willie found herself pulled forward so swiftly, she barely had time to bob and say, "Your ladyship."

"She is your servant, Katherine. You must learn to distinguish." Lady Jacomena turned a sharp eye on Willie. "Come closer."

Willie hurried to where the imperious woman sat.

"What is her given name, Katherine?" she said, as if the minion were not present.

"Willie," Katy answered affectionately. "I named her that."

"That is an absurd name. No consequence to it. She shall be called Wilhemina." Lady Jacomena scrutinized Willie. "Tiny little thing. What are your qualifications?"

Broonie stepped alongside Willie, dwarfing her. "His grace brought the wee one to Gilfallen from a foundling home in Leeds."

"You are an orphan?" Steel blue eyes fixed on Willie.

"Yes, your ladyship," she answered, her gaze not wavering, though inside she felt her bones quake.

"Hmph! Sounds like Harcourt. Always was a nipcheese. Couldn't even go to a proper registry." Lady Jacomena addressed her niece. "There are many highborn young French women displaced by the war who would make excellent companions for you, Katherine. Someone more befitting your station."

A chill ran through Willie, and she clasped her hands to keep them from shaking. After the housekeeper's kind greeting, this was not what she had expected. She did not want Katy to be frightened, but if Lady Jacomena turned her out, where would she go? Confusion once more reigned, and Willie looked down at her feet. Things here were quite different from what they had been in Scotland. She prayed her ladyship would find another subject to pursue.

Lady Jacomena did and switched her attention back to her niece. "You, on the other hand, obviously inherited the Dalison height."

"Broonie told me my mother was very tall, too, and that she had red hair," Katy said wistfully.

"True, but you have the blue eyes and yellow hair of the Dalisons." Lady Jacomena's eyes narrowed and after a pause she asked, "Have you never seen a picture of your mother, Katherine?"

Broonie answered for her. "His Grace saw fit to have all portraits of the late baroness removed from the castle when he returned to England."

Lady Jacomena's eyes flashed, whether with indignation or anger, Willie couldn't tell. Tension hung in the air. Fortunately, Mrs. Butterworth chose that moment to knock on the door.

She stepped into the room and announced, "Beg pardon, your ladyship. Lady Katherine's chambers are ready."

"Your trunks arrived two days ago," Lady Jacomena said, looking at her niece. "I am astonished that addlepated brother of mine had the foresight to send a dressmaker to Scotland. I dreaded the task of having to haggle with a modiste over your wardrobe, for such nonsense seems foolish to me. However, that is neither here nor there. Your attire appears suitable, if somewhat extensive. Judging from the number of dresses, one would think you were planning to spend the entire year in London."

"M'darlin is so pretty she'll have hersel' a husband afore the Season is half oot," Broonie said. "We won't be botherin you any longer than that."

"Your confidence is admirable, Miss Abbot. I only pray it is not misplaced."

Mrs. Butterworth, looking at Katy with a broad smile and ignoring the glowering look from Lady Jacomena, agreed with Broonie. "Oh, I doubt we'll have a problem getting Lady Katherine off. She's a lovely gel."

Puzzled, Willie looked from one woman to the other. The housekeeper did not seem the least intimidated by her employer. Nor did her ladyship seem disturbed by her housekeeper's comments. She merely directed her to show Lady Katherine to her rooms, and to her niece added, "I have settled you in what were once my chambers."

"Oh, Auntie. I do not wish to inconvenience you."

Lady Jacomena seemed taken aback by Katy's concern. With a wave of her hand she said, "You are not. I seldom go abovestairs anymore. It may be unconventional, but my apartment has been on the ground floor for more than ten years now, where I have the library and all the public rooms to entertain. Much more sensible. I believe you will find your chambers quite adequate."

"Oh, I am certain we shall," she said, smiling at Willie.

"Miss Abbot," Jacomena said, "you are to have your own room on the third floor."

"That willna do," Broonie spoke up, like an old

warrior. "I'll no be climbin all those stairs, thank you."

Lady Jacomena started to say something, then evidently changed her mind. "Butterworth, give Miss Abbot the blue room you prepared for Wilhemina."

"Willie," interrupted Katherine. "Her name is not Wilhemina. 'Tis Willie."

Jacomena's chin thrust forward. *"Wilhemina* will move to the third floor. Have Tom check the bell pull, so she can be summoned whenever her mistress needs her."

Katy's eyes widened. "No!"

Willie could not stand to see Katy upset, and taking her hand, announced, "I always sleep in the same room with Lady Katherine."

Lady Jacomena's eyes narrowed. "Remember your place, gel. I give the orders here."

Willie looked down at the floor.

"Auntie?" Katy pleaded, "I want Willie with me."

"Well! I can see my life is no longer my own." Lady Jacomena turned to her housekeeper. "Butterworth! See that a cot is brought in for the gel."

"There is no need," Katy said, her cheerful nature restored.

"You wish your abigail to sleep on the floor?"

"I only meant—" Katy began when Willie stopped her with a sharp look.

"See to it then, Butterworth," Lady Jacomena said. After the housekeeper nodded, she turned again to her niece. "I have arranged a number of invitations and acquired vouchers to some of the most sought after balls of the season, Katherine. Of course, I do not plan to go to the tedious affairs myself except for those necessary few to introduce you to the leaders of the *ton.* I socialize with my own group of friends here at Dalison Hall, but that is need not concern you. Most of my entertaining is done on this floor in the library and salons across the hall. Since your quarters are abovestairs, you may use those sitting rooms. That is why I insisted on you bringing your own chaperone." She glanced at Broonie. "I can see that you will be quite well protected."

Lady Jacomena was relieved to see her guests go. She had not asked for this assignment, and she could see this was just the beginning of the aggravation she would be forced to endure.

She must have been temporarily insane to let Harcourt talk her into sponsoring his daughter. Her insatiable curiosity was to blame. She'd wanted a look at Katherine, and now that she'd seen the gel, she regretted her impulse. Her niece was a beauty, and sweet-tempered to boot. Harcourt didn't deserve her.

Jacomena had not spoken to her brother in over eighteen years. She was twelve years his senior and the last time she had seen him was just before his wedding. He had been a most disagreeable little boy and an even more disagreeable young man. She had not wanted to stay around to watch him grow into a disagreeable adult.

She'd much preferred their brother, Adrian, a rapscallion at heart, but a true gentleman. She had adored Adrian and bitterly regretted his death. She still held Harcourt to blame, feeling he could have prevented the duel had he but tried.

Soon after Adrian's murder, for that is how she thought of it, Jacomena had left with some of her literary friends for a grand tour of the Continent. While the short peace with France lasted, their travels had taken them as far as the exotic lands in northern Africa. She had even ridden a camel in Egypt. Nasty animals, but she was not one to give up a chance to see the great pyramids just because of the foul smell and lack of manners of the beasts that were their means of conveyance. That, of course, had been the beginning of her aches and pains.

Well, it was her own folly which now faced her. Heaven forbid, she hoped she wasn't going to become agreeable in her old age.

Duncan Fairchild spent three weeks in London before paying a visit to Dalison Hall. He would have delayed longer were it not for the arrival of the third letter in as many weeks from his mother, reminding him of his promise to call on Lady Jacomena. In a family of six children, he was the middle child and the only son, and he knew it his duty to marry and carry on the family name, yet he balked at being pushed— even toward so beautiful a lady as the Baroness of Gilfallen.

Lady Katherine possessed the requisite breeding, charm and temperament a man of his station sought in a wife. If she would have him, he could not hope to do better than to wed the only daughter of the duke of Hammerfield. Why then, was he so reluctant? Feeling he was behaving unreasonably, he resolved to call on Lady Jacomena without further procrastination.

The decision made, he rang for his man. "Charles, I shall be making a call this afternoon."

"Very good, my lord." Well-trained servant that he was, he made no further comment and laid out his master's clothes.

For the first time, Duncan looked with a critical eye at his wardrobe. All blacks and grays or shades of buff.

"Must you always drape me in drab colors, Charles?"

"My lord?"

"I'd prefer something with a little more color. I'm calling on a lady."

The servant raised his hands helplessly. "You don't own anything with more color. May I remind you that you choose your own clothes, my lord?"

That was true. He also recalled several occasions when Charles had tactfully suggested a blue coat or a paisley vest. Trying to ignore his servant's blatant smile, he muttered, "Must you fuss so much with my neckcloth?"

Charles said nothing, but his raised chin and pinched set of his lips, adequately conveyed that he thought his master was indulging in a fit of the sullens.

Ruefully, Duncan owned his man was right. And it was not just the thought of his intended marriage that put him out of sorts, but that bloody girl who'd had the audacity, the unmitigated cheek, to steal his watch. After generously refraining from calling the authorities, she had blatantly betrayed his trust. How could a man start out a courtship when he distrusted the lady's own servants? Of course, he could not prove the little magpie had taken his timepiece, but it seemed to him that no one else had the opportunity. The girl appeared to have a good position with a kind and generous employer. What need prompted her to steal? Was it bad blood or pure devilment, he wondered, recalling the fire in her violet eyes.

Upon his arrival at Dalison Hall, a cheerful woman greeted him at the door. After giving his name and enquiring for Lady Jacomena she ushered him in.

"I'm Mrs. Butterworth, the housekeepr. I'll take your wraps, my lord. The mistress don't have any men servants. 'Cept Old Jack, Cook's husband, who takes care of the horse and carriage, and li'l Johnny who runs errands when we need a fast pair of legs," she finished, leading him down the hallway until she came to a Greek columned portal.

"Your ladyship," she called in, "another nice young man to see our Lady Katherine. Lord Wakeford." Mrs. Butterworth turned and started to retrace her steps. "The salon is small, so I shall carry your cloak and hat across the hall into the library, my lord."

Although it was the most unorthodox introduction Duncan had ever received, his composure remained unruffled and he stepped with cool confidence into the room.

He cared little for the goings-on of the *ton,* but of late it proved impossible to avoid hearing the gossip about the latest arrival in town for the season. Everywhere he turned, it seemed someone was singing the praises of the beautiful baroness of Gilfallen. Young dandies, gazetted fortune-hunters, and gentlemen of good lineage and fortune had placed her at the top of their lists.

As he glanced about the crowded room, he noticed at least four gentlemen already seated amidst half a dozen ladies. But it was an older woman with exceptionally strong features who dominated the room. Her piercing blue eyes met his, and Duncan had the feeling he'd been weighed and found wanting.

"Over here, young man. I am Lady Jacomena Dalison."

Duncan bowed. "My pleasure, your ladyship."

As he was introduced to the others, Lady Katherine said little, but blushed prettily when he mentioned their encounter at the Landed Gull. Before he found a seat, two identical serving maids entered carrying a tea service and tray of refreshments, which they placed upon a low round table beside Lady Jacomena.

Her ladyship looked down disdainfully at the decorative *petits fours* and tiny sandwiches and motioned to one of the maids. "Pansy, push me over to the alcove and then bring two cups of tea. Don't bother with any of those ridiculous tidbits. They're an insult to a good appetite."

"Yes, my lady."

Jacomena turned toward her niece. "Katherine, serve your guests. I want to talk to Lord Wakeford." So saying, she crooked her finger in Duncan's direction, then indicated a chair across from her. "Turn me around, young man, then you may sit by me. Another time you can do the pretty with Lady Katherine."

When her back was to the others in the room, he sat down opposite her. Frankly bored with the frivolous world of fluttering fans and flirtatious innuendos, Duncan did not object. It would have been impossible to hold any serious discussion with Lady Katherine with others about. But he could learn much from Lady Jacomena, and eyed her with interest.

"Now, tell me what your mother has been up to these last few years. She had undoubtedly told you that we were cellmates at Madame LaFarge's Academy for Young Ladies." She laughed suddenly. "Alice Duncan Fairchild. I never thought she would rusticate in the country. She had more wits in one of her little fingers than all of those silly girls at school had in their entire heads—wrote beautiful, thoughtful poetry. Too bad she wasted it having babies." Jacomena raised her quizzing glass to survey Duncan. It was a thorough appraisal from his polished boots to the top of his well-coiffed head.

"At least you're not one of those puffed-up poppinjays who strut about Town passing themselves off as men. I suppose Alice might have done worse," she said, bestowing grudging approval.

"Thank you," Duncan murmured, much amused. To one who was accustomed to being described as the most eligible bachelor in town, her remarks were diverting. He sat back and listened while Lady Jacomena informed him what she considered wrong with society—which seemed to encompass almost everything from the current style of dress to manners and morals.

Her opinions were stated as fact, and she did not pause for him to comment. She left him little to say without directly contradicting her.

His attention wandered and he glanced idly over her shoulder, then stared rudely as he spotted the elfin maid. Dressed in a black bombazine gown which emphasized her slender figure, she moved with unconscious grace across the hardwood floor, then stepped unobtrusively from the room.

Duncan felt the sharp rap of a fan on his arm.

"What is so interesting?" Lady Jacomena barked. "Didn't Alice teach you it's impolite to stare?"

Fairly caught, Duncan felt the blood rush to his face.

"Have to find that gel a husband before the Season is out," she said. "I couldn't abide another year of this nonsense."

Duncan said nothing. Far better she think he was watching Lady Katherine than to admit who had really been the target of his interest.

Jacomena fixed her critical gaze on Duncan. "I am giving a small dinner party tomorrow evening. Half past eight."

Evidently her ladyship did not think it necessary to issue an invitation or expect a refusal, although Duncan was searching for an acceptable excuse until she said, "I do believe you will know some of my guests. I have invited two old friends of mine, Jeremy Betham, the economist, and Hannah More. Also, that young rascal Robert Peel will be here. I believe it will prove to be an interesting evening. He is being accused of wanting to go easy on our criminals while crime is rising at an unprecedented rate in Town."

At the mention of Peel, Duncan reconsidered. Representative of Oxford University, Peel was one of the few men in Parliament whom he admired, and another outspoken champion for the need of changes in the penal code. What better chance, he thought, to advocate his own views?

"I have a few artists and writers to round out the table. Benjamin Haydon is about your age. He helped persuade the government to buy the Elgin Marbles. And William Blake is bringing the watercolorist, John Varley, who believes in astrology and thinks the stars control one's destiny." Jacomena laughed with gusto. "I cannot abide dull dinner conversation. Nothing like a good argument to get the digestive juices flowing, heh? I hope you're not one of those namby-pamby types who thinks courtesy precludes an honest difference of opinion?"

"My mother would be insulted to hear you suggest such a possibility," he replied with an amused smile. "I shall look forward to the occasion."

He *would* call today, Willie thought the moment she saw Lord Wakeford enter the room. At any other time she could have slipped quietly from the room, but today her presence was required to chaperone Katy. Poor Broonie, exhausted by the endless round of balls and teas, and the late hours kept by the stylish members of the *ton,* had fallen asleep after luncheon.

Willie had not wanted to awaken her, and surprisingly, Lady Jacomena had agreed, but had delegated

Willie to accompany Lady Katherine in place of her nurse. To accommodate Lady Jacomena, visitors were received on the ground floor salon, and there had been a steady stream of callers.

Willie had not minded her duties. She had even taken pleasure in watching Katy take her proper place in society. Despite her nervousness, Katy behaved beautifully. Her deportment during the last three weeks did them proud. It was true, a few things had been taken, but thank the Lord, nothing of great value. A pair of scissors from Mrs. Butterworth and a ribbon Willie later discovered belonged to Daisy had both been replaced without incident. The other incidentals were in a drawer in the bedroom waiting to be returned when their owners were found.

If only she could return Lord Wakeford's watch as easily as Daisy's ribbon. She had racked her brain to come up with some scheme, but to no avail.

Now, as luck would have it, he had appeared on their doorstep.

She glanced at Katy, talking to Sir Phillip Norton, a stiff-rumped, older man and young Mr. Harding. Surely it would be safe to leave her for a few moments. Deciding to risk it, Willie slipped from the room.

Mrs. Butterworth always placed the men's wraps in the library. Willie prayed she could retrieve the watch, slip it into the lining of Lord Wakeford's cloak and get back to the parlor before the guests were ready to take their leave. Then, when he found it, he would think it had fallen there by accident.

Willie flew up to her room and searched in the drawer where she had placed the watch. Palming it, she ran back downstairs.

In the library she was confronted with the realization that there were five gentlemen's outer garments laid carefully over the backs of the chairs. Which one belonged to Lord Wakeford? She picked up one and was going through it for some sign of its owner, when she heard voices in the hallway. Quickly, she dropped the coat and ran for the door, just as Mrs. Butterworth opened it.

Willie tumbled into the hall and would have sprawled on the floor except for the strong pair of male arms which caught her. Fearfully, she glanced up into Lord Wakeford's eyes.

Chapter Four

The watch burned in Willie's fist. Certain the earl's stern eyes saw the guilt written all over her face, she broke away and dashed for the stairs.

As she turned and fled, Duncan found himself staring, not at the maid's hands, but at the delectable swishing of her skirts. More disturbing was what he'd felt at the touch of her. One look into those violet eyes and something happened to him.

Anger! It had to be anger, for he had never felt so hot before, except when he was in a high dudgeon. She was at it again. Robbing the guests. He was tempted to chase after her and bring her back, but he was faced with the same dilemma as before. He would have no choice but to turn her over to the law. For some reason that idea left him quite shaken.

Duncan automatically reached into his watch pocket, then cursed under his breath at his lapse. He consulted the tall wall clock beside the library door. Certainly all the time pieces in Lady Jacomena's house were correct to the minute, and if he didn't hurry, he'd be late for his appointment. That would never do. Slapping his beaver hat on his head, he quickly left the house.

The next evening, Duncan presented himself at

Dalison House. He soon realized that Lady Jacomena's dinner party was like none other he had ever attended. She sat at the head of the table like a queen holding court. The small dining room easily seated the sixteen people, some from titled families, all well connected, acclaimed in political or academic circles. No gossip, no social trivialities. Like gunfire, strong opinions shot across the table. Duncan could just as well have been on the floor of Parliament or in a court of law. Obviously, her ladyship made her own rules when it came to her house, for no proper member of the *ton* would permit her guests to speak to another across the table. But then he realized there were no barriers, either, no large flower arrangements or epergnes, those high tiered dishes of fruits, to obstruct one's view.

Duncan was seated to Lady Jacomena's right and Lady Katherine on his other side. The significance did not escape him. None of the dandies who'd called the day before were present, which he hoped meant his acceptance as a suitor for the baroness's hand. Although she did not seem to take an aversion to him, she sat quietly, a white dove in the midst of hawks and owls, her hands clutched in her lap.

As another remove stilled the conversation for a moment, he glanced down the long table. At the beginning of the evening, he had been surprised to find Miss Abbot included in the assembly. Nurse? Friend? Relative? He could not tell, though *warrior* seemed a more appropriate description of the barrel-chested woman. He'd heard her quote the Scottish poets with a better deliverance than the British, but he noticed she kept a watchful vigil on Lady Katherine.

Next to Miss Abbot sat Tobias Trunnion, a gentleman whose Scottish brogue and bright kilt identified him immediately as from the north country. Two chairs down from them was Trunnion's host in London, a rotund young man, Mr. John Teagardner, whom Duncan knew well. The Teagardners were near neighbors to his mother in Cambridgeshire, their lands marching along the northern border of Wakeford. The timid John, whom he had known since childhood, couldn't see beyond his nose, wore a perpetual squint, and at present focused on his plate.

When Lady Jacomena introduced the dour-faced Miss Abbot as the granddaughter of Sir Phineas of Bothwell Bridge fame, Mr. Trunnion claimed he was delighted to be her table companion. Duncan, who could not imagine the old nurse being the delight of any man, heard her lusty voice happily reciting the words of several ballads about her grandfather.

Across the table was Miss Hannah More. She was a religious writer who believed in educating the poor, but only in skills which befitted their station, and was now in a heated discussion with her contemporary, Jeremy Bentham, one of the early pioneers of prison reform.

"A plan is needed, I tell you," Bentham shouted. "Those titled scoundrels who get themselves assigned to King's Bench Prison, and have the means to do so, live in relative leisure serving their term, while those of the lower class are transported for stealing a loaf of bread."

Duncan lent an ear to the discussion. He'd read Bentham's *The Panopticon,* an idea for a model prison.

Opposite Duncan, the Parliamentarian Robert Peel, whom the earl hoped would prove to be an ally in his fight for fairer treatment of the common man, laughed and spoke in an undertone. "The old man has been working on his scheme for years and done nothing.

'Tis too bizarre and spoiled by the elaborate detail he loves. Nothing will be done unless action is taken."

"Perhaps a new approach is needed," the earl said. "One of prevention, not punishment. But how do you answer opponents who say there is no evidence that more lenient sentences reduce the amount of crime on the streets, or that humane treatment redeems the criminally minded?"

"I believe you and I think much alike. One has only to look at the inequality in justice between the poor and the rich," Peel countered. "For the wealthy, there are money-greedy sheriffs who can be bribed into providing every conceivable luxury. Outsiders are even allowed in to amuse the prisoners with games of chance. But the poor—the gaolers treat them cruelly."

Like a frightened rabbit surrounded by baying hunters, the baroness looked back and forth between the two men. Duncan gave her a reassuring smile, which in turn brought a look of gratitude to her large eyes. Of course the gently bred girl would find the conversation distressing, but her gratefulness seemed out of proportion. He felt much as he did when rescuing one of his little sisters. The imps were always in trouble, never taking the time to think before plunging into one escapade after another. When possible, Duncan intervened to save them from punishment. He used the term lightly, for the restrictions imposed on his sisters were nothing compared to the harsh treatment meted out to female prisoners in London's gaols. Thought of a dark-haired minx with light fingers intruded. If the girl didn't mind her ways, she'd soon find herself in Newgate. The thought was vastly disturbing.

Remembering his manners, Duncan brought his attention back to his dinner partner. Lady Katherine looked distinctly uncomfortable.

"Piety is the answer," Miss More said, her voice outdistancing any of the men's. "Teach the poor to accept their station, to serve God and their masters well, and there would be no crime."

Such a lively discussion ensued from her remark that only Duncan noticed Lady Jacomena shake her finger at her niece and say in a deep whisper, "Is that not what I told you, Katherine? I am afraid that if your abigail does not learn to act with the proper respect for your position, I shall have to replace her. I cannot have you embarrassed in front of the *ton*. They may be a bunch of last year's cabbages, but their power is strong. 'Tis your first appearance in London and very important for you to make the proper impression."

Katy answered her with a wide-eyed stare.

"However, I am certain a word of rebuke from you should suffice to remind her of her place." Her duty done, Jacomena turned her attention back to the more interesting discourse on present harsh methods of punishment for wayward souls.

Horror showing on her face, Lady Katherine retreated further into silence.

Pity for her plight moved Duncan to speak. "Forgive my insensitivity, Lady Katherine. Of course such references to the unseemly side of life would upset one of your tender upbringing. Shall we speak of something else?"

Her look of appreciation answered him.

She asked in a near whisper, "Are you going to the Bellrumple Ball?"

Every year, Duncan received an invitation to this most august occasion. Usually he found an excuse for not attending the crush, but this year he doubted he could avoid it. The ball would introduce Lord and Lady Bellrumple's only daughter, Helena, to Society.

He considered it his duty to make a short appearance, and nodded pleasantly. "Why, yes, I daresay I will."

She sighed and leaned closer. "I am so glad. I am quite nervous."

"About what, my lady? From the *on-dits* going about, I should think you would have become quite accustomed to such affairs."

"Oh, no, my lord. I don't believe I ever shall, for I always fear no one will ask me to dance."

Duncan sat back to have a better look at her. "You, my lady? Why, a gentleman would consider it a privilege to stand up with you."

Katy clasp her hands and gave the earl a radiant smile. "You would? Oh, thank you, my lord. I am most grateful for your offer. If you escort me for the opening dance, I am sure others may be led to ask me, too."

Duncan blinked, trying to fathom what he had said for her to believe he would lead her out, but he recovered quickly and replied, "It would be my honor, Lady Katherine. You may put my initials on your dance card."

Lady Jacomena too had overheard the exchange. Although she gave no outward sign, she was inwardly delighted. Perhaps this tedious affair of finding a suitable mate for her niece would end sooner than she had hoped. If Katherine caught a *nonpareil* like the earl in the parson's trap, it wouldn't be necessary to give a ball for the girl.

Jacomena had scant patience for the tiresome business of bringing a girl out, an expensive and foolish procedure that cost the world. To her mind, it would be faster for Harcourt just to put his daughter up for auction at Tattersall's and take the highest bid. From Jacomena's observations of the way men neglected their wives, Katherine would have a better chance at happiness if she received half the attention gentlemen devoted to their horses.

At that moment the pudding arrived, signaling the end of the meal.

Duncan ate his with mixed feelings. His suit was getting off to a faster start than he'd planned. Whereas he had hoped to come late and stay at the Bellrumple's ball only long enough to pay his respects in case the prince regent made an appearance, he was now committed to an early arrival.

After dinner, the men did not linger long over their cigars and port, for before the women left the table, Lady Jacomena had announced, "Wine will also be available in the music room, gentlemen. You may join us when you will."

While some of the guests stayed to view the paintings and statues in the hallway and others made their way to the retiring rooms on the floor above to refresh themselves, Duncan confronted Peel. "A most remarkable dinner, do you not agree, sir?"

Peel smiled. "Lady Jacomena's reputation is widespread. One may be certain of encountering a diversity of opinions on any number of subjects. She seems to have chosen prison reform tonight, which of course interests me tremendously, as I am sure you are aware, my lord."

"Yes, I have been waging my own small efforts in that direction. I, too, strongly believe that prevention, not harsher punishment, is the answer to the problem of rising crime. I may be able to produce an example to prove my point."

"I am intrigued. Pray continue."

"I am acquainted with a young woman—a servant to a lady of quality—who stole a valuable piece of jewelry right from under the noses of dozens of onlookers. Judging from the expertise with which she performed the feat, she has become quite adept at her profession."

"A most audacious thief. Is she awaiting trial?"

"No, I . . . er . . . didn't report her to the authorities. There were circumstances which persuaded me it would be more effective to handle the matter privately. Of course, I made certain the jewelry was returned to its rightful owner."

"Well, I am certain you did what you thought right. But 'tis a pity the girl got away with it. Don't you fear it will lead to her being more brazen in the future?"

"That is just the sort of thing I wish to stop—I strongly believe an effort should be made to reform the girl's habits before punishment is enacted."

"Most interesting concept. You know, I feel many sentences exacted on the less fortunate are too harsh and do no lasting good," Peel said. "Are you planning to test your theory?"

Duncan now saw his encounter with the little thief as an opportunity to gain Peel as an ally. It was too good to pass up. "Yes, I am."

Peel held out his hand. "Well, my good man, if you can give me some proof that a better solution can be found than incarceration, I will welcome the information before I address Parliament again."

Hours earlier while the guests were eating dinner, Willie had finished her own meal in the warm kitchen. Old Tom was pressed into service as footman and to serve the men their port and cigars after the meal. Johnny was set to scrubbing pots and pans, and helped carry the dishes to the butler's pantry. Mrs. Butterworth supervised, while Daisy and Pansy served the guests. Willie would have helped too, had not Mrs.

Butterworth put down her foot and said she would have none of it.

" 'Tis not your place and t'would set a poor example for Pansy and Daisy. A lady's maid don't do a serving girl's work. The mistress is very particular on what's proper and what ain't."

Willie frowned. What was her place? Mrs. Butterworth took care of running the household and served Lady Jacomena's personal needs. Pansy and Daisy cleaned the house and served the table, and the laundress and scullery maid were a mother and daughter who came in during the day.

Although Cook would not let Willie dirty her hands, she ate in the kitchen and was served with Mrs. Butterworth. On the other hand, Broonie was found acceptable to eat at Lady Jacomena's table. Willie thanked providence for that, because one of them had to make certain Katy did not make off with the tableware.

Her dinner finished, Willie knew she had hours ahead of her before Katy would return to her room. Because she thought Willie was taking books for Katy, Lady Jacomena had granted Willie permission to use the enormous library, and she now decided to select a new volume to take upstairs. As she passed the portal into the dining room, she kept to the shadows on the far side of the hall. A jumble of animated voices drifted out, and for a moment she paused to listen. The conversations were centered on the most fascinating subjects; strange countries, wars, the stars, things she had read about in the books at Gilfallen, but never had anyone with whom she could converse. For a moment she lingered, wishing passionately that she could have attended the dinner along with Katy, for had Katy any say in the matter, Willie would have been treated as a guest.

Before the others arrived, Katy had pouted and said, "I want you to sit beside me at dinner, Willie. There will be all those people I do not know."

Willie reminded her, "Remember, dear? Your aunt told us that it was not a lady's maid's place to mingle with the guests." Katy still looked forlorn, so Willie patted her hand and said, "Broonie will be there to give you encouragement."

"I don't understand why you cannot be," Katy had wailed.

Willie didn't understand either. She reckoned it had to do with parents. Parentage seemed very important, and according to Lady Jacomena, the rules in England were very strict.

Willie thought back to earlier in the evening when Katy, a vision in blue, had descended the stairs to greet her guests. The grand hallway had been awash with strange faces, all turned upward, but Willie saw only Lord Wakeford's. Had he seen her? She thought for a moment that he had. But then, elegant in his black evening attire, a white cravat around his throat, the earl stepped forward. His dark brows knit together, shadowing those telling eyes. "Lady Katherine," he said, extending his hand.

Katy, forgetting her fears, had laughed and run down the steps to place her fingers in his.

Leaning heavily on her cane, Lady Jacomena slowly followed. With a satisfied smile, she announced, "Ladies and gentlemen, may I present my niece, Lady Katherine Dalison, Baroness of Gilfallen."

Lord Wakeford raised Katy's gloved hand to his lips and she, a butterfly in motion, curtsied prettily.

On the balcony above, Willie pretended she faced the only other lord she had ever met, the Duke of Hammerfield, and turned to a potted plant and curtsied. Then she tiptoed to the bannister and peeking through, watched the party go in to dinner. With a tug at her heart, she admitted to herself that Katy and Lord Wakeford made a very attractive couple.

As soon as the hallway was empty, Willie had crept down the stairs into the library. She couldn't help but reflect on what had happened yesterday when she'd run into the earl. From the way he had scowled at her, she knew he didn't hold her in the highest regard. Heavens! She shivered to think what he'd have done if he'd caught her with his gold watch. And yet she knew she'd chance his disapproval just to be back in those strong arms again.

Willie shook herself to clear the wool from her head and looked about at the books lining the walls. Lady Jacomena had collected a treasure trove of old and recent editions, the latest research, and knowledge garnered from numerous countries. The library at Gilfallen was extensive, but no new volumes had been added for the past fifteen years. Here was the world at her beck and call. Willie decided an interesting book was just what she needed to help her forget her troubles.

Willie had let her ladyship believe that she carried all those books to their room for Katy to read. Thinking that her niece read extensively had brought the first hint of a smile to the stern noblewoman's face, and Willie had not corrected her. A little flummery couldn't hurt—not when it cast her sweet Katy in a more satisfactory light with her aunt.

Willie herself only earned frowns from the mistress of the house. Willie felt she must be sadly lacking in what it took to be a good lady's maid. A pity she could not find a book which would tell her how to go about the business, then perhaps she could improve her own standing with Lady Jacomena.

Willie climbed the ladder to the little balcony where

more shelves ran around the upper half of the room. She was not looking for anything in particular, for the adventure was in finding something quite unexpected. One by one her pile of books grew. A book of law caught her attention, and she seated herself near the candlelight from a sconce on the wall and opened it. The treatises on the British legal system in the Gilfallen library had been old, and the date on this was quite recent. Soon she was so engrossed that she lost all sense of time, until she heard high-pitched voices outside in the hall.

"Oh, dear, I have stayed overlong," she said, gathering her books and descending the ladder.

The women's voices were soon joined by the low murmur of men's. Sighing, Willie realized she would have to wait until the guests retired to one of the salons before she could slip out of the library.

At that moment, Benjamin Haydon and Mr. Blake stood in the hall, fully engrossed in one of the smaller paintings on the wall. Mr. Haydon held his quizzing glass an inch away from the canvas. "I say, Blake, look at this."

Duncan studied the talented pair. He did not often frequent art galleries, but he was quite aware that Haydon, a brilliant historical artist, had experienced the humiliation of being sent to debtor's prison. Mr. Blake, too, struggled to earn a meagre living as an engraver while illustrating his own poems.

Lady Jacomena approached them. "The dampness in this place has turned all my pictures dark. Nothing like they used to be."

"How did you come by this oil, your ladyship?"

"Found it in the Netherlands, in an old shop in Utrecht. No, I believe it was Leyden. So many years ago, I can't recall—but it was when I took the grand tour of the Continent," she answered.

"Do you know who painted it? I can barely make it out."

"Haven't the faintest," she said, coming closer to see it better. "The painting caught my fancy, so I bought it. I liked the figure with all those books and papers about—reminds me of my own room."

"Incredible, but I do believe you bought yourself a Heems."

"Heems lived in Antwerp and painted flowers and fruit," she said knowingly.

"Not always," Blake countered. "It is known that on rare occasions, when he was in a melancholy, he painted figures. You may have a rare treasure here, my lady. You must get an expert opinion."

Somewhere down the corridor, the musical laughter of Lady Katherine's voice drew the attention of all.

"I have asked my niece to sing for us this evening," Jacomena said. "Shall we proceed to the music room?"

Blake held his arm out to her. "I will ask a friend of mine, Jacob Tellerman, an art dealer, to call on you. I am certain he can recommend someone to restore your paintings."

When they moved away, Peel went with them. On the pretext of inspecting the painting, Duncan remained in the hall. He had little interest in the piece of art. His mind dwelt on his boastful promise to reform his little magpie. It had occurred to him that perhaps he could solve two problems with one stroke.

Who better than a lady's maid to know her mistress's innermost desires? If he convinced the abigail of his good intentions toward her lady, would she not receive him more amiably? Consequently he would have the opportunity to persuade her to mend her wicked ways. And perhaps return his beloved watch. A sudden uncomfortable thought crossed his mind.

What if she had fenced his timepiece for a mere pittance? Duncan clenched his fists.

He would have to face that problem later. For now, he knew he should make haste to join the others in the music room. But as he strode past the library, he glimpsed a dark figure through the half-opened door. The guests' coats! Was that pickpocket at it again? Earlier in the evening when Lady Katherine had stood at the top of the stairs, the curly-haired pixie's face had appeared behind her. Now he knew it had not been an illusion. The little thief had only been awaiting the chance to rifle the guests' pockets.

From inside the room, Willie listened to the voices fade away. Time for her escape. Clasping the books to her bosom, she started for the door. Abruptly, she found her arm grabbed and looked up into the angry eyes of Lord Wakeford. "My lord!" Blood rushed to her face. She dropped the books, then quickly bent to retrieve them.

Duncan leaned over with the same intent, and banged her forehead with his.

Willie's cap popped off in one direction, and she would have gone the other had not his strong hands steadied her.

Head throbbing, Duncan was saved from making an embarassed apology by a voice from the doorway.

"Oh, I say now!"

Good God! The man stood only a few feet away, squinting at him. "Teagardner?"

"Lord Wakeford?"

Duncan realized his hands still grasped the girl's shoulders. What a coil. He tried to block her from view with his body.

"Afraid I failed to catch the lady's name at dinner," Mr. Teagardner managed to say, peering over Duncan's shoulder. When Duncan did not respond, Mr.

Teagardner coughed. "I was looking for the music room. Went abovestairs for a few minutes, you know, to . . . "

The man again raised his quizzing glass and leaned forward for another glimpse, but by now Duncan held Willie's face firmly against his chest.

"That is . . . " the man stammered, "Lady Jacomena asked if I'd oblige and accompany the baroness on the pianoforte while she sang. Hope I didn't interrupt anything."

"No, no, you did not," Duncan said, trying to keep his voice casual and at the same time attempting to keep Willie's face covered. He hoped the chit had sense enough to keep her mouth shut. "May I show you the way?"

"Most kind of you, my lord. And the lady?"

Duncan pointed toward the door. "You did say Lady Katherine is awaiting you in the music room, did you not?"

"Oh, yes. Well, I suppose I must hurry along. Are you not joining us, my lord?"

"Oh, shortly, but do not wait for me."

Mr. Teagardner started out the door, then turned back and stared into the dimly lit room.

"By your leave, Lady . . . Lady . . . ?"

Duncan barely heard her muffled voice.

"I am not a 'Lady', sir. My name is . . . " Willie thought quickly. "My name is . . . Miss Winkie."

Duncan choked, too stunned for a moment to speak. Then releasing the abigail, he turned and stared at the empty spot where Teagardner had been. Hearing a rustle of skirts behind him, he whirled, but before he could stop her, Willie grabbed a book and was out the door.

"Wait!" Duncan called, "I wish a word with you." By the time he hurried into the hallway she was al-

ready halfway up the stairs. Oh, she was a sharp one.
His task of taming the little vixen was going to be
difficult, but along with the exasperation came a surge
of excitement. He only hoped the short-sighted Teagardner was not a gossipmonger, for if it were bandied
about that Lord Wakeford had been found dallying
with a woman in the library, his courtship of the baroness could be ruined before it started. Duncan
scooped up one of the volumes from where it had
fallen on the floor. He opened the front page. A first
edition. Was the magpie up to stealing valuable books
now? Duncan turned the old leatherbound volume
over in his hands. It would be worth a fortune to some
unscrupulous collector. He gathered the other books
and stacked them on a table. The evidence of her
presence, the mob cap, he placed beside the books.
Her employment was on the line as well as his reputation.

When Katy tiptoed into their room hours later and
began to undress, Willie was in bed reading. Throwing
off the comforter, she started to rise. "No need to be
quiet, dear. I'm awake."

Katy jumped.

"I'm sorry. I didn't mean to startle you," Willie
said, noticing that Katy held her left arm stiffly, making it difficult for her to remove her long gloves.

Alarmed, Willie quickly set her book on the bed
table. "Here, let me help you. Did you injure yourself?"

"No!" Katy insisted, turning her back. "My arm is
just a little sore from holding it out to so many people." In a flurry, she pulled off the glove and tried to
stuff it into the drawer.

But Willie was quicker. "It is your right hand you hold out. Now show me what you took."

Reluctantly, Katy turned, her hand open.

"Oh, Katy! That sweet Mr. Teagardner's quizzing glass."

"I just borrowed it," she cried, holding it to her bosom. "And it is so much fun to look at things and watch them get bigger."

Willie took the eyepiece. Walking over to a small bureau, she opened the top drawer and dropped it in. "We shall put it with the other things." With a sigh, she looked helplessly at the number of items: a feather from a hat, a leather glove, a lace handkerchief, a pearl pin. Day by day, the mounting pile was beginning to take on the appearance of a novelty shop.

A wave of despair washed over Willie. There was a possibility that she would never encounter Mr. Teagardner again. How was she to get his quizzing glass back to him? Perhaps she could leave it somewhere in one of the sitting rooms where it could be found.

Lord, getting Katy safely married was going to be more difficult than she'd guessed.

Chapter Five

Early the next morning, Willie slipped out of bed and dressed. After writing a note for Katy, she hurried downstairs. If she did not place Mr. Teagardner's quizzing glass in one of the sitting rooms before the others were about, it would become a permanent part of Katy's growing collection of articles. The sound of tittering voices coming from the dining room alerted Willie that the twins were already tidying up after the party. In the green salon, she placed the eyepiece on a table where it could easily be found, then headed for the library.

An image of Lord Wakeford arose in her mind as she approached the room. That gentleman was forever popping up in the most unexpected places, which made her think of all those books she had dropped. It would not do to leave them on the floor. Half expecting the earl to be waiting to pounce upon her, she cautiously entered the room. The heady aroma of old bindings, ink and oiled wood filled her senses. To her surprise, she found the books neatly stacked on a table, her cap beside them.

Since Katy liked to dilly-dally over her hot chocolate before dressing each morning, Willie decided she would have time to look at the book of law again. She had found some strange tales of adoptions, but not exactly anything that she could tell Katy. With a little shiver of anticipation, she climbed the ladder to the narrow balcony and soon became engrossed in her studies.

Half an hour later, Duncan presented himself at the front door of Dalison Hall. It was far too early to call, but he hoped to persuade Lady Katherine to drive with him through Hyde Park later that afternoon. In bold, black lettering, he'd written the invitation on the back of his calling card, and turned down the corner to show he'd delivered it personally. There was no reason to believe a lady of quality would have arisen this early, but he felt leaving his card would be far more advantageous to his suit than an impersonal note delivered by messenger. Besides, he had business to attend to at his solicitors and would not be at his residence to receive a reply if Lady Katherine sent one.

Mrs. Butterworth asked him to wait in the library, indicating that room.

"Daisy will find out if the baroness is engaged for the afternoon. I'm certain she will be up, my lord," the housekeeper said, laughing. "Lady Katherine cannot break herself of country hours. Says she likes to hear the birds in the morning, even though we don't have much to offer 'cept sparrows and pidgeons."

Duncan was pleased to hear this bit of information about his intended. An early riser himself, he enjoyed morning rides at his country estates. While Duncan waited, he browsed over a shelf of books. A rustle of cloth made him glance up to see a dainty foot feeling about for the next step of the ladder. A glimpse of leg momentarily left him speechless. Recognition shot like a flash of fire through him. At it again! The most valuable books were kept on the upper tiers. Too

angry to look away, his voice exploded. "By God! Do
you never quit?"

A cannon going off could not have startled Willie
more. She lost her balance, slid down the ladder and
tumbled to the floor. For a moment she sat dazed, her
legs spread in a very unladylike fashion, her skirts
showing a great deal more than was seemly.

Enticed by the sight, Duncan forgot the lecture he
intended to give her. He could not tell if it was guilt or
exasperation written across his magpie's face. Here the
subject of his proposed rehabilitation lay sprawled at
his feet, looking deceptively vulnerable, almost child-
like, her expression unreadable. He wondered if she
felt contrite enough to be willing to listen to him.

He also wanted to know what she had done with his
gold watch. Duncan considered himself a reasonable
man, but his immediate impulse now was to wring a
confession from her. With an effort he restrained himself. Honey attracted faster than vinegar. He would
never have a better opportunity than this to start his
experiment. Patience was the wiser virtue.

Taking a deep breath, he forced a smile and held out
his hand to her. "I did not mean to startle you."

Willie was inclined to ignore his offer, but the alter-
native would be a very awkward attempt to rise. Pulling her skirt down over her knees she reluctantly
accepted his hand.

"That was very unfair of you, my lord," she said,
not feeling in the least charitable.

Willie watched a myriad of emotions play across his
face. Never before had she met anyone with such a
penchant for upsetting people. Perhaps he was prone
to accidents. Heaven knew her own emotions had just
about reached their limits from being tumbled about
by this man. Willie felt the heat rush to her cheeks.

"I agree. Most unchivalrous," he said, flattered to

have made her blush. He could be agreeable when he set his mind to it. "I ask that you accept my apologies." Duncan stooped to pick up the book. Turning it over in his hands, he frowned. Another first edition, a priceless old volume on mathematics. He knew Lady Jacomena wouldn't allow so valuable a book to be removed. Besides, he reasoned, it couldn't possibly be of any interest to a servant, but he handed it back to see if she had the nerve to take it. She did.

"Thank you, my lord," she said.

Brazen chit. Duncan scowled and counted to ten before indicating that she should be seated in one of the straight-backed chairs.

Willie remained standing, her lower lip pushed forward.

"Sit down," Duncan said, doing his best to look pleasant, but feeling he was failing miserably. "Please."

Willie eyed him warily before seating herself on the edge of the chair. What was it about the nobility to look perpetually out of sorts? But he had said "Please." She wriggled into a more comfortable position. "A word about what, your lordship?"

Duncan, trying to ignore the distracting motion of her hips, took the chair opposite her and rubbed his chin. Oh, she was a conniving little piece of baggage all right, throwing the challenge back into his face. He knew the warm affection Lady Katherine exhibited toward her abigail and was saddened to think that loyalty was misplaced. He tried to think of how to tactfully question her.

"Are you happy serving Lady Katherine?"

"Oh, yes, my lord."

"You are satisfied with your living?" he asked.

"Ka . . . Lady Katherine is more than generous and most kind."

"But you like pretty things. You wish to possess them."

Willie looked down at her plain black frock and thought of the lovely gowns she saw at the parties. At Gilfallen, she had practiced and practiced with Katy to help her learn the steps of all the dances. But here in London, Willie had to sit and watch others have all the fun. Katy would return from the balls humming the music until she fell asleep. Willie would then rise and waltz around the dark room imagining herself in the arms of a handsome man. Perhaps it was wicked to have such selfish ideas.

Afraid that her thoughts were being read, she looked up shyly. "Am I in for a scold?"

Duncan sat as far back from her as he could. The desire shining in those violet eyes could make a man forget his purpose, and her devious questions had an unsettling effect. This angered him. What had driven her to such dangerous habits? Upbringing? No, from what Lady Katherine had told him, they had been raised in a castle with servants of the highest standing. Ten was not a high enough count when it came to this vagabond. "Eleven, twelve . . . " he said, between clenched teeth.

Willie did not mean to, but because his manner of speaking reminded her of the gruff matron in the orphanage calling all the girls by number, she giggled.

Duncan was accustomed to having his remarks received with a sobriety befitting the situation. To have this magpie laugh at him stung deeply. "What do you find so amusing?" he demanded.

"When you said the number *twelve,* I thought of a fat old lady."

Duncan's mouth fell open. Taking a deep breath, he sucked in his stomach. Never had he been accused of any resemblance to a fat old lady. In fact, he was quite

proud that he'd not let himself go to flesh like so many
of his cohorts.

Willie's voice mimicked a raspy-voiced harridan.
"Number twelve, 'tis your turn to empty the slush
pots." She then went into gales of laughter. Wiping a
tear from her eye, Willie grinned. "Number twelve.
That was what they used to call me."

"They called you 'twelve' at Gilfallen?" As his own
privileged childhood came to mind, guilt crept into
Duncan's thoughts. How humiliating to be called a
number, and she spoke of slush pots. Was she also
made to feed the swine? There had to be more to her
story than had first been revealed. Sympathy compelled Duncan to take her hands in his.

The warm sensation of his flesh against hers nearly
undid Willie, and she blurted, "Oh, no. That was at
the orphanage before I was taken to Gilfallen."

"You were not born there?"

"I don't know where I was born," Willie said, strug-
gling to recover her wits. She did not know why it
should disturb her to have her hands held, but the
sensation clouded her mind. She explained how Lady
Katherine had been the one to name her Willie.
"Broonie—that is, Miss Abbott—said I came from a
foundling home in Leeds. Lots of little angels, she said,
get left on their doorsteps every day. But at the orphanage a big *twelve* was carved into the wood on the
footboard of my bed. My hair was shorn, and they
gave me a heavy woven garment with a *twelve* embroi-
dered on the front." Willie's expressive hands sketched
an imaginary twelve across her bodice.

Duncan looked at the two rising and falling mounds
under her modest, black dress. Angel? Hah! Devil was
more like it. He swallowed hard and with difficulty
brought his gaze back up to her face.

"I remember when I first put on that scratchy gown,

it reached the floor. When I left, it came to my knees.
I must have been about four, or no more than five."

Duncan gave her hands a squeeze. He was getting a
picture of a world he knew little about, and frankly felt
surprised to find he wanted to hear more.

Unable to suppress the little feeling of shyness, Willie looked down at his fingers completely engulfing
hers. "Then came the magical night when my prince
came and carried me away to the castle in Scotland."
She slowly focused her eyes on Duncan's face.

He looked at her closely. He'd never thought before
that serving girls might dream of princes. Of course, if
she'd overheard some of the fairy tales such as his
sisters read their children, she might pick up such fan-
ciful notions. With a nod he encouraged Willie to go
on.

"I remember a big woman, who always smelled of
oil and sweat, calling me." Willie's voice dropped
again. " 'Come, number twelve. One of the quality
wishes to employ a serving wench.'

"I was lined up with four other girls in front of a
splendidly-dressed gentleman. I was the smallest." As
if bemoaning her shortcomings, Willie removed her
hands from Wakeford's and lifted her skirt to reveal
two tiny feet which barely reached the floor. "I was so
afraid of being found wanting, that I stood on tiptoe
and stretched as tall as I could."

Her little heart-shaped face turned up to his and
that familiar impulse tempted Duncan once more to
take her into his embrace and kiss away the misery he
saw in her eyes. Aghast at the impropriety of what he
was thinking, he folded his arms and sat back.

Willie, her mood changing as swiftly as the English
weather, contorted her features and mimicked the old
lady. With her cheeks puffed out and her lips pursed,

she intoned, " 'Keep your eyes down and don't be uppish.' "

She looked so like a saucy squirrel with nuts stuffed in its mouth, Duncan threw back his head and laughed aloud.

Willie cupped her face with her hands and grinned. "Goodness knows, I tried, but I couldn't resist a peek. He was the most awesome personage I had ever encountered, and the most beautiful. That old lady kept addressing him as 'Your Grace.' " Willie's eyes grew dreamy. *"My* Grace. Isn't that a lovely name?" she said, gazing into Duncan's eyes.

For a moment, he forgot time. Then she spoke again.

"I didn't find out until I arrived at Gilfallen that he was also called the Duke of Hammerfield."

At first, the significance of her statement eluded him. "Ah, I see. Being raised as you were, there are some things you do not understand about our ways here in England."

"Oh, you are right—and I do so want to learn to be a proper lady's maid." She clasped her hands and sat forward. "Only there has been no one to show me how to go about it."

Here was his chance to gain her confidence, he thought, and smiled at her gently. "Then, perhaps, we can help each other."

"How, my lord?"

"You wish to learn to be a proper lady's maid. And if I am to successfully court your mistress, I must know what pleases her. Perhaps we can assist each other. If you will confide in me what Lady Katherine likes or dislikes, I will do my best to try to instruct you in your proper duties."

"Oh, that is a splendid idea," Willie said, clapping

her hands. "I know everything that pleases Ka . . . Lady Katherine."

"First, if you wish to be a good servant, you do not take valuable things which do not belong to you," he said, pointing to the volume in his hands.

"But I was fetching books for Lady Katherine."

This bit of information sent a surge of hope through Duncan. If true, it indicated that the soft-spoken baroness hid interests which paralleled his own. He would be a most fortunate man if she proved as intelligent as she was beautiful. These promising thoughts made him doubly resolve to reform Lady Katherine's maid.

"Did she tell you to come to the library?"

"Not exactly."

"There, you see? A proper lady's maid waits for orders, and she never takes anything which does not belong to her. Do you understand what I am saying?" However, the little abigail's mind seemed to be floating about in the attic, and he was disappointed when he realized she'd missed his frown.

Willie was thinking that if she had to wait for orders from Katy, nothing would ever get done, but she couldn't tell Lord Wakeford that. Nor did she dare mention that it was Katy who took things which didn't belong to her.

Speaking to her as to a child, Duncan lowered his voice, "Now return this book to its place on the shelf. See here inside the front cover, these letters mean it is very old and valuable."

Willie looked at the Roman numerals. "Fourteen thirty-five," she whispered softly. Many of the books in the Gilfallen library had much earlier dates than that, and she had carried them all about the castle. She was of a mind to tell him so, until she noticed the humor had disappeared from his eyes. She judged it wiser to hold her tongue. Hiking up her skirt, she started to climb the ladder.

Duncan, on the other hand, had been dealt another puzzling question. Who had taught her to read Roman numerals? Her voice had been barely audible, but he had heard. This presented another possibility—the little minion could have an educated accomplice.

Willie had climbed no more than three steps on the ladder when she heard a cough behind her.

Duncan looked at the trim little derrière in front of him. "On second thought, mayhaps it would be best to leave the book with the others." He'd no sooner helped her down than Mrs. Butterworth stuck her head in the door.

"My lord, Lady Katherine instructed me to tell you she will be most happy to ride with you this afternoon at four o'clock."

"Thank you, Mrs. Butterworth. Tell Lady Katherine I shall look forward to it." As soon as she had withdrawn, Duncan turned once more to Willie. "Do you have anyone you can talk to about this impulse of yours?" Remembering what Lady Jacomena had said about insubordination of servants, Duncan dismissed her as a confidant. He was not sure about the Scotswoman. "Your mistress, perhaps?" he asked. "She seems a sympathetic and forgiving person."

Panic struck Willie. "Oh, please, your lordship. I beg you, don't mention our conversation to Lady Katherine."

Surely she wasn't afraid of that gentle creature, Duncan thought. However, gaining her trust was uppermost in his mind, so for now he would go along with her whims. Reaching into his pocket, he handed Willie a card. "I want to help you. If at any time you feel tempted . . . that is, you feel the urge to do something naughty and would like to talk to someone, send a message to me at this address." He thought he saw a spark of trust in her eyes. "Is there anything else you'd like to tell me? Any secret which proves to be a burden? Trust me, I shan't condemn you. I want you to think of me as a friend."

"Friend, my lord?"

"Exactly. Now, is there anything you'd like to say to me?"

Her pink lips pursed. "No, I can think of nothing." She thought she heard him counting again, but that was ridiculous. Lord Wakeford turned and walked into the foyer when Willie remembered something and ran after him.

"Wait!" she called.

"Yes?" he asked expectantly.

She stood on tiptoe and whispered, "Lady Katherine is very fond of chocolates with rum cherry fillings."

Duncan, afraid his disappointment threatened to show itself, tried to cover up with a smile. "Thank you for the confidence, Willie." For a few moments, he felt she was going to admit stealing his watch, but now he saw it was going to take longer than he thought to get a confession from her. He only hoped that when she did, it would not be too late to redeem it. Why had he made such a shuttleheaded pledge to Peel?

As soon as the front door closed, Willie hurried back into the library, picked up the books which she had previously chosen, and one by one opened them to their front pages. At the thought of his lordship's kind offer, she felt a warmth in her heart. She wanted more than anything to become a proper lady's maid, so she would do her best to follow his instructions. Leaving only the two first editions, she carried the others upstairs. Opening the door and seeing Katy standing before the mirror, she called, "Look what I've found for you, dear."

*　*　*

That afternoon, exactly one minute before the library clock struck four, Lord Wakeford, a box of chocolates tucked under his arm, stepped down from his fashionable little curricle in front of Dalison Hall. He questioned the wisdom of bringing his newly acquired, untried pair of blacks, but Duncan was eager to impress the baroness. Surely the daughter of a duke was used to seeing the best of horseflesh, and he thought Lady Katherine couldn't help but admire this magnificent pair. As he jumped down to steady the horses, he tossed a coin to the young boy standing there.

"Thank y' guv," the youngster piped. "Me name's Johnny, Lady Jacomena's houseboy."

Duncan handed him the reins. "Thank you, Johnny. Do you think you can handle these devils?"

"Do it all the time, yer lordship," the audacious little fellow said, grabbing the reins of both horses from the earl.

The boy's boastful declaration seemed unlikely, but seeing that the wide-eyed horses seemed to recognize that they were in the hands of someone as stubborn as they, Duncan confidently started up the steps.

Punctuality was not considered a virtue for young ladies of society, so he was considerably surprised when the door was opened by Mrs. Butterworth, and he observed Lady Katherine skipping down the hallway to greet him. The huge brown hen, Miss Abbot, descended the stairs behind her, huffing and puffing, all the while imploring her charge to slow her pace.

While gratified that the object of his attention was as punctual as he, Duncan had to stifle his disappointment when he realized Lady Jacomena obviously didn't trust him to escort her niece without a chaperone. With dismay, he wondered how they all three were to fit into his stylish little carriage. However was he to hoist the heavy older woman up into the high seat without tipping it over?

He need not have worried. One look at the two-wheeled conveyance and Broonie balked. "I will noo set foot in that wee basket," she said, turning back to the housekeeper. "Have one of the girls fetch Willie."

Willie, listening behind the bannisters on the stairway, scurried back to her chamber to get her cape and little black bonnet. Her excitement was so fierce, her fingers fumbled trying to tie a tidy bow under her chin. She was going for a ride in the park!

No more than fifteen minutes had passed after their departure when Mr. Jacob Tellerman, art dealer of considerable repute, presented himself to Lady Jacomena in the green salon. Behind him stood a slightly built young man. His coat, shiny at the elbows, hung loosely on his thin frame. His neckcloth, though of a common fabric, was nonetheless carefully tied, brown hair neatly combed.

"May I introduce my assistant, Mr. Nathaniel Penbrooke," Tellerman said.

"Your servant, my lady." Nathaniel bowed politely, studying the wheeled chair and the proud carriage of the older woman, while the art dealer continued to discuss their purpose. "We have been most interested in seeing the painting Mr. Haydon mentioned."

"It is in the hallway," Jacomena said. "Butterworth, call one of the girls to push my chair."

Nathaniel stepped forward. "Please, allow me."

Jacomena did not usually take to young men. For the most part, she considered they had inflated estimates of their own importance, but Mr. Penbrooke struck her as having none of these traits. In fact, an uncommon sensitivity showed in his soft grey eyes. "As you wish," she said, leaning back. "To the right outside the door."

It did not take long for Tellerman to come to the conclusion that Lady Jacomena had indeed purchased a true Heems and that she should have it restored. He also persuaded her to let him take several of her other oils to be cleaned and revarnished.

While the art dealer supervised his workmen in crating and carrying the paintings to his coach, Lady Jacomena, ever happy to show the collection of artifacts she'd collected from around the world, found an eager and surprisingly intelligent audience in the shy Mr. Penbrooke. Under her pointed inquisition, she discovered he was the grandson of Sir Henry Penbrooke, an acquaintance from her past. A handsome devil, if she remembered correctly. Proud of his large stable, member of the Whip Club, or Four-in-hand, as they called it now. So Mr. Penbrooke was well connected, she mused, but from the shiny, threadbare condition of his clothes, it didn't look as though the young man had a feather to fly with. Puzzles intrigued Jacomena, and she wasn't beyond probing for more information.

"Grandfather married twice and had twelve children," Nathaniel explained in answer to her questions. "Quite truthfully, his generosity far outdistanced his livelihood and by the time he died, his estate was substantially reduced. As the sixth son, my father received only a small legacy and a bit of land in Sussex."

"Sussex, heh?" Lady Jacomena sniffed. "How came you to London?"

"Father sent me to be tutored by Mr. Mims, the vicar's son, in Crawley Down, with the understanding that as soon as I was able, I was to try to obtain a position to help pay for the education of my younger brothers." Nathaniel stopped to watch one of the pictures being wrapped. "Painting and writing poetry were what I liked best, but Father said they were not practical, and he obtained a position for me to keep accounts for the local squire." Nathaniel looked at her shyly. "Then one day I met Mr. Blake in the village."

"Good lord!" Jacomena expostulated, "Blake is the one who said, *The Sussex men are noted fools, and weak in their brain-pan.* Why would he stop in such an out-of-the-way place as Crawley Down?"

A hint of a smile brightened the young apprentice's face, which Jacomena noted transformed Mr. Penbrooke's otherwise plain features into quite pleasing ones.

"He is a friend of the vicar's and stopped on his way to Brighton. Mr. Blake read some of my poems," Nathaniel continued. "I'd given Mr. Mim's a little book which I'd illustrated with watercolors. After seeing it, Mr. Blake suggested I come to London to prove wrong the statement he had made about the Sussex men. It was he who acquired my appointment with Mr. Tellerman and he has encouraged me to write. Even offered to help get some of my poems printed."

"Well, if Blake thinks you have talent—" Jacomena paused. "By the by, I am giving a *conversation,* next week. Blake is coming. I shall send a note around to him asking that he bring you. A reading will be expected. Hope you don't write any of that mishmash you hear at those social soirees."

"Oh, no, your ladyship. I am inspired by men who pen a simple style, such as Wordsworth, and of course, Mr. Blake."

"Good! Bring some of your work. We'll see what you can do." With a flourish of her hand, Jacomena orchestrated the end of their conversation. "Mr. Tellerman is motioning to you. I shall expect you next week."

Before Nathanial could thank her, Jacomena called, "Butterworth, the men have finished. See them out."

Half an hour later a blue-deviled Duncan tooled his curricle off Piccadilly and through the eastern entrance to Hyde Park.

Disappointment had started his downward mood when he found Lady Katherine wasn't seated next to him. Then the doll-sized abigail sandwiched between them began bumping his elbow every time she enthusiastically pointed to a statue or building. This caused him to jerk the ribbons, setting his blacks prancing out of control. His misery increased every time the top of her bonnet tickled his nose when he turned his head to converse with the baroness. Compounding his frustration, the two women were so totally absorbed in their own conversation that they ignored him completely, and he felt his skills as a crack whip weren't being fully appreciated.

It wasn't until they were riding down Rotten Row that he realized the advantage of having the beautiful baroness on the outside in full view of the fashionable crowd, and his good humor returned. Duncan smiled condescendingly toward several young blades who tried to waylay him for an introduction, but his spirited team gave him an excuse not to stop. He thought his *coup* complete until a smart little French cabriolet, pulled by a pretty chestnut mare, blocked his way. A full liveried tiger graced the small platform in the rear. Recognizing the driver immediately, Duncan eyed him warily. Count on the Marquis of Wainscotte to bring back one of the smart little two-wheeled carriages with him from France, Duncan thought. Several years previously, when barely past his majority, the marquis had married a wealthy heiress old enough to be his mother. It took years for her to die, but the word at the clubs was that eleven months ago, as soon as his marchioness had been laid in her grave, he had taken off for the continent.

The marquis raised his hand. "Wakeford, I insist on an introduction."

There was nothing to do but comply. "Wainscotte, may I present Lady Katherine Dalison, Baroness of Gilfallen."

The marquis inclined his head toward the baroness, but it was on Willie that his gaze narrowed. "And the pretty lady in mourning?"

Willie looked up, wide-eyed. He was speaking to her. She had not thought that her dark frock could be taken for widow's crepe.

With silver tongue, his hand over his heart, the marquis continued, "I, too, have just recovered from the passing of a dear one, my lady."

Duncan choked back a smashing jest, but it was the baroness herself who provided the setdown he wanted to give.

"Oh, this is Willie," she said, smiling proudly at her companion, "my abigail and my best friend."

The fleeting flush which colored the marquis's cheeks was worth more than Duncan could hope for. Then like lightning, Wainscotte turned his attention back to Lady Katherine so smoothly that Duncan wondered if he had imagined the marquis suffered at all from his *faux pas.* Duncan looked down at the tiny girl beside him, anticipating her amusement at being taken for one of the quality. But damn if his sense of triumph wasn't erased when he saw the tears glistening in those large, violet eyes. What had the little magpie expected? While trying to cipher her reaction, Duncan

missed the marquis's next statement. Anger pulsed
through him as he heard the baroness ask, "Oh, can I
see them? Are there really white crows?"

"They are partial albinos, my lady. Very rare," the
marquis answered smoothly. "Hyde Park is home to
several."

Duncan glowered at the man. "Can't we see them
from the cart path?"

"Afraid not," Wainscotte replied, alighting from his
vehicle and handing the reins to his coach boy. "Right
now they are in the trees along the banks of the Long
Water section, and they may fly away if we do hurry.
Jimmy will hold the horses for us."

Katy rose unexpectedly, turning her expressive face
to Duncan. "Oh, may we go, my lord? I have never
seen a white crow."

The delicately balanced curricle rocked precariously, and pictures of them all being tipped out onto
their heads shot through his mind.

The baroness, quite used to doing as she pleased,
had already started to step down from the high seat
and was in danger of landing upside down, until Lord
Wainscotte caught her by the waist and lowered her to
the ground.

Duncan would have called the scoundrel out for
such unseemly behavior had he not been fully occupied with controlling his impatient cattle.

The marquis grinned up at the earl. "Surely his
lordship does not want to deprive you of such pleasure, my dear." Laughing, he started down the path on
the southside of the lake, Lady Katherine, her hand
upon his arm, skipped beside him. They were nearly
out of sight among the trees before Duncan was out of
his carriage trying to calm his horses enough to hand
over the ribbons to Wainscotte's tiger. But it was soon
clear to Duncan that his high-spirited blacks were too

much for one small boy. A conclusion that he was certain the marquis had come to much sooner. *Blast the man!*

Willie, trying to keep her balance in the high-wheeled conveyance, looked after Katy and Lord Wainscotte. There was something about the marquis that made her feel uneasy. She wanted to follow them, but her legs were too short to get her out of the curricle without embarrassing herself.

Meanwhile, Duncan's thoughts of murder and mayhem were interrupted by a voice from the carriage.

"I'll be glad to hold the horses for you, if you want to go after Ka . . . Lady Katherine," she offered.

That rang a bark of laughter from Duncan.

Willie glared at him. "That was not called for, my lord." She might be short, but she was not helpless. Hadn't she and Katy raced across the Scottish moors in their little donkey carts? Everyone knew that it was much more difficult to control a unpredictable donkey than a wellbred horse. She reached for the reins in front of her.

"Don't you dare!" he shouted. Duncan dropped his hold on the horses' bridles and leaped for the carriage. Too late. The minute the prime bits of blood felt their freedom, off they raced across the bridge to open fields, scattering all who happened to be their path. He saw the little black bonnet fly off Willie's head. "She'll be killed—if I don't kill her first." Duncan's gaze fell on the marquis's chestnut. Grabbing the reins from the unsuspecting tiger, he leaped upon the horse's back and took off after his runaway curricle, unmindful of the pretty little carriage bouncing wildly behind him.

Anticipating the direction his blacks would take, Duncan managed to intercept them on their turn around the Serpentine, almost back at their starting

point near the bridge. Leaning over, he grabbed a
bridle. Both horses, their sweaty bodies too tired to go
much farther, came to a halt.

Wainscotte's tiger came running up. Duncan leaped
off the chestnut, ran back, and hauled Willie out of his
carriage. Had not they drawn such a crowd of onlookers, there was no telling what he would have done to
her. He looked down into her flushed face, but the fear
he saw in those wide eyes made him pause.

"I lost my bonnet," she whispered. "Lady
Jacomena will have my head."

Duncan listened to the wheezing of his horses and
glanced at the disreputable condition of the other carriage. *Oh, God!* he thought, battling the impulse to
crush her to his chest. *My cattle are fighting for their
breath, Wainscotte's cabriolet will never be the same,
and the brat is concerned about her hat.*

At that moment, they were interrupted by a cheerful
voice, and everyone's attention turned to the pleasing
sight of the lovely baroness running toward them.
"Oh, Willie, I saw the albino crows. Why didn't you
and Lord Wakeford come with us?"

The horror and disbelief which froze the smile on
the marquis's handsome features when he viewed his
carriage made the whole fiasco worthwhile as far as
Duncan was concerned. One wheel on the stylish little
vehicle was bent inward, and a deep scratch made by
contact with some bramble bushes marred the lovely
lacquered finish on the left side.

"Did you have a good time, Wainscotte?" Duncan
asked jovially. "I decided to rest up a bit and let you
do the walking. Hope you enjoyed yourself." With
that, he offered his hand to Katy. "May I help you up,
Lady Katherine? 'Tis time I returned you home."

Once they were seated, Duncan tipped his hat to the

marquis, and smiling broadly, started his team out of the park.

"Oh, Willie," Katy said. "I am so sorry you did not get to see the beautiful paths along the water. It was selfish of me not to have waited. I hope you were not too bored. Why, whatever happened to your bonnet?"

"The wind blew it away."

"Well, never you mind. We will get you another."

The horses, strangely submissive, took a long time to carry them back. After Duncan left the two women at Dalison Hall, he jumped up into his curricle and cracked the whip over his team. The former fiery pair obeyed as meekly as lambs. He threw back his head and laughed. Perhaps when he'd completely reformed the little thief, he'd set her to training his horses.

Chapter Six

On the evening of the Bellrumple ball, Broonie took to her bed with a nasty cold. Poor Broonie, thought Willie. She could not adjust to city hours. All her life she had had a little clock in her head which said to get up and go to bed with the sun.

"All me wheels be rusted into place," she lamented. "They willna change."

This presented an unexpected and unwelcome predicament for Lady Jacomena, for Mrs. Butterworth was already dressing her mistress's hair in preparation for the festivities. When Katy and Willie came to inform her of the Scotswoman's ailment, Jacomena complained, "Time is too short to acquire the services of a respectable, mature chaperone. Wilhemina, I shall have to depend upon you to attend both of us."

"I thought you said Lord and Lady Bellrumple always had an army of servants about, my lady," Mrs. Butterworth commented. "Certainly they will take care of you."

"I can never get the attention of one when I need it," Lady Jacomena said. "Well, Wilhemina, do you think you can do your duty?"

Willie's eyes lit up. "Oh, yes, your ladyship!" She could not believe she was going to the ball.

"Oh, Willie," Katy said. "We must find you a pretty dress."

"Nonsense, Katherine," Lady Jacomena interjected, looking Willie up and down. "She will be going as your chaperone. I agree her clothes are plain, but that may work into my scheme. If anyone inquires about the absence of Miss Abbot, I shall say Wilhemina is a poor relation—a young widow still in mourning, who has agreed to accompany you. It will lend more to her consequence and explain her being so young."

As soon as the girls left, Lady Jacomena settled back down at her dressing table. "Always did dislike Julia Bellrumple," she said, knowing full well her servant never gossiped. "She's nothing but a light-headed peahen, but have to admit, that husband of hers, old Perky, can be a good hoot now and then."

"Now, your ladyship," fussed her housekeeper, trying to hide a smile. "You jest go and have yerself a good time. Don't you be worryin' about a thing. Lady Katherine will do fine."

"I counted on that old woman's stern countenance to deter any of the young bucks from coaxing her outside. Although for the likes of me, I cannot see the concern. Isn't that what these affairs are for, Butterworth? To find a husband? Improper advances only hurry up the process of getting the man to come up to snuff."

"You wait and see," Mrs. Butterworth soothed as she patted her mistress' waves into place. "That lovely young lady is such a toast, she'll be kept busy dancing all evening."

Jacomena knew her problem was not a lack of beaux for her niece, but trying to weed them out so that she could make a comprehensive list of prospects to send to her brother. "Posh and bother! Why did I agree to this farradiddle? I should have told Harcourt to tend to his own business and leave me at peace. I am just too generous." Jacomena chose to ignore her housekeeper's good-natured *Harrumph.* "But we shall prevail," she said, slapping her servant's hand away. "Don't fuss so, Butterworth. If you make me too attractive, I shall turn all the young men's heads from my niece."

In their chambers abovestairs, Willie withdrew Katy's lovely, white ball gown from the clothes press. As she did so, a violet-colored frock, made of fine sarcenet, fell to the floor.

"Oh, dear!" Willie said, quickly placing the white gown upon the bed and picking up the fallen dress. "I have never seen this before. I hope it didn't get soiled."

"I've never worn it because it's too short for me." Katy's expression of indifference turned to delight as soon as she looked at Willie. " 'Tis the color of your eyes. Mayhaps if Aunt Jacomena sees it on you, she will change her mind about you playing the poor widow. I don't know why my father had all those dull black dresses made for you." She fingered the soft, purple gown.

"You take this one."

"I can't do that," Willie said wistfully, but she could not resist the temptation to stand in front of the cheval glass, holding the dress before her.

"At Gilfallen, you always wore my outgrown clothes." Katy laughed. "If you had been the one to grow taller, I would probably have worn your hand-me-downs."

That was true. At Gilfallen they had shared everything. Willie wondered why, since they had come to

London, their lives had turned topsy-turvy. 'Twas a puzzle.

Willie put the gown on the bed and began to dress Katy.

"I like Miss Bellrumple," Katy chattered. "I met her at the Lady Elizabeth's tea, two weeks, ago. Several of the ladies remarked that she and I looked so much alike, we could be sisters. I always wanted a sister," she said. "So it is almost like I shall be among family this evening."

Katy turned to let Willie button the back of her gown. "I don't know why you cannot have a come-out with me, but I suppose it is not done that way." Her eyes fell on the gown and she mused, "Willie, if you wore the purple dress to the ball tonight, every young man there would ask you to stand up with him for a dance."

Willie handed Katy the delicate strip of lace which Lady Jacomena had insisted her niece use to cover an overly generous display of bosom. "I'm afraid her ladyship would not consider it proper attire for me," she answered sadly.

"I don't know why. Miss Bellrumple's personal maid wears quite the loveliest of dresses."

Willie remembered Lady Jacomena's threat to hire a new lady's maid for Katy if Willie's impudent attitude did not make a turnabout. "Most likely she is one of those French women your aunt spoke of. One who lost her family and fortune in the war with Napoleon."

"What does that signify? She is an orphan like you," Katy said.

"Miss Bellrumple's maid did not come from a foundling home. She has a name. Antoinette DeBoyer. They address her as Mademoiselle DeBoyer."

Katy thought on that a moment. "I'll be your family. We can call you, Miss Willie."

"That will not do, dear. A baby is given the name of the family it is born into. That makes it legal." Willie knew that Katy would not understand what she had read in the old law books she had found at Gilfallen. Instead, she thought of what she had blurted out to Mr. Teagardner in the library. "My name is Miss Winkie." She wondered if she could be charged with taking a false name. It was the first thing that had come to her mind before Lord Wakeford held her to his chest. A little shiver went through her as she thought of the long, lean lines of his body, and for a moment she completely forgot the purple sarcenet.

Katy looked at her strangely. "Well, keep the dress anyway," she insisted. "You can wear it here in our room whenever you like. Aunt Jacomena never comes abovestairs. If she doesn't see you, she cannot criticize."

Picking up the silk gown, Willie held it to her cheek, then carefully hung it in the clothes press before dressing Katy's hair.

"I still do not see why you have to go about looking like a blackbird, while I have so many lovely ensembles," Katy fussed. "I cannot wear them all in an age." However, she forgot her complaint when one of the twins came to tell them their carriage had arrived to take them to the ball.

As the three women were helped up into the Dalison family coach, Lady Jacomena addressed Willie. "You will have to fetch and carry for the both of us this evening, gel."

"I shall do my best, your ladyship," Willie said, with more assurance than she felt, wondering how in the world she could cope without Broonie.

Mumbling to herself, Lady Jacomena accepted her cane and settled back into the soft squabs. Even if Miss Abbot had not fallen ill at the last moment, it

would still have been up to her to attend. After all,
Julia Bellrumple had been an acquaintance at boarding school. Took her two seasons to catch her husband, a baron, in the parson's trap. Percival was an
ineffectual blunderbuss, but exceedingly wealthy.
Each year, they gave one of the most sought-after balls
of the year, which Jacomena seldom attended, but this
being the come-out for their only daughter, Helena,
she could not very well refuse the invitation. She acknowledged that her presence at such a prestigious
affair would lend a great deal of credibility to her
niece's acceptance by the *ton*.

The Bellrumple Ball was always an insufferable
crush and once inside, Jacomena expected she would
have to find a seat and sit for the entire evening. The
ballroom was on the second floor, opened to terraced
balconies and therefore impossible to take her wheeled
chair. Now that her mind was set, Jacomena looked
forward to being miserable all evening.

Katherine's abigail was another thorn in her side.
The gel was far too young and pretty to lend significance to her niece's station. Jacomena was not so blind
to have missed several young dandies' glances which
strayed toward the little maid when they called at
Dalison Hall. A gel's looks were none of her own
doing, Jacomena admitted—and she could not fault
the maid's devotion to her mistress—but she still had
her doubts about the lowly beginnings of her niece's
maid.

As she'd anticipated, all the streets leading to the
Bellrumple residence were backed up for blocks.
Young boys ran along the sidewalks carrying lanterns
to light the way. A reception at the royal residence,
Carlton House, could not have been more popular.
Indeed it was rumored that the Prince Regent himself
might make an appearance.

Once inside the grand mansion, the receiving line was long, extending down the stairs from the upper floors. As soon as their little party entered the great hall, Lady Jacomena banged her cane on the marble floor and clearly made it known that she would not be kept waiting. Two footmen carried her up in a chair and took her immediately to the head of the crowd.

Candles from the great chandeliers hanging overhead glowed down upon thousands of flowers, while the ostentatious costumes of the *haute ton* echoed the colors of the frescoed ceilings. To Willie it was a fairy land, and the dazzling light blanketed the chattering assembly. While Lady Jacomena and Katy greeted their hosts, Willie stood to one side, near enough to catch their conversation.

"Oh, but you must call me Helena," the young debutante insisted, "for I do hope we are to be the best of friends."

The two tall girls were indeed much alike with their blonde curls and white dresses. Only instead of the simple strand of pearls and eardrops, which Jacomena insisted were proper for Katy to wear, Willie was certain that Miss Bellrumple was bedecked with every bit of the family jewels which were not already hanging from her mother's neck and ears. In addition to the diamond and emerald necklace and eardrops, a matching bracelet dangled from each of Helena's wrists.

Trouble was written everywhere Willie looked. Oh my! She knew she dared not let Katy out of her sight tonight. The flickering lights challenged the glitter of the largest collection of jewels she had ever seen. All of society, it appeared, were determined not to leave any of their treasures at home.

As Lady Jacomena emerged from the receiving line, she refused to relinquish her wraps to a servant, but

sent Willie with them to one of the rooms set aside for
such purpose. "Remember where you put them," she
said. "I may want you to fetch something for me
later."

Willie scurried on the errand and returned in time to
accompany the two ladies into the Grand Ballroom.
As soon as Lady Jacomena was seated, gentlemen
surrounded her, pleading for an introduction or the
promise of a dance with her niece.

Only when Mr. Trunnion and John Teagardner
made themselves known, did a smile appear on Lady
Jacomena's face. Afraid Mr. Teagardner would recognize her as the woman in the library, Willie ducked her
head and stood behind Katy until they moved on. But
she had overheard Mr. Trunnion express his disappointment that Miss Abbot had not attended, and
Willie reminded herself to be sure to tell Broonie.

"Bedlam cannot be worse!" Lady Jacomena complained to Willie. "I could be dying, and you would
not see me in this zoo. If I want you, I shall wave my
cane in the air. Like this!" Her ladyship promptly
raised her stick like a sword, knocking the wig off the
head of an unsuspecting footman. Jacomena shot him
an impatient look. "Make certain you find a seat
where you can see my signal, gel."

"Yes, your ladyship," Willie said, finding it terribly
hard not to laugh at the befuddled footman's predicament. She could understand now why the servants
avoided Lady Jacomena.

Duncan arrived at the Bellrumple residence well
before the fashionable hour though it was later than he
wished, for he was well aware of his promise to stand
up with Lady Katherine for the first set.

When he entered the ballroom a few minutes later,

the musicians had begun the theme for the opening dance. Duncan made his way directly toward the group surrounding the tall, blonde baroness, pausing only to give his regards to Lady Jacomena.

Willie waited until Lord Wakeford bowed to Katy before thinking of leaving. A sense of safe haven surrounded the earl, and she felt Katy would be in good hands. "I shall be near your aunt," Willie whispered.

Eyes shining, Katy clasped her hands and kissed her on the cheek. "You'll sit where I can see you, won't you?"

"Yes, dear," Willie said, patting her hand, all the while keeping a lookout for the tip of the cane waving above the crowd. "Your aunt is signalling me. I must go."

Duncan took Lady Katherine's gloved hand to lead her out, but she would not turn aside. It disturbed him that her attention should be addressed elsewhere for he expected to be the focus of admiration to any lady he escorted. He let his gaze follow hers and saw that it was her little abigail whom she watched. As the maid reached Lady Jacomena's side, she straightened her black lace cap and gave a twist to her skirt, sending a disturbing heat throughout Duncan's body.

Lady Katherine waved, but it wasn't until the little magpie waved back, that the baroness gave her attention over to him.

"It isn't fair, is it?"

"Fair, my lady?" Duncan's thoughts were brought back abruptly to the woman beside him. "I don't believe I quite understand," he said, escorting her to her place in the set.

"It isn't Willie's fault that she has no family," Katy said, turning her blue eyes up to him. "As soon as I am married, I am going to adopt Willie and give her a come-out. Then she can wear pretty clothes and find herself a husband. Do you think I shall have to wear black if I chaperone her? I really do not like dark colors."

The music had started which saved Duncan from making a reply, for he could think of none.

Standing among the potted ferns where she could keep a sharp eye on both Lady Jacomena and Katy, Willie drew a deep breath. Her feet ached fiercely and she could not have been more tired than if she danced every set like Katy.

"Please give me a rest, Lord," she prayed. But a second later Lady Jacomena's cane flashed in the air. Willie hurried to her side. "Yes, my lady?"

"Took you long enough, gel. I will be playing whist in the gold salon. Fetch me a couple of footmen to move my chair."

Willie obeyed. While she supervised Lady Jacomena's removal, she also tried to keep a sharp eye on Katy. What was she to do? Now, she would have to run back and forth between the salon and the ballroom. Oh, if only Broonie were here!

However, Katy was so busy whirling about the dance floor, set after set, that Willie began to think her fears were foolish.

Relief came when Katy was asked by Miss Bellrumple, who seemed set on making a bosom friend of the baroness, to retire to a small alcove for a bit of refreshment. "It will give our weary feet a rest," she said, laughing, as she slipped an arm around Katy's waist.

As soon as she had asked a footman to bring over his tray of refreshing drinks to the young ladies' table, Willie sank into a chair alongside the wall and closed her eyes, thankful for some respite.

A few moments later, a servant tapped her on the shoulder.

"Lady Jacomena says she wishes you to attend her, miss."

Willie jumped up and hurried into the salon.

"Where have you been?" she demanded. "Been waving this infernal cane for five minutes. With all these ridiculous head dresses, you cannot see my signal when I want you. Go to the cloak room and bring my red lace kerchief from my inside pocket. I shall tie it on the end of my cane like a flag." Willie was halfway to the door when Lady Jacomena called out, "Wait! Before you go upstairs, tell Lady Katherine I wish to speak to her."

On her way past the alcove, Willie gave the message to Katy and showed the girls to the salon where her aunt was playing cards. It took no more than a matter of minutes for Willie to run upstairs, but when she returned to the card room, Katy was nowhere to be seen. She handed Lady Jacomena her scarf and hurried by the alcove to the ballroom. No trace of her in either place.

It was then Willie heard the scream.

"The bracelet was on my wrist but a short time ago," Miss Bellrumple's high-pitched words carried over the cacophony of voices. "I know I had it on when Lady Katherine's abigail led us into the card room."

An alarm rang in Willie's head. Many of the guests stopped dancing, but Lord Bellrumple insisted the music continue. While servants and many of the guests searched for the missing jewelry, Willie investigated outside on the terrace and glanced down into the garden below. Where could Katy be? Then, recalling the room on the upper floor set aside for the ladies to refresh themselves, Willie scurried up the stairs. With a sigh of relief, she found Katy primping in front of a looking glass.

"Don't you ever go off by yourself like that again," Willie scolded.

She was so thankful to find Katy safely away from the trouble below, that it wasn't until she heard a collective gasp that she realized there were others in the room.

"Well I never!" one of the ladies said. "If a servant spoke to me in such a disrespectful manner she'd be out on the street in no time."

" Tis a poor relative, I hear, that Lady Jacomena has taken in out of the cold. Tch, tch. And Lady Katherine is such a sweet child."

"Ill-bred and ungrateful, I would say."

The realization that her outburst had been observed by several ladies of the *ton* sealed Willie's lips from further utterances, but Katy was not so observant. "I'm sorry, Willie," she said, her eyes downcast.

"I didn't mean to ring a peal over you, dear, but you must not run about unattended." Willie waited for the other women to leave the room. "Now," she said, fluffing up the sleeves of Katy's dress, "stand up and let me see how you look."

Obediently, Katy rose.

"Your ribbons are playing peek-a-boo down your bodice," Willie said, knowing full well that a reminder of the earlier episode when Lady Jacomena insisted her niece cover her bosom, would tease Katy back into a lighter mood. "That will never do now, will it?"

Katy looked down. She giggled and made an effort to straighten her bodice.

"Let me do that," Willie said.

Katy shrieked and tried to cover her chest, but Willie was quicker. Brushing Katy's hands aside, she reached unceremoniously down the front of her dress and pulled the laces out. With them came the unmistakable glitter of Miss Bellrumple's diamond bracelet.

"I couldn't help it," Katy said, contritely. "It sparkled so."

Her heart pounding, Willie stuffed the jewelry down the neck of her own dress, just as another group of women entered the room. One was Lady Elizabeth.

"Lady Katherine," she said. "There is a gentleman, a Mr. Trunnion, below with your aunt. Says he has permission to escort you and Lady Jacomena into supper."

Katy turned questioning eyes to Willie.

Willie knew she must plant the bracelet somewhere where it would be found and therefore thought to have fallen off Miss Bellrumple's wrist accidentally. It was imperative that she get Katy situated as quickly as possible. Knowing she would be safe from mischief with Mr. Trunnion and her aunt, Willie nodded her approval.

"We shall talk about this later. Come, dear, you must not keep your escort waiting."

It was midnight and Lord Wakeford watched the guests head for the dining room. Although the Bellrumples' banquets were known to be feasts worthy of a king, Duncan was preparing to leave, for the prospect of overeating did not tempt him. Since he had already danced twice with the baroness, his serious intentions toward that lady were most assuredly known. He saw no further reason to stay and had asked a servant to fetch his cloak.

However, he found his thoughts did not dwell long on Lady Katherine, but kept returning to the strange antics of her maid. He had caught glimpses of her all evening, which had not been hard to do. She did not sit sedately upon a chair with the other chaperones, but flitted about among the throng like a field mouse scurrying in and out of a field of cornstalks. Didn't the little minion understand that there were several servants about to do the bidding of the guests? No, he could see she really did not know, as she put it, *how to go about being a proper lady's maid.* Duncan would make it his first priority the next time he called at Dalison Hall, to instruct her further on some of the finer points of serving.

Now as he waited for his cloak in the empty hallway, he chanced to see that very same character, peeking into the gold salon in the most peculiar way. She did not return, but skittered through and out onto the terrace. What mischief was the little magpie up to now?

He followed her to find out . . .

It was Willie's intention to take the bracelet directly into the card room, but having entered, she found it still occupied by a table of players intent on finishing their hand. Slipping out to the balcony, she hid in the shadows beneath the casement window where they sat. As soon as the foursome left, she would enter and leave the bracelet. Surely a servant would find it and return it to Miss Bellrumple.

Her patience soon paid off and the players exited. But she saw the dark figure of a man silhouetted in the doorway, turning this way, then that. She decided her only recourse to get back inside the room unnoticed was for her to go through the window. The sill was not so high that she entertained any qualms about her ability to enter easily from the outside. She and Katy had climbed into enough windows at the castle. Clutching the bracelet in her fist, she threw one leg up and over the sill, and was about to leap, when her skirt caught, leaving her dangling half in and half out of the room. She heard a ripping sound and had not strong hands caught her from behind, she would have pitched forward onto her head. The muffled voice behind her ear was strangely familiar.

"Willie, Willie, what am I going to do with you?"

She felt herself being lifted back out the window. The sensation so befuddled her, she dropped the bracelet inside the room. But she knew he had seen it, because he made a fruitless grab for the jewelry nearly squashing her in the attempt. "You won't believe it if I say I found it on the floor?"

Still holding her down, Duncan peered helplessly over her shoulder at the rosewood drum table beneath the window. The glittering gems lay draped over the gilt brass mount covering one of its splayed legs.

"No!" he growled. This was outside of enough, he thought. Perhaps the magistrates were right. A professional criminal could not be rehabilitated. He should report her, but he hated the thought of failure, and he was not a man to give up a quest so easily. He would have to double his efforts to reform her.

Just when he thought he would have to crawl through the window to redeem the bracelet, two chattering maids entered the room with brooms and baskets.

The devil take it! "We've got to get out of here before they see you," Duncan said.

"My skirt is still hooked on something—" Willie didn't get to finish before she heard a final rip, and she was pulled with such force against his lordship, they tumbled onto the flagstone.

"Coo, what was that?" came a voice from inside the room.

"It come from over here by the window. I'll be a beggar! Will y'look at this?"

The speakers were no more than a few inches above Duncan's head. Hunkering down, his arm still around the little abigail, he flattened himself against the wall underneath the window. Pulling Willie up against him, he hoped to God she had sense enough to keep quiet.

"Look what I found," came the same voice from inside the room.

"Lud, if it ain't Miss Bellrumple's bracelet. Won't she be 'appy to be gettin' that back."

"The master is such a goodun, he'll give us a reward for finding the young mistress's trinket, now, won't he?" The voices slowly faded away.

Chapter Seven

Held in the hard embrace of Lord Wakeford's arms with his lips whispering, "Shh," in her ear, Willie felt an ecstasy she had never known before.

Duncan let out a sigh of relief. He was safely out of that net, but he found himself faced with another problem. The little chit was practically sitting in his lap and he heard shuffling footsteps coming toward them. "Oh, hell!" he said under his breath, and rising quickly, pushed her back into the vines covering the wall.

Instead of hiding her from detection, her resultant, "Ouch!" only pinpointed their position.

It was not difficult for Duncan to identify the rotund silhouette of John Teagardner against the backdrop of the lanterns.

Obviously startled by the woman's squeal, the short-sighted man yanked out his quizzing glass and peered right into Willie's face.

"Oh, I say, it is Miss Winkie, is it not?" He then looked past her to her companion. "Ho! 'Tis you again, your lordship."

"Evening, Teagardner," Duncan said, with resignation. "What on earth are you doing out here?"

"Don't dance, y'know, so took a walk in the garden.

Got lost in the maze. Hope I haven't missed dinner."

The earl tried to keep up with his neighbor's hop-scotching excuses. "You won't miss it, if you hurry," he said wearily, but much to his annoyance, Teagardner didn't move. Knowing the young man's propensity for being easily distracted, Duncan said, "John, I do believe I heard your mother asking for you."

Willie saw the man's mouth form a silent *Oh*. "By Jove, now that you mention it—I did promise to escort her into the dining room."

Duncan grasped at the straw. "Good, good. Give her my warmest regards."

Teagardner bowed. "Indeed, will do that. Thank you for mentioning it. Well, won't disturb you any longer. Miss Winkie. Wakeford," he said cheerfully, before making his way back into the house.

When Teagardner had disappeared, Duncan, maintaining a strong grip on her arm, pulled Willie into the card room. His eyes sternly rebuking her, his voice ominous, he warned, "Now, my little magpie, we are going to have a talk, and I expect some honest answers from you."

Willie gazed up at him with wide, deceptively innocent eyes.

Before she could answer, a footman stepped into the room and exclaimed, "Ah, there you are, Lord Wakeford."

Exasperated, the earl sighed. "Yes, Parsons, what is it?"

"Excuse me, your lordship, but I brung your cloak as you asked."

"Thank you," Duncan replied, reining in his temper with difficulty. He released his hold on Willie to accept the voluminous coat. In an instant she'd twisted away from him.

She stepped around the footman, dropped a swift

curtsy, and said sweetly, "Good evening, your lord-ship."

Short of knocking the servant over and chasing after her, there was nothing Wakeford could do but watch her disappear down the hall.

"Bloody hell," he murmured.

During the days which followed, the social activities at Dalison Hall continued unabated. Broonie recovered from her indisposition, and since Katy was putting forth extra effort to be good, Willie saw no reason to inform the old nurse of their near disaster at the ball.

A steady stream of suitors called. Some were admitted, some not. Passionate letters arrived daily declaring undying love for the beautiful Lady Katherine. Flowers filled every vase in the house, and each time the bell rang, the silver salver overflowed with new invitations. The household staff were kept so busy attending the door and providing refreshments for the visitors that their regular duties were neglected.

"I cannot do m'job and be running hither and yon all the time," Mrs. Butterworth finally complained.

"It's just like my brother to shuffle all the responsibility onto someone else's shoulders," Jacomena remonstrated.

"What we need, my lady, are extra servants," Mrs. Butterworth proclaimed.

"More bodies will only clutter up the house," Jacomena grumbled, but by week's end an assistant housekeeper was added and old Tom was fitted with a fine black suit and permitted in the front of the house to answer the door. A registry office sent over a social secretary to help Katherine write her acceptances and sort out her busy schedule.

In the meantime, Jacomena sat in her room composing a list of men whom she thought her brother would consider worthy of marrying his daughter. As yet, Harcourt had not asked for a report on Katherine's progress in London. But, knowing her brother's wily ways, she suspected he had his own netherworld of informants. Of course, Jacomena kept a separate list of her own, which was nothing like the one she prepared for her brother. Harky's priorities had never been hers.

Harky, she thought. Odd how that old nickname came to mind—she hadn't called her younger brother that in years, not since he was a little tyke stumbling after her and Adrian. She laid her pen down, looking back into that old book of her past. Adrian had christened their brother Harky. Jacomena had called him less affectionate names—pest, nodhead, nincompoop. She gave a bark of laughter. She'd had a good vocabulary even as a child, but she'd had scant patience in those days—not like Adrian, who'd treated everyone with an unruffled aplomb. Thoughts of her cherished brother stirred the pain of his loss. Lord, she missed him.

But this was no time for sentimentality. Picking up her pen, Jacomena determinedly concentrated on her lists. There was only one *nonpareil* whose name appeared on both. Duncan Fairchild, practical young man not given to frivolity. In fact, the more she considered, the more the earl appeared the ideal solution. Business came first with him, and yet his behavior was quite propitious toward Katherine. Fortunately for the woman he chose, he would certainly not be a husband who was underfoot all the time. Jacomena thought him well-looking enough, and he circulated as easily with the intelligentsia as he did with *le beau monde.* Yes, indeed, he did have all the desired qualifications.

Therefore, on Wednesday, when Duncan arrived to take Katherine for a drive about Hyde Park, and mentioned that he would be leaving London on the weekend to attend to affairs in Cambridgeshire, Jacomena knew she had to act swiftly if she was to bring him up to snuff. She told him to come to her gathering at Dalison Hall that evening.

"Katherine will sing," she said, with dictatorial authority.

Her niece's lack of a reaction to that statement worried Jacomena, but she decided to save her frown until their guests left. Was there no substance to the child? Thus far, Katherine had shown no particular interest in fashion or parties, but obligingly accepted whatever was planned for her. While disappointed in the child's indifference to the *conversations* she held, Jacomena was surprised that she showed no marked preference either toward carriage rides in the park, shopping or balls.

That evening, punctually at the designated hour, Duncan ascended the steps to the blue door of Dalison Hall. He was becoming accustomed to Lady Jacomena's acrimonious tongue, and had taken no offense at what amounted to a summons. He'd planned nothing more exciting than spending a dull evening at one of his clubs, so obliging her was no hardship. More guests were arriving behind him, and after a short exchange of pleasantries with Lady Katherine, he drifted off to stand by the window observing the interesting variety of people as they assembled.

Duncan decided that over all others, the baroness' clear, sweet voice was in itself a delight to the ear, but he was finding that they had very little to say to each other. After a few minutes of conversation, he found himself at a loss. She seemed to hold no personal opinions. Perhaps that was best, he thought. Heaven forbid he should have a chatterbox for a wife.

"Mr. Penbrooke, may I present my niece, Lady Katherine, Baroness of Gilfallen," Lady Jacomena said when that gentleman arrived with Mr. Blake.

Nathaniel stepped forward, tugging at his too-short sleeves, more conscious than ever of his mean coat and common shoes. One look into Lady Katherine's eyes and a peal of church bells chimed in the young man's head, blocking out all thoughts except that of the lovely girl before him.

In that instant, Nathaniel Penbrooke lay down his heart, and he knew he would never recover it again. He dared not speak, for his bumbling tongue would only make him appear more foolish than he felt, so he bowed low over her gloved hand and said nothing.

When he was called upon to recite, Nathaniel agonized over the poem he had chosen for the occasion. He even doubted it was his voice which spoke the words. The applause and the kind praise heaped on him afterwards were nothing compared to the heavenly music he heard when Lady Katherine took her place beside the pianoforte and began to sing.

Katy looked at the young man shifting back and forth on long legs. His lips were silent, but his eyes spoke a message which she had never seen before. He looked like none of the young dandies or sophisticated gentlemen who had danced attendance on her the last few weeks. As she watched him walk away, she wondered curiously where Mr. Penbrooke was from. As she performed, Katy searched the faces for the one who had piqued her interest. When he'd read aloud his poem about the birds of the fields, she, for the first time in her life, made a decision without asking for Willie's advice. She was going to find a way to see Mr. Penbrooke again.

After her solo, the group of admirers surrounding Lady Katherine encouraged Duncan to remain where he was. She embodied everything he pictured a perfect countess to be, an accomplished musician, gracious, lovely to behold. No man would tire of seeing her every day, or so he told himself. But no matter how many times he said it, the thought of marriage to her left him strangely reluctant.

As the baroness now stood with a small group, Duncan's eyes strayed to her shadow, the little abigail, who always seemed to be nearby. He had observed on previous occasions how Lady Katherine often turned and conferred with her maid before making a decision or voicing an opinion. Judging from the amount of books he'd seen the abigail take to the baroness, she had to be well read in a wide variety of subjects. Her dependence on her servant remained a mystery to Duncan, an intriguing one. This evening, though, Lady Katherine seemed oddly distracted. She listened politely to Sir Andrew Barkley, who was dominating the conversation. The discussion had proceeded from the Elgin marbles to Greek mythology, a subject Duncan never pursued with any great enthusiasm.

But it was the little minion who continued to draw his attention. Whereas the baroness' gaze wandered, Willie was a picture of rapture, hanging on to every word Sir Andrew spoke. Duncan laughed inwardly when he saw her pretty head nod in agreement, her delicate mouth mimicking everything the old codger decried in his loud, trumpeting voice. Barkley, in Duncan's opinion, was a fat walrus who, having made one trip around the Mediterranean Sea, considered himself a world traveler.

Sir Andrew twirled his mustache and with a superior nod, said, "Lady Katherine, you remind me of a statue of Hera I saw in Greece. Tell me, have you found your match yet?"

Katy looked at him blankly and blushed.

"The husband of the queen of the gods, my dear," he said condescendingly. "Of course, you would not know, but it is Jupiter of whom I speak."

"Of course," Katherine answered, lowering her gaze.

Willie looked up in surprise. It was not like Katy to mix up her mythical characters, for she loved the stories of the ancient gods and goddesses. "He's wrong," she whispered to Katy without thinking. "You know Hera's husband was Zeus. Jupiter was a Roman god."

She had not meant for her words to be heard by any other, but Sir Andrew, his face a florid red, stared at her in astonishment.

"Step forward, gel," Lady Jacomena ordered.

Still sputtering, the man looked down at Willie. "Why 'tis only . . . a servant. How impertinent of it!"

Indignation tempered Willie's backbone into a rod of steel. She had never been referred to as an 'it,' before. Even a number was better than that. Looking him straight in the eyes, her little chin jutting forward, she said, "Is it impertinent to speak the true facts, sir? Jupiter's wife was Juno."

The walrus puffed out his chest. "You dare to contradict me?"

"Wilhemina, I've warned you before to mind your manners," Lady Jacomena said ominously. "I knew it was a mistake when Katherine insisted you attend her this afternoon. Apologize to Sir Andrew for your offensive behavior, then leave the room. I shall tend to you later."

Willie stuck out her lower lip. "Beg pardon, sir. I apologize for my impertinence in correcting you," she repeated, then ran from the room.

Duncan saw the startled look upon Lady Katherine's face. Fearing she intended to chase after her abigail, he stepped quickly to her side. Placing a restraining hand on her arm, he said quietly, "Better that you don't anger your aunt more than she is, my dear."

Miss Abbot, too, he noticed, had hurried across the room and positioned herself between Lady Jacomena and her niece.

Katherine looked up into Duncan's face, then at her nurse. "But Willie is always right."

"Aye, that she is," Broonie cooed. "Don't ye be worryin' yirself about her comin' to harm," she continued, frowning her darkest at Sir Andrew until the man seemed to shrivel to half his size. "Broonie will see to that."

Katherine seemed soothed by the big woman's answer, but Duncan had no doubts that Lady Jacomena meant to carry out her threat. Trying to assess what had just happened, he looked toward the doorway. Willie was gone. He speculated that his redemption of her might never get started. Did he dare speak on her behalf or reveal his plans for her turnabout to Lady Jacomena? Unless there was divine intervention, he had the feeling that the little abigail's employment in the Dalison household was about to end. The thought sent a surge of sadness through him.

Surprisingly, the altercation had not attracted as much attention as Duncan feared. He found intellectuals to be of a singular mind when it came to concentrating on their own fields of thought, and the incident soon passed over, but a sense of foreboding clung to him. He stayed close to Lady Katherine until a few guests began to take their leave.

Across the room, Mr. Blake spoke to Nathaniel. "Will you fetch our hats, Mr. Penbrooke. I would like one more word with Mr. Haydon before we go."

Nathaniel entered the long hallway, but not seeing any sign of the butler, proceeded to the library.

Lady Katherine, noticing the poet's departure, asked to be excused for a few minutes, and hastily went after him.

Duncan contemplated following her . . . to what? He didn't want to admit his thoughts were more on whether or not the little minion, Willie, had obeyed her ladyship's instructions to go to her room, than where Lady Katherine was going.

Willie, in defiance of Lady Jacomena's orders, had not gone directly to her room. She stayed in the great hallway. Trying to shake her fidgets that Broonie would have to tend her charge alone, she studied the statues of the Greek philosophers. Then she saw Katy, in a most suspicious manner, slip into the library. Katy would be upset, of course, and Willie knew that when the baroness was nervous or overly excited, she would be apt to *borrow* something. Fearful that her charge intended to search through the guests' coats, Willie followed her into the library, and slid behind a statue near the door.

Katy was seated on a sofa watching Mr. Penbrooke search the table covered with hats. Willie decided to stay out of sight.

"You must be a noted writer, Mr. Penbrooke," Katy said breathlessly.

"Oh, no, my lady. I am employed by Mr. Tellerman, the art dealer."

"But your poem . . . it was so extraordinary."

A flush broke out on the young man's cheeks. "Thank you, my lady. It's kind of you to say so, and I must thank Lady Jacomena for allowing me to read."

Katy looked at him with unconcealed admiration. "Oh, no, Mr. Penbrooke, it is she who should thank you."

Nathaniel shook his head. "I am much indebted to her, and to Mr. Blake for their encouragement. He is even using his influence to see that some of my work is published."

Katy nodded solicitously. "There now, see—it is as I said. I am certain 'twill not be long before you are famous and quite wealthy."

The young man paused, while he made a serious production of separating one of the hats from the others. "I'm afraid writing will not make me rich. Poets are paid little for their efforts, and even with the generous salary Mr. Tellerman pays me, I am obliged to send most of my wages home to help defray the expense of my brothers' education. By the time I pay for my board and room, there is little left."

"How honourable you are, Mr. Penbrooke. Your family must be very proud of you."

He turned and stared at her, brows raised in surprise. "What? For helping my brothers?"

"Yes, that, and for the way you write poetry. I . . . I admire poets. Robert Burns stayed at our castle one time and wrote a poem under a tree while looking down over the Loch of Tay. They say he became very well known."

"Tell me about it," Nathaniel said, his face breaking into a shy smile.

Katy tried, but she couldn't speak past the sudden lump in her throat. Silent tears brimmed in her eyes and ran down her cheeks.

"Dear Lady Katherine, whatever did I do to distress you?" Nathaniel cried, so overcome with emotion he knelt before her and offered his handkerchief.

"Oh, Mr. Penbrooke, do not think it something you said." Katy sniffed, taking the handkerchief and blowing her nose. "Really, you have been most kind. It's just . . . when I talk about Gilfallen, something happens to me." Looking at his kneeling figure, she patted the sofa beside her and asked, "Isn't your position quite uncomfortable?"

"It is some," he said quite seriously. Rising, he brushed off his breeches, then seated himself on the edge of the couch.

"Do you ever get homesick?" she asked.

"Aye," he said. "I miss Mama and Papa, and my six brothers and sisters. They're a lively bunch, and the city gets very lonely."

"Your poem about the birds arriving in spring was lovely," Katy said. "It reminded me of the meadows near Gilfallen." Her eyes were wide with unshed tears. "Oh, Mr. Penbrooke, I don't think anyone else would understand, but I do so want to go home."

"Please don't cry again," he pleaded. "Tell me exactly what you see, for I would like to envision it. Do the birds sing as prettily as in England? What do the pine forests and the sun on the earth smell like? Which fairy tales do you think of when you picture Gilfallen Castle?" Quite forgetting himself in his breathless concern, the young man moved closer. "I beg you, leave out nothing. I shall write you an ode and when you feel sad and long for your home, you can read it—or sing it to a tune you know—and picture yourself there. Perhaps it will ease the pain."

"Would you do that for me?" Katy said, placing her hand on his.

Nathaniel looked at her delicate fingers. If he could enshrine his hand and never again allow it to touch anything mortal, he would. But Nathaniel had a sensible side, and although reason was nearly impossible for him at that moment, he knew he could never hope that she would love him as he loved her.

Hearing the voices outside in the hallway, Willie coughed and stepped into view. Katy blushed, and the spell was broken.

Nathaniel jumped to his feet, just as Mr. Blake stuck his head into the room.

"Are you ready, Mr. Penbrooke?"

Nathaniel grabbed their hats and sped through the door, not daring to look back.

No sooner had he gone than Broonie appeared. A sigh of relief escaped her when she saw Willie standing guard. "There you are, lamb," she said to Katy. "Come, Lady Jacomena wishes you to say goodbye to your guests."

Clutching Mr. Penbrooke's handkerchief as if it were a rare jewel, Katy did her nurse's bidding.

Curiosity finally overcame Duncan's sense of propriety and a short time later, he made his way from the drawing room in time to see Miss Abbot nudging the baroness toward where he stood. At the other end of the great hallway, the butler was opening the door for Mr. Blake and Mr. Penbrooke to make their exit. All seemed normal. The earl smiled at Lady Katherine as she passed and was flattered with a becoming blush. He had turned to re-enter the salon when from the corner of his eye he spied a dark-clothed figure emerge from the library. Willie! Her gaze darted furtively this way and that.

Hidden by the tall statues and potted plants alongside the wall, Duncan knew she hadn't seen him, for she made a dash for the stairs. *The little minx,* he thought as his arm shot out to catch her.

"My lord!" Willie gasped, looking up with guilt written all over her flushed face.

Too furious to think what he was doing, Duncan grasped both her hands and held them up.

Willie's mouth fell open. He still held her wrists firmly, but it was her lips, only a few inches from his, which caught his attention. Again, Duncan was forced to fight the terrible desire to kiss her. He forced himself to shift his gaze to her hands. Empty. Relief flooded through him, and steeling his most improper emotions, he said in as gruff a tone as he could muster, "I am glad to see you have kept your promise to keep out of mischief."

He felt a shiver go through her body, but the look she gave him made him wonder if she questioned his sanity more than she feared him. At that moment Duncan heard voices behind them and quickly stepped away from her.

As soon as he dropped her hands, Willie turned and ran down the hallway, giving him only one last glance over her shoulder, just as Lady Jacomena emerged with some guests from the salon.

Breathlessly, Willie ran up to her room. Thank goodness her ladyship's attention was concentrated on her friends and she hadn't seen that she had disobeyed her orders.

What a twist. Willie was still shaking from her encounter with Lord Wakeford, her near apprehension by her ladyship—and what was meant by the strange conversation she had overheard between Katy and Mr. Penbrooke? She had so much to think about!

Later when all were in bed and the house quiet, Jacomena picked up her cane and made her way to the library. Luckily the book she was looking for was on a lower shelf and within her reach. Settling in the chair, she ran through several pages until she found what she wanted.

A smile slowly crept across her face and she let out a bark of laughter. "Hah! The gel was right. I'd love to see your face, you old coot, when you find out you've been bested by a common abigail." Then she frowned and tapped her chin with her finger. How did the chit come by her information? Wilhemina evidently had more in her head than the usual minion. Hannah More had the right of it. Over-educating the masses could prove dangerous, a bad example to other servants. Next they would want less work, better wages, and then expect to sit at the same table with their employers. It was evidently what had gone on in that castle in Scotland. However smart, the gel had made a singular breach of decorum and would have to be punished. Nevertheless, a certain amount of satisfaction rolled over Jacomena, and she slapped her knee as she recalled the mortification on Sir Andrew's face.

Strangely, although Willie, Katy and Broonie expected the worst, nothing further was heard about the incident with the venerable Sir Andrew and the new week commenced with the usual round of activities.

However, along with the delivery of flowers and invitations, several packets in brown paper arrived daily for Lady Katherine. These she quickly separated from the other correspondence and retired to her chambers to open. Willie waited for Katy to tell her who the letters were from, but to no avail.

Katherine also showed a surprising willingness to accompany her aunt to intellectual gatherings. In fact, she asked to go. Now delight was not an emotion Lady Jacomena would admit to, but her niece's sudden enthusiasm did bring about an exclamation from her ladyship.

"Something may come of the gel yet, Butterworth," she said.

At the beginning of the week, Duncan arrived at Wakeford Manor, where he discovered his mother bursting with news of plans for a country party in seven days' time.

Duncan tried to hide his exasperation. "But, Mother, I returned home to take care of business, not to entertain the countryside."

"Nonsense, my boy. Your Aunt Hespah wrote to say she and Calvin are coming for a visit. Of course, your cousin Cecil will be with them. It would be remiss of us not to provide some sort of entertainment."

It was not that Duncan did not care about his aunt. He was quite fond of her, in fact. Twenty-four years ago she had married a baron, Calvin Fultonhouse, who possessed an old estate and not much else. Duncan liked him as well, but his opinion of their only child, Cecil, was a different matter altogether. Three years younger than himself, his cousin, a self-indulging rakehell, would have thrown Uncle Calvin into dun territory if Duncan had not paid off his debts. He groaned at the thought of having to put up with his cousin.

Lady Wakeford tapped his arm with her fan. "Surely you can arrange a few hours for socializing, dear. I have invited several of the local gentry."

"Can't you put it off awhile longer?"

"I'm afraid the invitations were delivered this morning, and I wrote to a dear friend in London, inviting her to visit."

"London? Who?" Duncan asked suspiciously.

She looked at him innocently. "Oh, just Lady Jacomena Dalison and her niece."

Duncan shook his head. She'd done it again. "Touché, Mother. You should take up dueling."

Her eyes twinkled. "I knew you'd see it my way, dear."

Lady Jacomena was in the music room with her niece when the letter arrived from the Countess of Wakeford. Katherine, in the middle of rehearsing a song which she was to sing at a musicale in four days time, obediently put down her music and gave her attention to her aunt.

"We are invited to a country party at Wakeford Manor," Jacomena announced. "Wouldn't go if it were anyone else but Alice." She then began to count on her fingers. "Have Wilhemina pack your trunks and tell Miss Abbot we will leave in three days."

"But the musicale—" Katy interjected, her eyes growing wide.

"—will have to be cancelled," Jacomena finished. "I cannot make the journey in one day." She pulled the bellpull. "Get that secretary to send our regrets."

The housekeeper appeared at the door.

"Butterworth, we shall be journeying to Cambridgeshire for a country party at Wakeford

Manor. Pack my trunks and one for yourself. Tell Old Tom I wish to see him."

Jacomena then turned to instruct Katy, but the dratted gel had disappeared.

Chapter Eight

Katy's eyes were red-rimmed the evening before their departure, but she insisted she only had a summer cold. Willie found it hard to believe she showed so little interest in the trip, for she thought Katy would be excited at the prospect of seeing Lord Wakeford. Mrs. Butterworth was plainly taken with him, and Lady Jacomena's rigid disposition mellowed considerably when he addressed her. She said she liked earnest young men. Even Willie had to admit that although Lord Wakeford looked grim-faced a great deal of the time, he could be very charming when he put his mind to it.

I want to be your friend, he had said, which proved he could be kind, too. That made her think of how warm his hands had felt when they held hers, and a little shiver went up her spine.

Confused, Willie tried to concentrate on the journey and Katy. As she packed her valise, she wondered if perhaps Katy was scared of meeting the countess, and smiled at her. "Just think, you will be introduced to Lord Wakeford's mama."

"I know," Katy said, looking up from where she sat writing at the little cherrywood escritoire.

"Are you not curious to see where he was raised? You can learn a lot about a man from his home."

"I suppose," Katy said with a wan smile, then leaned back over her paper.

Willie was not quite certain she had pinpointed her friend's reticence, but until Katy decided to confide in her, she would not press the issue. More to the point, Willie thought, the visit could provide an opportunity to return Lord Wakeford's watch. How she was to execute the hoax she didn't know, but her good spirits rose at the prospect, making her feel a bit reckless. On impulse, she folded the lovely purple dress Katy had given her and packed it with her plain black frocks.

The following morning, the five women prepared to leave for Cambridgeshire. Just as they were entering the Dalison family coach, a little brown packet arrived by messenger for the baroness. Her eyes glistening, Katy held it tightly in her hand but did not open it.

Willie, with the gold watch safely in her reticule, squeezed into the forward seat with Broonie and Mrs. Butterworth. Katy and Lady Jacomena faced them. Katy said little during the two days journey, and Willie began to suspect the mysterious packet had more to do with her melancholy than any fear of meeting the Countess of Wakeford.

No one else seemed to notice Katy's reluctance. Lady Jacomena napped for most of the journey. When she was awake, she complained of the tedious drive, the poor state of the roads, and the weather. Broonie and Mrs. Butterworth, who seemed to be kindred spirits, chatted incessantly until even Willie was lulled to sleep.

It was well into the afternoon of the second day when they drove through the ornate iron gates of Wakeford Park. They traveled along an impeccably maintained road lined with stately elms. Then the slate roof of the manor house came into view, a great sprawling brick and stone edifice set upon a slight rise, surrounded by terraced gardens.

Broonie, with unbridled enthusiasm, expressed the admiration Willie felt. "Look you noo, Katy darling. Ain't that a grand hoose?"

Just then a doe and her fawn bounded across the road in front of the coach.

"They have deer!" the baroness cried, at sight of the animals. "I am so happy to see them—and look!" she said, pointing toward the gardens. "I saw a rabbit hop into that rose bush. Oh, thank you for bringing me, Auntie."

It was the first enthusiasm from Katy that Willie had heard since they left London.

"Humph!" spouted her ladyship, with a wave of her hand. But the spark of pride in her eyes as she looked away from her niece did not escape Willie.

The coach soon came to a halt on the circular drive in front of the mansion.

"Go ahead without me," Jacomena said to Katherine. "Butterworth and I will wait until the footmen unload my chair."

At the top on the broad stone terrace stood a gray-haired woman dressed in bright pink, upright in carriage, her face so animated it belied being old or young. She enthusiastically waved a handkerchief. Beside her stood Lord Wakeford, calm, sedate, dressed in a black riding coat, buff pantaloons and Hessian boots. How elegant he looked in country attire. Willie's eyes misted over and she swallowed hard. What a wonderful husband he would make for her Katy.

The baroness was gazing about in such a whimsical fashion, that it took another command from her aunt to get her started up the path. Broonie and Willie followed.

As Duncan observed the little procession, a wave of relief broke over him. His little magpie had not been turned out of the Dalison household after all. Giving his attention back to the baroness, he saw that he needn't have worried about his mother's reaction when she saw Lady Katherine. However, he was concerned with that young lady's response to his ancestral home. She approached hesitantly, head down, as if her feet needed to be told their direction, eyes hidden by the rim of her bonnet.

"Welcome to Wakeford Manor, my dear," Lady Wakeford called out, long before her guests reached the top of the steps.

Katherine looked up shyly through her long lashes.

"I see that you brought your family nurse—Miss Abbot, I believe," she said pleasantly to the large Scotswoman. "Lady Dalison wrote about you."

Before Broonie could answer, Lady Wakeford returned her remarks to Katherine. "And did I understand her to say you were bringing your own abigail, dear?"

"Yes, my lady." Katy, who had reached the terrace, curtsied low, revealing the tiny, black-frocked figure which had been hidden behind her. Encouraged by the countess' kind voice, the baroness raised her face, her lovely blue eyes clear and innocent, to smile sweetly.

Duncan had just stepped forward, when he was startled by a gasp from his mother. He looked in time to see her sway, her face pale. Before he could do more than take her arm and say, "Mother?" she brushed his hand away and laughed.

"You needn't worry that I shall swoon, Duncan."

Her gaze went once more to the baroness whose face showed genuine concern. "Just a foolish woman's sentimental remembrances, my dear," the countess said.

Still puzzled by his mother's response, Duncan took Lady Katherine's gloved hand and bowed.

Lady Wakeford nodded her approval. "Welcome to Wakeford Manor," she said, holding out her arms.

Like a love-starved child, Katy went willingly.

"For a moment I was taken aback by your strong resemblance to your father," Lady Wakeford said, brushing Katy's hair back from her face. "Of course I have not seen him for years, but I remember well what a fine looking young man he was. You have his hair and eyes." She held her away from her. "How tall you are, but then, both of your parents were. Weren't they?"

"You knew my mother?" Katy didn't wait for an answer but rushed on. "Broonie says my temperament is more like hers."

"Oh, I do hope so, dear," Lady Wakeford replied a little vaguely.

For a second, Duncan feared his mother was off in that never-never-land she frequented so often, but she recovered quickly, her good spirits returned.

"I didn't get to know her well, but I can tell you, she set London on its ear. A lovely girl. Your father was not the only young buck to notice, you know," she said, a slight wavering in her voice, "but he was the one who won her hand. She must have been about your age, Katherine," Lady Wakeford said, throwing a knowing look at her son. "Love at first sight," they say.

"Perhaps sometime you will tell me about my parents. I know very little about what their life was like."

"Of course, my dear," Lady Wakeford said, taking the young woman's hand in hers. "I'd be delighted and you shall tell me all about your life in Scotland. My sister and her family are here, but the other guests won't begin to arrive until tomorrow, so we will have some time to ourselves. I was hoping my two youngest daughters would be here to meet you. They are about your age, but they will not be home from Brighton for some three weeks, yet." The countess then turned and looked doubtfully at the tiny figure standing in her shadow. "Now, who is this?"

Katy turned and drew Willie up beside her. "This is Willie."

"Her name is Wilhemina," came a voice behind them. Jacomena, carried in her chair like an East Indian potentate, was set upon the terrace by four footmen. "I have told you, Katherine, that calling your maid by that silly name adds no substance to your consequence."

"Jaco! Is it really you?" the countess cried, hurrying toward her friend. She looked at the chair and brought her hand to her throat. "Oh, I didn't know——"

"Butterworth, my cane." Jacomena alighted and walked toward her hostess. "Lady Wakeford."

"What a scare you gave me," the countess said, embracing her. "But why the chair, for heavens sakes?"

"Can't get up and down the stairs like I used to. That's all."

"Well, thank goodness it is nothing worse. Now none of this Lady Wakeford twaddle. It will always be Alice to you."

"As you wish," Jacomena said. "You received my reply to your letter?"

"Yes. Your man delivered it when your wagon arrived with your luggage. But let us discuss that later. You must be tired from your journey and wishing to refresh yourself." The countess looked doubtfully at the small figure beside the baroness. "Could you use another attendant, my dear?"

"Oh, no. Willie . . . ," she said, giving a surreptitious

glance at Lady Jacomena, "Willie does everything for me."

"If you are certain," the countess said, and that ended the matter. She turned and clapped her hands, signaling a servant. "I do hope you like the accommodations I have chosen for you, Jaco. I have given Miss Abbot and you rooms in a front wing on the first floor. Mrs. Butterworth is nearby."

They all watched as Jacomena's chair was carried to the stairs where a footman helped her be seated.

"And," the countess continued, "a cot has been placed in Lady Katherine's room for her abigail, as you requested."

Surprised, Willie's gaze darted to Lady Jacomena.

Her ladyship did not return the look. "My niece seems to prefer that arrangement. Can't make heads or tails of how the young think today."

"Some of us do try to stay a jump ahead." Lady Wakeford glanced slyly at her son before adding, "When you are rested we will have to have a coze, Jaco. I can hardly wait to catch you up."

Suddenly a dozen assorted chimes sounded, a gong rang five times, and a cuckoo's call echoed through the halls, making it nigh to impossible for any further conversation.

Willie saw Lord Wakeford smile with repressed amusement. To her discerning eyes, he appeared more relaxed here than he had in town. Evidently neither he nor any of the servants were disturbed by the symphonic cacophony. Taking Lady Wakeford's lead, the other women followed her up the stairs, trying to appear unconcerned by the startling performance of dozens of clocks.

* * *

After the baroness and her party retired to their rooms, Duncan sought out his mother. He found her in her sitting room staring out the window, as though lost in thought.

"Mother? Is there anything I can do?" he asked, crossing to her side. "If Lady Katherine's visit here disturbs you—"

The countess shook her head, interrupting his statement.

"You said that it was because she looked so much like her father, but that was not the whole story, was it?" he continued.

"For someone so practical, you are surprisingly astute in ascertaining my moods, Duncan." Lady Wakefield motioned for him to sit in the chair opposite her. "No, though there is a striking likeness, I was overcome by the vivid recollection of a time of sadness, of memories that I thought I had set aside away years ago."

Puzzled by his mother's uncharacteristic, melancholy mood, Duncan said no more, but waited for her to continue in her own good time.

"It is outside of enough that her father has not seen her for fourteen years. The poor child," she said.

Duncan thought of his own large, close-knit family. Even though he had only sisters, they were a lively lot, eager to fish, race their donkeys, and plot all sorts of mischief against unsuspecting servants with him. He had not realized what a lonely childhood the baroness must have had.

"I will of course tell her about her mother and father—to a certain degree—but I want you to know the whole story so you can understand."

"You do like her, then?" Duncan said.

"Very much."

"If she accepts me, I shall do all I can to make her happy, Mother."

"I'm certain you will, dear. That is how I raised you. But when you do decide to marry, make certain you find someone you love. Without it, life could be a desert. Your father and I had special bond, and from what I observed of them, I believe the baroness' parents shared it too. It would not be fair to offer Lady Katherine less. However, there are certain . . . circumstances you should be aware of."

For a moment, Lady Wakefield's whimsies flew out the window again. Duncan thought perhaps he should take his leave, when she began to speak.

"The war did so many things to so many people. Husbands and sons marched off, some never to be seen again." She turned then to look at Duncan. "I had a very good friend. Her name was Patricia Grayson, a lovely creature, full of life and gaiety. Her husband, Sir John, was knighted after his part in the sea battle of Abukir Bay under Lord Nelson."

Lady Wakeford poured a cup of tea and handed it to Duncan. "It is difficult being a navy officer's wife, especially so, I think, because she was one of the most popular young women in London. Patricia's husband was away for months at a time. Once she did not see him for over a year. Oh, there were plenty of willing escorts, acceptable gentlemen, but she fell in with a reckless group, and I was very disturbed. Patricia began going to more and more affairs with the late marquis, Adrian Dalison. I told you that young Harcourt had attached himself to his brother's band of Corinthians, didn't I?"

The countess poured Duncan another cup of tea and absentmindedly stirred in three spoons of sugar before he could stop her. He never used sugar, but he accepted the cup from her hand without a word.

"Whenever Adrian was away, Harcourt tried to outdo him in recklessness. Thank heavens, he met the Baroness of Gilfallen. One look was all it took for Harcourt to fall madly in love and forget all about his brother's ways." Lady Wakeford looked her son directly in the eye. "It takes an exceptional woman to save a man from a life of debauchery, do you not agree?"

"Yes, Mother," Duncan said, trying desperately to keep a straight face.

"As I was saying, about the time the late Lady Katherine and Harcourt announced their betrothal, Adrian and Patricia both disappeared from town. It was rumoured that they had run off together. Of course, he returned for Harcourt's wedding but only stayed briefly, then was not seen again. The stories grew."

"Take your time, Mother," Duncan said, as his mother paused to sip her tea. He realized the extent of her distress by the way she clutched the fragile tea cup in her hands.

"Well, now, you see, I was very disturbed about Patricia," she continued, as though she'd not heard him. "We had been bosom friends since childhood, and I grieved with her over her husband's long absences. I was greatly relieved when I finally received a letter from her. It was brought by a messenger who left before I could question him about her direction. Patricia assured me that she was all right, only in the dismals and said that she had decided to travel. It wasn't until later that I realized the seriousness of the situation."

"What situation?" Duncan asked, intrigued.

"Patricia's husband returned from sea. Harcourt was advised of the danger Adrian was in, and set out to warn him." Lady Wakeford stopped a minute to place her cup on the table.

Duncan steepled his fingers and waited.

"He was too late. The marquis had been killed in a duel and Patricia and Sir John were missing."

"Where had they gone?"

"No one knew. Three days later, their bodies washed ashore on the Kent coast. The authorities called it a double suicide."

Introducing Cousin Cecil to Lady Katherine and her aunt was an inevitability Duncan was glad to have over and done with the first evening of their visit. How such a placid and kindly couple as his Aunt Hespah and his Uncle Calvin could have given birth to such an out-and-outer, he would never understand.

Cecil, cocksure of his unquestionable charm, changed costumes several times a day. His wardrobe was never over-stated, yet he dressed in the first stare of elegance. In polite society his manner of speaking was flawless, and he had a certain wit which the ladies seemed to find irresistible. But there was another side to Cecil only seen in secluded gardens or dark bedchambers. He was known for never keeping a mistress of his own, for to him the forbidden fruit of someone else's wife or ladybird was far more exciting. Any female was fair game to the rakehell. Duncan begrudgingly admitted there were women who found such men exciting.

What his cousin did in Town was his own business, but whenever Cecil visited Wakeford Manor, anger and frustration were Duncan's constant companions. He did not want to see his mother humiliated by his cousin's indiscretions or any of his female staff compromised. And now he had the added responsibility of

Lady Katherine to consider. Such an innocent would have no defense against a libertine like Cecil.

Duncan realized he'd have to forego his work on the estate until his mother's party was over. He would have to be satisfied with going over the jumbled account books in the office, which he'd established in the rear wing of the house. Bellamy was an honest steward, but the old man was a little slow now and his eyes were getting as bad as John Teagardner's. Duncan would have hired another overseer, but he could not turn out a man who had served his family faithfully for so many years—not until Bellamy was ready to step down.

After six days, Willie felt they'd settled well into the routine of the household. The countess was an outstanding hostess, providing her guests with an endless round of music, games, picnics and company. Several houseguests arrived, the Thurstons among the throng, and near neighbors rode over each day to join in the gaiety. John Teagardner was one of these. Willie noted that the shy young man did not often join a large group, perhaps because of his poor vision, but seemed content to engage in quiet conversation or wander about the gardens by himself. Nevertheless, she made it a point to stay out of his sight for fear he would recognize her.

She slipped through the hedges and joined the group of older guests seated comfortably in the shade of the tall oak trees. It had become their habit to sit there after nuncheon, sipping lemonade and watching the younger people playing a game of shuttlecocks.

Willie sat down on the blanket next to Broonie. She noted that his lordship too, seemed to prefer observing to joining in the games. More often than not, he would appear from inside the house, watch for a while as if making certain all was well, then disappear back into the mansion. From the corner of her eye, she saw he was still there, his lean muscular legs spread apart, arms folded across his chest, his dark brooding eyes taking in the entire picture. Did they stop for a moment when they came her way?

Feeling a flush burn up her neck and spread across her face, Willie quickly shifted her gaze back to the field where Katy eagerly pursued the game. In her light muslin dress, the baroness looked like a piece of afternoon sky fallen to earth.

"The bloom is back in m'darlin's cheeks," Broonie said. "And she's been a good lass. She hasn't borrowed anything that don't belong to her since we arrived."

Willie heard a burst of laughter from the field and rose so she could see better. Katy's excitement when she soundly whacked the bird with her paddle was irresistible to watch and Willie couldn't help but call out, "Splendidly done, Katy!"

Happiness filled the little maid's heart, for she wanted to believe that the fresh country air and friendly company had put the music back in Katy's voice. "Oh," Willie whispered to herself, "I hope I am wrong when my senses detect a sharp edge to that gaiety." But no matter how much Willie wanted to believe that Katy was enjoying herself, she had to admit there was a new seriousness about her which she'd never seen before.

Duncan, who felt he did not have time for what he considered childish sports like bowls or shuttlecocks, stood on the terrace outside the library. Steps slowly wound upward to a balcony off the ballroom on the floor above, where craftsmen and servants had labored for several days, preparing the decorations for the ball tomorrow.

He had come out to observe Lady Katherine, but his eyes kept straying to the little abigail. Amused, he noticed that each time someone readied to hit the bird, Willie swung her own arm right along with the player. She played no favorites, he noted, and when a racket hit its mark, she clapped enthusiastically. Until now, his mother was the only person he knew to express such unrestrained joy.

It was a relief for Duncan to know that Lady Katherine was safely under the watchful eye of both her chaperones, and cousin Cecil nowhere to be seen. Duncan had no doubts that the rake was indulging himself somewhere in a hayloft with a village maid, or had found an accommodating crofter's wife. Satisfied that his guests were occupied for the next hour or so, Duncan decided he could return to his office.

Willie was still watching the game on the lawn, but she was thinking of how Lord Wakeford had looked standing on the terrace. Nearly a week had passed and she was no nearer returning his watch than she had been in London. She knew from taking note of his habits the last few days, that very likely Lord Wakeford had returned to his office, where he would spend the rest of the afternoon. Perhaps now was her chance. She knew that Charles, his lordship's valet, would be in the kitchen having a cup of tea with Anna, the countess's maid, for whom he seemed to be developing a tendre. While Broonie watched Katy, Willie could fetch the timepiece and take it to his chambers. She'd think of someplace to hide the watch once she saw his room.

"Broonie, will it be all right if I run up to my room for a minute?"

"Take all the time you need, dear."

Willie hurried off to get the gold watch. His lordship's apartment was in another wing of the manor, one which she was not familiar, but surely she could find her way. If someone asked where she was going she could always say she was on an errand for Lady Katherine or Lady Jacomena.

Her quest proved more difficult than she thought, but after making several wrong turns, Willie finally located the earl's rooms. Nervousness and apprehension made her hesitate outside the high-arched wooden door. But knowing she must protect Katy at all costs, Willie took a deep breath, then slipped inside.

The room surprised her, though she didn't know why. It was a comfortable room, definitely a man's room. The furniture was like the earl—masculine, solid and serviceable. The colors not foppish, but plain like the clothes he wore. Forest-green velvet curtains were pulled back from both the dark mahogany bed and the mullioned windows letting in as much light as possible. An ancient tapestry of mounted hunters and woodland creatures covered one wall and on another, medieval weapons were arranged in a circular pattern.

His huge canopied bed sat high above the floor, the ruffled skirt around the bottom, concealing much of the wooden-planked floor. A strange, fluttering feeling came over her as she observed the bed—*his* bed. Then the flounce caught her attention. It occurred to her that if something were dropped and kicked underneath, it could easily get caught in that skirt.

With great effort, she moved the sturdy bedside table a hair off center, then placed the gold watch against the leg, half concealed by the flounce. If she knew the earl's nature as well as she thought she was beginning to, he would move the table back to sit square with the bed. In so doing, the leg would nudge the watch into sight. Hopefully he would think it had been there all this time, pushed back by a careless maid. Feeling quite clever with herself she took one last look, then hurried to the door.

Stealthfully, she sneaked into the hallway to see if the coast was clear and found herself staring into the face of the Honorable Cecil Fultonhouse. Before she could protest, the man grabbed her and pulled her to him.

"Well, what have we here?" he asked, laughing in such an insidious way that a sense of doom engulfed Willie. "So my pattern-saint cousin hides a doxy in his room." He cupped her chin with his hand and brought his mouth within an inch of hers.

Willie glared at him. What an odious man, she thought.

"Lady Katherine's abigail, are you not?" he asked, smirking. "Playing games behind your ladyship's back, while his lordship has you on yours?"

Shocked by his ungentlemanly accusations, Willie could think of no response strong enough, until she found her lips crushed by those of Mr. Fultonhouse. She didn't like it. Not at all. He should have asked if she wanted to kiss him, which she didn't. Exasperation quickly replaced complacency and she tried to push him away. Solid as a rock. In fact, it took but one of his arms to hold her against his chest, while he pulled up her skirt.

"Shall I show you how a real man can play?" he whispered against her cheek before capturing her lips again.

Chapter Nine

Willie could not fathom how Mr. Fultonhouse managed to hoist her into his arms, kiss her and carry her down steps at the end of the corridor, all at one time. This was an entirely new experience for Willie, and she could see that men certainly had the advantage there. Thus imprisoned, she couldn't free her mouth long enough to call for help, but when she felt a breeze tickle the top of her bare legs, the seriousness of the matter hit her and she began to cry. Helplessness has a way of creating new responses, and Willie was not one to give in to such a weakness without a fight. She used what defenses she had and bit down hard on his lip.

"Why you little she-devil!" he yelled, tumbling backwards with her onto the stairs.

Willie, the wind knocked from her by the fall, watched as confusion turned into pandemonium. Feeling quite dizzy, she blinked as she saw a large fist grasp Mr. Fultonhouse's shoulder and rip him away from her. The resounding crack which followed sounded like bones breaking. Mr. Fultonhouse sat down hard beside her, blood pouring from his mouth and nose. She did not like the odious lecher sitting next to her after what he had done, so she rose, made a hammer of her fists and popped him soundly on the top his head. Mr. Fultonhouse's expression looked decidedly glazed before he tumbled head over heels onto the floor, unconscious. She looked down at his prostrate body. Yes, indeed, it certainly served him right.

Willie's gaze then traveled up the long, muscular legs in front of her until she came to Lord Wakeford's face. Heart pounding, she raised her chin and spoke more boldly than she felt. "I reckon that will teach him a thing or two." She tried to rise, but her legs buckled. The earl caught her, but as soon as he had set her upon her feet, he dropped his hands and stepped back. She wished he hadn't.

His eyes stark, he asked, "Did he hurt you?"

She liked him better when he smiled. But now, her own eyes threatened to betray her and to keep back the tears, she shook her head.

Saying no more, Lord Wakeford took her hand gently and led her down another flight of stairs to a door which opened out onto a back courtyard.

"Go to the left at the corner of the kitchen, through the herb garden, and you will find yourself just off the terrace. You are certain you are all right?"

"Yes," she replied, though her chin quivered a little. She would have liked to ask him to hold her again, just for a moment or two until her legs felt less like cream pudding, but she didn't dare. His jaw was set in a hard, unrelenting line and anger sparked in his dark eyes. She nodded again, then glanced anxiously back at the house.

As if interpreting her thoughts, Duncan said tersely. "I shall take care of Mr. Fultonhouse. He shan't bother you again."

"Well, I dare say not," she said, with a toss of her head. "Not after the thumping I gave him."

Duncan watched her turn and march across the

cobblestone yard, fists clenched at her sides, determination showing in every wobbly step. It was all he could do to keep from laughing. "You brave little chit," he murmured, as he observed her efforts to walk a straight path on the bumpy cobblestone. She really thought she'd knocked Cecil unconscious. Duncan waited until she'd turned the corner, then went back to collect his unscrupulous cousin. All amusement left Duncan as he thought of the way his blackguard of a relative had forced himself on an innocent girl. It might have been different if she had welcomed his advances, but Duncan knew she had not. Willie had fought him valiantly, using every resource at her command. But given Cecil's lack of conscience and superior strength, Duncan shuddered to think what might've happened had he not interfered.

The hallway was empty. Two spots of blood on a step were the only evidence that there had been an encounter. Anger and disappointment mangled his composure, and after giving the bannister a few whacks with his fist, Duncan climbed the stairs to look for Cecil.

Luck was on Duncan's side. He caught Cecil in his room, throwing a few garments into a portmanteau. Duncan didn't waste time on formalities and gripped the front of the scoundrel's shirt.

Cecil threw up his hands in supplication. "No need to be violent, cousin. I'm leaving."

"Damned right, you are," Duncan growled, using all his control not to strangle the bounder.

Cecil, however, laughed. "As enticing as she was, I leave your little doxy to you. I'm certain I shall find other entertainment. Didn't mean to trespass on your territory."

Fury turned Duncan's eyes the color of coal, and his fist slammed into Cecil's face, sending him once more to the floor. Afraid he would be tempted to do something worse, Duncan stomped out of the room and headed for his own apartment.

Splatters of blood decorated the front of his coat. He couldn't chance encountering his mother, or aunt, in his present state. They would, of course, want to know why Cecil left before the ball, but Duncan was certain he could dredge up an acceptable explanation. After all, Cecil was not known for being dependable.

Entering his room, Duncan threw the offending garment down on the bed. Charles would make a fuss, of course, and wonder what had possessed his master to engage in fisticuffs, but Duncan had every faith his valet would remove the stains.

He'd started to unbutton his shirt when he noticed the bedside table was slightly out of place. Automatically, he twisted it square with the bed and was astonished to see something shiny pop out from under the bedskirt.

"Jupiter! Father's gold watch!" Duncan claimed the timepiece, turning it over in his hands with great care. It had been there all this time and he had falsely accused Lady Katherine's maid.

For an agonizing moment, Duncan wondered if his other assumptions about her were wrong, as well. There was something about the little magpie that did not entirely match with the notion of her as a thief. But discounting the gold watch, he had caught her on two other occasions . . . and try as he would, he could think of no other acceptable explanation. What he needed to do, he decided, was get to know Willie better. The idea parodoxically both worried and pleased him.

* * *

By the time Willie returned to the terrace, she found most of the guests had departed. Broonie sat alone under the trees, looking too tired to move.

"Where is Katy?" Willie asked, concern edging her voice.

"Don't you be worryin'," Broonie answered. "The others went off to take a nap and Katy wanted to go to the library to find a book. I saw no harm in it."

Praying Broonie was right, Willie hurried across the lawn and through the casement window which led into the library. Fear gripped her when she looked around and there was no sign of her charge. She willed herself to think rationally about where Katy might be. Willie decided to make certain she was not in their room, and had turned to leave when she heard the sound of sobbing. She found Katy a moment later, curled up in a large wingbacked chair crying as though her heart would break.

Willie's own troubles quickly flew away. "Why," she said, "whatever is the matter, dear?"

"Oh, Willie, I am so unhappy."

"But I thought you were having such a splendid time. Broonie and I have been so proud of you, dear. You haven't taken anything that is not yours for ever so long."

Katy said, with great determination, "I shall never steal anything again." With a sniff, she stared at her hands. "I know what it is like now to have something which I treasure a great deal taken from me."

"Why, whatever do you mean, Katy? Has someone stolen some of your jewelry?"

"Worse than that," Katy said, her eyes pleading for understanding. "I have lost my heart, and I shall never get it back."

"But isn't that what we hoped would happen?" Willie asked, with a catch in her voice. "You won't have a loveless marriage, for I know that Lord Wakeford harbors the most tender feelings toward you."

Katy wiped a tear from her cheek. "It is not the earl I care for."

Willie didn't know whether to laugh or cry. Her own station made it impossible for her to have any dreams in that direction, but the thought that Katy did not want Lord Wakeford lifted a heavy load off her own shoulders. Willie had not put it into words before, but she'd been dreading the day Katy accepted Lord Wakeford. The notion of living here, in *his* house, seeing him every day, watching Katy fall deeply in love with him—for how could anyone not help loving such a wonderful gentleman—had troubled Willie greatly.

Now feeling tremendously light-headed, she laughed. "Don't be a goose, Katy. Lord Wakeford has not offered yet, and even if he does, you don't have to accept him. But tell me, dear, whom do you want to marry?"

"Mr. Penbrooke."

"Oh, dear!" Willie said, putting her hand over her mouth. "Surely, Lady Jacomena wouldn't allow . . ." She couldn't say what she knew, that her ladyship would find a poor art dealer's assistant a most unsuitable match for her niece.

Katy did not seem to notice her unfinished sentence. "He has been writing me beautiful poems."

"The little brown packages?"

Katy nodded. "We have been meeting at Aunt Jacomena's gatherings. I told him how homesick I was for Scotland, and he understood at once. Just before we left London, he sent me a lovely ode about Gilfallen, and he painted a little watercolor of mountains." She dabbed at her eyes with the handkerchief. "Oh, Willie, it is as if he can see right into my mind."

"Does he love you?" Willie asked.

"He says he dare not say what is in his heart, but I know he does," Katy said, beginning to cry again.

"Well, we shall have to think on this a bit, won't we?" Willie said.

"You will help me? You'll make Nathaniel see that things can work out, won't you, Willie?"

Willie started to say she thought it impossible, but the worshipful trust in Katy's eyes made her fudge the issue. "Cheer up, dear. I'm certain we shall find the right solution."

"I do hope so," she said and reached out to clasp her friend's hand. "We don't laugh much anymore, do we, Willie?"

"I thought you were enjoying yourself. You always acted delighted with everything."

"I smile a lot, but that is not the same as laughing, is it?"

Willie realized that it was going to take herculean efforts to reassure Katy. She rose, stuck her nose in the air, and glided across the room.

"Pray tell me why I find you in such dismals, Lady Katherine?" she began.

Katy giggled. "Oh, Willie, it sounds so funny when you call me that. You sound just like Lady Thurston."

Willie pursed her lips and made a grand sweep with her hand. "Lady Katherine!" she said, dramatically. "Remember, you are a baroness."

"How can I forget," Katy pouted, "when I am reminded a hundred times a day."

"Then act like one. I should think a baroness could do pretty much as she pleases—that is, if she really wants something badly enough. Now, put a feather in your cap and hold your head up." Willie looked cross-eyed at the tip of her nose until they doubled over with laughter.

* * *

Duncan, trying to take his mind off his confrontation with his rapscallion cousin, headed for the library. He was about to enter when he was certain he heard the voice of Lady Thurston coming from inside. An encounter with that formidable lady was the last thing he wanted. He had just turned on his heel when he was caught up short by a giggle. Lady Thurston did not giggle. That woman didn't even laugh. She brayed like a donkey. Puzzled, he stopped, then against all his scruples, peeked through the crack in the door opening.

The little magpie was strutting across the room in such a proud fashion that it was all Duncan could do to keep silent. Willie had told him she didn't know how to be a proper lady's maid, but in her simple, black dress, she could pass for a member of *le beau monde* dressed in mourning.

Although Duncan couldn't see Lady Katherine, he recognized her voice. "But if I walk like that I would only see the end of my nose. I couldn't see the birds in the trees or the flowers on the ground, and I'd get a kink in my neck. Oh, Willie—I don't want to be a lady. You do it so much better than I."

"I know," Willie sighed, collapsing into the nearest chair. "But you can climb trees faster than I, dear, and you sing like a nightingale."

"I wish we could trade places," Katy said with a sigh.

Willie hopped off the chair and with hands clasped behind her back, began to pace. "When we used to read all those fairy tales, I wished that I was highborn, but now that I have seen what unhappy creatures constitute society, I'm thankful I am an orphan."

Creatures? Duncan was caught up short. What did

the chit mean by *unhappy creatures?* Curiosity was a dangerous ally to befriend, but nonetheless, Duncan succumbed to temptation. He flattened himself against the wall outside the door and hoped to God that no one found him playing the eavesdropper.

For the next half hour, Duncan was entertained by imitations of practically every one of his guests, including himself, and some of his servants. When Willie mimicked him, it was plain as a pikestaff whom the ingrate meant, for she frowned and drew her lips into a straight line and repeated outrageous exaggerations of what he considered his most profound statements.

"I enjoy a jest as well as any man, and I do not frown all the time," Duncan muttered. As if to prove to himself how smooth it was, he drew his hand across his forehead, only to find his brows were indeed nearly meeting over his nose.

The ungrateful wench! Hadn't he saved her life from ruin only an hour ago? Duncan was all for ringing a peal over her curly head, but he couldn't go charging in without admitting he was eavesdropping. An ignoble act, if there ever was one. What a coil! The only person Willie refused to imitate was his mother.

"No one can be as gracious as she," Willie said, when Katy asked her to do Lady Wakeford. "The countess is a true lady, Katy, and you would do well to follow her example."

Warmed by her sincerity, all the cobwebs left Duncan's mind, and hard as it was to swallow, reason returned. But just as he thought he was putting it all together, the clock in the hallway began to toll, then another and another. He tried to ponder the maid's remarks over the noise.

Was it as she said? Were they all merely actors playing roles? And doing it badly, according to the little mimic. Before his eyes, she had become a lady. Walked like a lady, talked like a lady and yet she was no more than a servant.

Duncan held his hands over his ears until the chimes stopped, only to hear another clock begin a plaintive jingle from a distant room. He shook his head. He was tired. The day had been distinctly out of the ordinary. Before he lost all reason, he decided that a long ride on a fast horse would be the only thing to keep him from losing his sanity.

While her son headed for the stables determined to regain his composure, the Countess of Wakeford entertained Lady Jacomena in her sitting room. They faced each other across an oval tea table covered with trays of succulent biscuits, cinnamon tarts, sandwiches and seed cakes.

Lady Wakeford sat sedately, poured them each a cup of tea, then waited for the servants to leave. As soon as the door closed, she looked quickly over at her friend. "I was beginning to wonder if we would ever find time for a coze. Once I reveled in these week-long country parties, but now I look forward to passing on the household responsibilities to a younger woman." She looked innocently across at her friend. "Do you take sugar in your tea?"

Jacomena waved away the sugar and took the cup. "And you think my niece would fill that position," she stated, without ceremony.

Lady Wakeford laughed. "You always were one to aim right for the target, Jaco. I find it so refreshing not to have to go round Robin Hood's barn to find out what one wants."

"So shall we get right to the point, Alice? I have a niece who needs a husband. You have a son who should be starting his nursery, or else the family fortune will pass on to your late husband's ne'er-do-well nephew, who, if I am any judge of character—and I believe I am—would have the entire family in dun country before a year of inheriting."

"I fear you are right," Lady Wakeford said, with a sigh. "Is it that obvious?"

"Sufficient that I believe we must hurry," Jacomena said. "Now, Lord Wakeford has been devoted in his attendance on Katherine. At the Bellrumple Ball, he led her out for the opening dance, and I gave my consent for him to stand up with her again."

"Goodness, that certainly was an announcement to the *ton* of his intentions, wasn't it? He was quite anxious for my approval of her, you know, and I have given it."

"Which leads to the next step," Jacomena said. "He must ask my brother for permission to address her."

Lady Wakeford glanced quizzically at her friend. "Surely, his grace will not object?"

"How should I know? I haven't talked to the man in eighteen years."

The countess gasped. "Well, for heavens sakes, why then did you agree to sponsor his daughter?"

"Curiosity. Wondered why he'd kept her hidden all those years up in Scotland. Must say I was pleasantly surprised. At first I thought she didn't have a pea brain in her head, but I've come to the conclusion that she is just shy."

"I find her sweet and very talented," the countess said. "If she were not a member of the peerage, she would do well on the stage with that lovely voice."

"Good heavens, do not suggest such a thing. I will have you know she was eager to attend the gatherings of my intellectual acquaintances, and she reads a great deal, too. She is continually sending that abigail of hers to the library for more books. I must hand it to

Harcourt. He made certain his daughter obtained as good an education as she would have had at any young ladies' academy here in England."

"But it must have been a lonely life. She told me of her upbringing at Gilfallen. The only other child she had to play with was the little orphan girl, Willie—"

"Wilhemina," corrected Jacomena.

"Katherine told me during one of our talks, that she named her Willie after the nursery rhyme, Wee Willie Winkie."

"That is an absurd name," Jacomena said.

"I think it charming," Lady Wakeford said cheerfully. "In fact, I find her quite bright, don't you? And she dresses and attends Katherine well."

Jacomena frowned. "Too precocious for her own good. I admit her devotion to Katherine is exemplary, only I fear she was given too much freedom in Scotland and often forgets her station."

"Miss Abbot said your brother chose her personally."

"Humph! Nothing but an afterthought. Harcourt's life was nothing but afterthoughts. Never questioned the consequences of his actions. He fetched her from an orphanage as he passed through Leeds. Too nipcheese to find a qualified lady's maid. Well, blood always tells." Jacomena shook a finger at her hostess. "I warn you that I am afraid if the reins are not drawn tightly now, trouble will follow. If you allow Wilhemina to come live here when Katherine and the earl are married, she will take advantage of your good nature and cause havoc with the other servants."

"She has no family, does she? What a pity it would be to send her away from the only people she has known. Besides, I never worry about what has not happened yet, Jaco. Now tell me, if you have not spoken to your brother in all these years, where is he?"

"I have no idea. I communicate with him through an agent. Periodically missives come by messenger. He wanted me to send him a list of ten eligible men for him to choose from."

"Oh, dear, then Duncan would be only one of many."

"Not necessarily," Jacomena said, tapping her forehead with a finger. "From the beginning I also made a list of my own. Your son was the only one I placed on both. Then as time went by, I'd struck everyone from my list except Wakeford."

"But the duke still has nine other men on his."

Jacomena gave a bark of laughter. "Harky never was very sharp in the attic. Always relies on others to do his dirty work. The other nine are so despicable in one way or another, they will be eliminated in no time at all."

"Why are you always so derogatory in your remarks about your brother, Jaco?"

Her mouth set in a firm line, she replied bitterly, "I always believed that if he had left sooner to warn Adrian, he could have saved his life. I can never forgive him for that."

"I think you are too hard on him—and on yourself." Lady Wakeford reached across the table and placed her hand over that of her friend. "I remember him as a very sad young man, lonely really, always trying to live up to a dashing older brother. The death of the marquis was terribly hard on him. Did he ever tell you what happened?"

"No. I stopped talking to him before his wedding."

"Then you never saw him with his lovely bride, Katherine's mother?"

"No. That is, I did see her from a distance once."

"With her, he was an entirely different man than you describe. Her death and that of his son must have been a terrible blow. It is quite sad that you and your brother are not on terms. Besides, what I wanted to tell you—" the countess paused, looked intently at her friend, then continued, "I was never satisfied with the story Harcourt told."

"What do you mean?" Jacomena said, her attention now fully awakened.

"Did you know Patricia Grayson?"

"That tart?"

"She was no such thing," said Lady Wakeford firmly. "She was my dearest friend, as close as any sister could be. Like so many women, she was caught up in the war as much as any man who went to battle."

"She caused the downfall of two men. My eldest brother as well as her husband."

"Did you ever meet her?"

"No! I did not attend the sort of soirés that my brothers frequented."

"If your brothers went to lively parties, why was it so wrong for her to go?"

"She was a married woman."

"And many of those men were married, too, and kind enough to escort those married women, so they would not have to go alone." At Jacomena's skeptical look, Lady Wakeford held up her hands. "Oh, I am not all that blind as to what went on. There were those, of course, who developed attachments. Do you remember the diaries we kept when we were at school?"

"Good heavens! I'd forgotten all about those," Jacomena said. "I thought someone, someday would want them to write my biography. I continued them for years until—"

"Yes, dear?"

"I stopped after Adrian died." She sat staring into space for a moment. "Hadn't thought about them for years. They must be packed away somewhere up in the attic."

The countess laughed gaily. "I quit the day after I married Wakeford. He found me writing in it on our wedding night and tore the page out." Lady Wakeford looked off into the distance, then continued. "Well, enough of that. I only brought up the diaries to illustrate a point. Patricia and I attended different boarding schools, but we wrote letters and during the summers we visited and would read each other's books. That is how close we were.

"We were living in London at the time, and that was why I was hurt when Patricia left town without letting me know. The fact that Adrian absented himself at the same time, of course, started all the rumours. He came back for Harcourt's wedding, but then we never saw him again."

Jacomena turned pale.

"Oh, I am sorry, dear," Lady Wakeford said. "I remember how close you were to Adrian, but do hear me out. I had one letter from Patricia, delivered by messenger, telling me she had not been feeling well. Nothing serious, she assured me, but she thought the clean sea air would set her straight in no time. She did not mention the place by name, but she alluded to what a pleasant time we had had on a picnic during one of our summer holidays. That was what prompted me to believe she was on the Dover coast somewhere. Once when we were still schoolgirls, she came with me to our estate in Kent, and I remembered we had eaten near St. Margarets-at-Cliffe."

"By Jove! That is where Adrian was killed. What is on your mind?"

Lady Wakeford stuffed a honey biscuit into her mouth. Then, patting her lips with her napkin, she said cheerfully, "You know, Jaco, I have developed a strong inclination to go to the seaside. Yes, indeed, the salt air is just what I need to lift my spirits. This party has exhausted me more than I realized. After the ball tomorrow night, I do believe nothing will do but for me to visit St. Margaret's-at-Cliffe.''

Chapter Ten

Lady Wakeford fluttered a long scroll of paper and laughed. "I can not imagine how my guest list got so out-of-hand for the assembly tonight. Wherever will we put all these people?"

Duncan smiled one of his rare smiles. He knew quite well how it came about, for it happened with every party his mother gave. Fearing she'd hurt someone's feelings, she always invited everyone within a twenty mile radius.

Lady Jacomena and Lady Katherine, accompanied by the little abigail, had also stopped by to watch the last touches being made to the decorations in the ballroom.

"If that is the case, Wilhemina, you are to remain in your chambers tonight," Lady Jacomena said, pointing her cane at Willie. "If Lady Katherine has need of your services, she can send for you. No sense adding one more body to the confusion."

Willie, trying to hide her disappointment, nodded. She had hoped she had proved her usefulness at the Bellrumple Ball. But after her humiliating *contretemp* with Sir Andrew, she knew she was definitely out of favor again with her ladyship.

Wakeford Hall had been all a hum for the last three

days. Delicious smells came from the kitchens, doubling everyone's appetites. Late in the afternoon, flowers were cut, decorations were hung, and an hour before a dinner for a select group of guests was to be served, the musicians arrived and began practicing in the ballroom.

Willie dressed Katy in a lovely green gown shot through with shimmering threads of silver. The stylish flounce around the neck and hem provided just the right touch to the simple lines. As before, Lady Jacomena allowed her niece to wear only a single strand of pearls and eardrops, and Willie agreed with her judgement. Katy, with her natural beauty, needed no glittering embellishments. Willie stood back to admire the effect.

"I wish you could come, Willie," Katy said, whirling about in front of the cheval mirror. "You wouldn't take up much room, and I know how much you love good music. Lord Wakeford said the orchestra his mother has hired is quite outstanding. Mayhaps, I can speak to him for you."

Willie blushed. "Don't fret, dear. I have an exciting book to read," she said, trying hard to put some enthusiasm into her voice, but she wished she could go to the ball, for Katy was a symphony all by herself when she danced, and a joy to watch.

Broonie had assured Willie that she would keep a watchful eye on Katy. They had both been so proud of her behavior this past week. Willie was truly beginning to believe that the baroness' promise not to take things again was sincere.

After an early supper, Willie went back to her room. It was a clear evening and the music from the ballroom climbed up the walls of the house and floated into the bedchamber. She sat on the window seat with her book in her lap, her feet tapping to the rhythm. This must be what it was like for a bird to view its world from a treetop, she thought. She rested her head against the window frame and gazed out over the moon-drenched rolling hills. Spicy aromas of flowers and herbs filled the warm air.

Nearer the manor house the terraced gardens became more formal, and right below was a view of a corner of the herb garden which she had run through yesterday after Lord Wakeford had rescued her from that odious Mr. Fultonhouse. Just as she was wishing she had wings to fly down to peek into the ballroom, inspiration struck.

"The herb garden!" she exclaimed, jumping down from her perch by the window. "Why didn't I think of it before?" If she were careful, she could hide behind the bushes below the terrace, perhaps even see some of the dancers through the tall windows of the great hall. Surely there could be no harm in it. Perhaps she could even catch a glimpse of Katy and his lordship.

As she hurried to the door, she envisioned herself as a grand lady clothed in a gown of gold and silver gossamer. Then she glanced down at her plain dress, and reality struck. She looked more like a little blackbird than a grand lady. What she needed was a fairy godmother—like Cinderella—to transform her for the ball. Unfortunately, such creatures seemed in short supply, and Willie knew she would have to rely on her own ingenuity. She ran to her trunk and flung open the lid. The lovely violet sarcenet gown Katy had given her was folded neatly on top. *Why not?* Willie thought. *Why not go to the ball?*

Oh, she wouldn't really. But she could slip down the back stairs to the herb garden. From there, she'd be able to hear the music clearly, and pretend she was one of the grand ladies. She could dance all by herself in the garden and perhaps peep into the tall windows and watch the others. As she quickly changed, Willie imagined her prince charming finding her in the garden. She grinned at the absurdity of it. Fairy tales and such foolishness were not for servants, but tonight, just this once, she could pretend otherwise. The night was made for magic. Slipping her black cape over her gown, she stepped into the hall.

Ten minutes later Willie stood among the sweet-scented plants, listening with delight to the strains of a waltz. The melody seduced her, and slipping off her wrap, she held out the corners at arms length. A pity she had no matching gloves to go with her dress, but it was a warm night, and Willie rather welcomed the fresh air on her bare arms. With her imaginary partner, she whirled round and round the narrow paths between the garden plots.

The music was clear, she could even hear the hum of voices, but her view was obstructed by the tall hedge of rhododendrons flanking the terrace. Willie remembered seeing a concrete bench surrounded by rosemary bushes. If she stood on that, perchance she could catch a better view of the party. Abandoning her dark-robed partner to the limb of a pear tree, she carefully picked her way along the path. The moon deserted her and darkness obscured that corner of the garden. Drawn by the sweet odor of the herbs, she soon found the bench, but her outstretched hands also felt the solid form of a person.

"Oh, my goodness!" she shrieked.

" 'Pon my soul!" came a deep response from a familiar voice.

Willie's eyes slowly became accustomed to the shadows. "Mr. Teagardner?"

The big man rose quickly, fumbling about until he pulled out his eyepiece. "Oh, dear! Oh, dear! Didn't mean to take up your spot," he said, peering over her shoulder as if expecting to see someone standing there.

"What in the world are you doing out here?" she gasped.

"Miss Winkie?" Mr. Teagardner sounded quite pleased and relieved with his discovery. "Where is . . . ? That is, are you alone, my lady?"

Heavens above, he thought her a lady. "Yes . . ." Willie caught her lower lip with her teeth. "That is, I stepped out for a breath of fresh air and quite lost my way." She fluttered her hand in what she hoped was a very maidenly way.

"Oh, that is so easily done at Wakeford's. Our place isn't nearly so grand. All these twists and turns do put one in a rattle, don't they?"

"But why are you not inside dancing?" she questioned.

"Well, I," he hesitated, running a finger around the top of his collar. "Truth is, never was very good at it. Doing the fancy, that is."

This threw Willie into the boughs for a moment. "I thought all the gentlemen knew how to dance."

"Not so, my lady." He shifted his big body clumsily from foot to foot. "Tried. Nothing came of it. My dance instructor said 'twas easier to teach a donkey."

As the moon rose above the clouds, she saw the despairing look on his face, and tried to console him. "Why, that was a very cruel thing for him to say."

"Thing is, he was right," he said woefully.

"Well, I do not believe it. Anyone can learn to dance. It is really very simple if you learn a few basic steps. I can show you how, if you would like." Lifting her skirt slightly so that he could see the way her slippered feet moved, Willie demonstrated a few steps. "Just go forward three steps, and then one back."

Mr. Teagardner concentrated on her feet. Then counting out loud, he imitated her.

"Jolly good, Mr. Teagardner! You did that quite well."

"Oh, I say now, do you think so?" he asked, surprise in his voice.

"I do, and it was easy, was it not?"

With a rumbling guffaw, he bowed, brought her bare fingers clumsily to his lips and asked, "May I have this dance, Miss Winkie?"

"No, you may not!" The deep angry voice erupted behind them from the shadows.

"Zounds, Wakeford! Thought you were the devil." Teagardner said, immediately dropping Willie's hand. "Enough to bring an elephant to his knees. I was just asking the lady to dance."

The earl took a menacing step forward. "Alone in the dark? Come now, John."

"Said she'd teach me . . ."

Duncan's brows snapped together. He was in no mood to hear what the minx was going to teach him. "You would take advantage of a . . . " Duncan was about to say *serving girl,* when he saw the pleading look in the little magpie's eyes. "A lady?" he finished.

"Indeed not, my lord!" John sounded insulted. "How could you suggest such a thing?"

Willie tried to slip away. The earl was furious, and he knew she'd disobeyed Lady Jacomena's orders to stay in her room. She was not afraid to face his wrath, but she hated the notion that he would realize she'd dressed in her finest gown and pretended to be a lady. She stumbled back a step, but strong fingers captured her wrist.

"No, you don't you little hellion," he whispered harshly. "I shall tend to you in a moment."

Duncan turned back to his belligerent houseguest. "That is enough, John! I suggest you go back to the house before you find yourself in more trouble than you can handle."

Mr. Teagardner turned so swiftly he whacked his shin on the corner of the bench, then hobbled as quickly as he was able toward the terrace.

Holding Willie at arm's length, Duncan looked her up and down. It was not his first glimpse of the dress, for he had seen it shimmering in the light of the moon, as he rounded the hedge. Finding the ball unbearably flat, he'd stepped out for a breath of air. When he'd heard the delightful sound of female chatter, he'd recognized her voice immediately. First pleasure warmed him, until anger spoiled that sensation when he heard a masculine voice answer her playful tone.

Duncan had been unduly hard on the bumbling Teagardner. He couldn't envision his neighbor behaving badly with any female, but an ungovernable rage had shot through him when he saw the fellow kiss Willie's hand. To see her slender figure next to the large, youthful Teagardner stirred feelings in Duncan he'd not known he possessed. He stared down at her, uncertain now what to say.

Willie sighed. "I meant no harm."

The devil within Duncan drove him. "Do you take dresses as well as jewelry?" he demanded, while thinking how beautiful and elfin-like she looked.

Willie looked at him apprehensively. "I swear, Lady Katherine gave me this dress. 'Twas too short for her. I wanted to hear the music better, and I . . . I was pretending to dance. I saw no harm in it."

"Hah, I saw you with Teagardner. You had no business leading him on—"

"Mr. Teagardner said he didn't know how to dance, and I offered to teach him a step or two. Is that a crime?" she said, twisting her arm from his grasp.

Lord, he wanted to believe her. She sounded so

convincing that once more guilt threaded through him. He smiled ruefully. "No crime, Willie, but I fear I owe you an apology."

"Why whatever do you mean, my lord?"

"I caused Mr. Teagardner to run off, and now you have no partner."

"I do not need one, my lord. I am quite accustomed to dancing by myself." Then she giggled. "I did have another partner before Mr. Teagardner."

His dark eyes scanning the shadows, Duncan growled, "There was someone here before John?"

"The gentleman is hanging in the pear tree near the terrace" she said, laughing at his startled expression. "He is dependable, warm and not in the least inclined to scold. His name is Mr. Mantle. Wait here, my lord, and I will introduce you." She whirled gracefully, then disappeared into the darkness.

Returning a few moments later, she held the black cape in front of her, and pirouetted as though dancing with a partner.

Apprehension filled her when he did not comment. In the pale moonlight she could not read his expression, but she knew humor was not one of the earl's outstanding qualities. She shivered as he stepped towards her and reached out a hand.

Duncan took the wrap from her and tossed it onto a bush. "Then I shall have to chase off Mr. Mantle the way I did poor John. Now, my lady, will you allow me the pleasure of this dance?" Not waiting for an answer, Duncan placed his hand lightly upon her waist and with the other took her hand. He felt her body quiver when they touched. Although he feigned indifference, he was keenly aware of her responses. It was not difficult to tell that this was the first time she'd danced intimately with a man, and Duncan willed himself to remain in control.

As the earl whirled Willie along the paths among the sweet-smelling plants, his touch rendered her speechless. Even if it had not, she still would've been afraid to speak for fear of breaking the spell. She felt like Cinderella dancing with her prince. She wished that he would kiss her, but he did not. And she certainly couldn't kiss him, because the top of her head reached no higher than his chin. Never had Willie wished so fervently to be taller. She looked up hungrily at the firm line of his lips. No, he would have to initiate the act, she thought, but to her great disappointment, he did not. He kept himself away from her, and it was only occasionally that his knee brushed against her skirt. The music ended before it had any right to. Lord Wakeford bowed low over her hand, then turned swiftly, leaving her alone in the moonlight. Willie stared after him. It wasn't even midnight, she thought wistfully.

Duncan kicked a stone out of his way. The moment he had taken Willie in his arms, he'd known it was a mistake. What was the matter with him? It was only a matter of days before he planned to offer for Lady Katherine, a tender, gracious lady with impeccable bloodlines. Yet, he had still felt an overwhelming compulsion to take a serving girl into his arms. No, not just any serving girl, but this one in particular. Another minute and he would have had her on the ground. He was no better than Cecil.

Disgusted with himself, the earl walked away from the house. He could not go back to the ballroom until his body cooled. Damn the girl, anyway. She had no right to be dressed as she was. She'd looked every inch a lady, and that nettled his conscience more.

He could no longer think of Willie as a mere servant. She was turning his well-ordered world upside down. Lady Jacomena claimed it was a dangerous thing for the working class to be educated, and he was beginning to see why. "You are extremely dangerous, my little magpie," he mused aloud.

It was time he married, and quickly. As soon as he returned to London, he would ask for an audience with the Duke of Hammerfield. That settled, Duncan returned to the ballroom, but his thoughts remained on Willie despite his efforts to set her from his mind.

He retired as soon as permissable, and found his valet waiting for him. Charles had done so for the past six years and Duncan had taken it for granted that his valet would be there when he wanted. Now he looked at the man and wondered.

"Charles . . . "

"Yes, my lord?"

"Have you ever thought of marrying?"

"Marrying, my lord?"

"That is what I believe I said," Duncan replied, wondering if other people conversed with one's servants. After all, Charles was . . . well, Charles was just Charles. It did not feel quite right, but with thoughts of Willie in mind, he persisted. "You know . . . is there any woman you've thought of in that way?"

Charles assisted his lordship in removing his coat, then stepped back. "How could I, my lord? 'Twould be very difficult to set up a household with you moving about so much the way that you do." There was a pause while he hung up the earl's coat. "Well—there was a lass once—but that was a long time ago."

"What happened?"

The valet shrugged. "She wouldn't have me, my lord."

Duncan frowned. "Because you had to move about too much?"

"No, my lord. She said I was too finicky."

"I would say you are meticulous, particular, exact-ing—not finicky, Charles. That is why I employ you. She did not value you properly."

"Thank you, my lord. I try my best." The valet produced a brocaded dressing gown and held it out for his lordship to slip into.

"I am quite certain she pined away."

"Oh, no, my lord. She chose the baker's son and now has six children."

"I say! Well . . . " Duncan let the matter drop. It was the longest conversation he'd had with his valet in all the years he'd known him, and it disturbed him to realize he'd never thought of the man as possibly hav-ing a life apart from serving him.

Duncan finished his drink and placed the glass on the side table.

It was all the fault of that nymph. She'd turned his world into a rigamarole. She made peers look like fustians and maids look like ladies. A thief who stole his reason and equanimity, and now she played havoc with his composure. If the little abigail had never been seen before by his guests, and he had dressed her in silks and satins, she could have walked into the ball-room tonight and convinced everyone that she was as grand and noble as any of them. For a moment, he was sorry she hadn't been able to attend the ball.

Suddenly, the room was too warm. He dismissed Charles, and stepped out onto the terrace. His eyes searched the dark gardens, but there was no sign of the sprite he'd danced with in the moonlight.

On Sunday, when they'd returned to Dalison Hall, Lady Jacomena announced she'd received a letter from her brother, the Duke of Hammerfield.

"Katherine, your father has leased an old country house called Odin's Woods just outside London. He wishes to see you," she said. "His coach will be here at twelve o'clock noon . . . " She read on silently a few minutes before continuing, " . . . on Tuesday. Good heavens! That is day after tomorrow. Leave it to Harcourt to think of no one but himself."

Katy clasped her hands. "Oh, I can be ready in no time at all, Auntie."

"It is of little consequence to me, for I shan't be going. But he wants to see Miss Abbot, too. Most likely wants a report from her."

Willie watched her eagerly, her eyes pleading to be included.

Lady Jacomena looked at her, then at the letter. "He doesn't mention your maid, but I am sure that is taken for granted. If the duke has orders to give, best you all hear them straight from the horse's mouth." She let out a bark of laughter, then stopped abruptly. "Well, what are you waiting for? Off with you. I have a gathering to go to tomorrow at Mrs. Vesey's. She's presenting a new member of the Royal Art Academy." Lady Jacomena dug around in the pile of opened letters before pulling out one particular note. "Blake wrote saying he will be there—says he saw my painting being restored at Tellerman's and will tell me how it goes."

"Mr. William Blake?" Katy asked breathlessly, showing the first spark of interest since they'd arrived at Dalison Hall.

Oh my, thought Willie, remembering their conversation at Wakeford Manor. Every time Katy had seen Mr. Blake, Nathaniel Penbrooke had accompanied him.

Lady Jacomena, busily concentrating on another

missive, didn't answer, but Willie saw the determination in Katy's eyes. "May I go with you, Auntie?"

"To Mrs. Vesey's?" Jacomena said, glancing up in surprise. "I'm certain you have several functions you would find more to your taste."

"I would much rather go with you," Katy insisted.

Lady Jacomena gave a wave of her hand, but she couldn't hide the gleam of pleasure in her eyes. "Well, do as you wish, but I have told Old Tom to have the chaise out front at four o'clock. Be ready, for I will not wait on you."

Later, when they were in their bedroom, Katy clasped her hands to her chest. Her face glowed and she seemed more beautiful than Willie had ever thought possible.

"Oh, Willie, Mr. Penbrooke will be at Mrs. Vesey's. I never knew being in love could be so wonderful. What could be more perfect? Then on Tuesday, when I shall see my dear father, I can tell him he need not worry any longer about finding a husband for me. I have found my own."

Katy spied Mr. Penbrooke conversing with a small group of people as soon as she, Aunt Jacomena, and Broonie entered Mrs. Vesey's the following late afternoon. She knew he saw her too, for his face changed from fair to a brilliant scarlet before he turned back to answer the gentleman standing next to him. Her aunt immediately deserted them to join a faction of her own cohorts, but Katy's interest was still centered on the young poet. If he was too shy to come to her, she would go to him. She had no sooner tried to manuever Broonie in Nathaniel's direction than she was approached by the Marquis of Wainscotte, the handsome man who'd shown her the albino crows in the park, but quite old, Katy decided, surely near his thirtieth year.

"Lady Katherine," he said with great assurance, bowing elegantly over her hand.

Katy was aware of the many eyes turned their way, for she had heard that the earl was much sought after since the death of his wife a year ago.

Lord Wainscotte chatted with her for a few moments, but seemed to become bored when they were joined by Lady Elizabeth and her daughter. Before he begged his reluctance to leave them, he turned to Katy and asked, "May I have the pleasure of accompanying you to partake of refreshments later, my lady?"

Trying to think of how she could manage to find a way to speak to Nathaniel alone, Katy was taken aback by the sudden request and could do no more than say, "Why . . . yes, my lord. Thank you."

The marquis had no sooner departed than she found herself hovered over by Sir Philip Norton, a portly man she had met at Aunt Jacomena's and had instantly disliked.

Katy glanced about wishing she could see Lord Wakeford, even though she knew he would be at an evening session of Parliament. Unfortunately for her, he seemed to take his duties in the House of Lords much more seriously than many of his peers, for his lordship was kindness itself, and she knew from the way he had looked at Sir Philip that he would rescue her from his unwanted attentions. In one last desperate attempt, she looked across the room at Nathaniel and smiled encouragingly. Relief ran through her as she saw him square his shoulders and start to make his way eagerly toward her. But just before he reached her side, she heard the smooth voice of the marquis of Wainscotte speak from behind her.

"If you will excuse us, Norton, refreshments are about to be served."

"See here, my lord, I was just about to ask the lady, m'self," Sir Philip sputtered belligerently, taking privilege of his advanced age as having precedence over rank.

Brushing aside Sir Philip's insult with self-assured aplomb, the marquis offered his arm to Katy. "I believe the baroness is promised to me."

Frantically, Katy turned her head to see Nathaniel standing behind her. The distressed look on his beloved face nearly undid her, but she slipped her hand into the crook of Lord Wainscotte's arm and smiled bravely up at him.

She didn't get another chance to be near Nathaniel the rest of the evening. Katy returned home disappointed but more determined than ever to fight the unfair circumstances which kept them apart.

Tuesday afternoon the Dalison coach passed through the gates of Odin's Woods and drew up before an isolated manor house. Neglect showed in the untrimmed gardens and dead vines climbing the walls. The three women were ushered inside by an angular, sour-faced man. "I am Sharp, the duke's man."

Broonie gave him an equally withering look. "Why is everything so blasted dark?"

"His Grace keeps the windows covered, madam. Now if you and the maid will wait in here—" he said, opening a door to an even more forbidding room, "His Grace wants to see Lady Katherine . . . alone."

Chapter Eleven

Willie stuck her head out the door and watched the butler lead Katy down the darkened hallway. "Perhaps we should go with her," she said anxiously.

Broonie removed one of the covers from a chair and settled down. "Our darlin' will be seein' her father for the first time in fourteen years. 'Tis fittin' they be alone. Come back noo and don't be worryin' yerself."

Willie returned to her chair, but she couldn't sit still. Her prince was near and she wanted so badly to tell him how grateful she was for all the wonderful years she'd had at Gilfallen. She remembered hearing Lady Jacomena say that the duke was a stingy man to have taken an orphan for his daughter's maid—that he should have hired a respectable young lady of good breeding and education. Well, she was wrong. She had been good for Katy. No one could be more devoted. And serving Katy had been a blessing for Willie. She dreaded to think what her life would have been like if the Duke of Hammerfield had not come to the foundling home years ago and taken a poor little girl to be maid to his daughter. Surely it showed him to be a man of most generous heart, not the pinchpenny that Lady Jacomena claimed him to be. Willie was determined to find a way to thank him.

* * *

Katy entered a large room through thick, oaken double-doors. Massive beams supported the high ceiling like ancient warriors. An immense stone fireplace covered much of the far wall, and even though it was midsummer, a fire was blazing. But its warmth did little to dispense the damp chill. She looked through the fog of heavy smoke to a figure seated in a wing-backed chair near the hearth. A candelabrum, set on a large round table beside him, silhouetted the man's gaunt features. She barely heard the butler withdraw, for her concentration was on the man.

"Father?" she said, in a half whisper.

"Come here, child," he commanded in a surprisingly strong voice.

Laughing, Katy ran across the flagstone floor to stand before the Duke of Hammerfield. In his hand, she saw he held a silver object no bigger than his palm. Katy smiled as she eagerly waited for her father to address her.

Steel blue eyes appraised her, then gazed down at the ornament in his hand. "You do not favor your mother," he said, caustically. "Not at all."

Disappointment unsettled Katy, until it dawned on her what he held. "Is that a picture of my mother?" she asked, eyes wide.

Hammerfield handed Katy the small painting, its frame a delicate, handcrafted filigree. She took it and gasped.

"She was lovely," he said, in words so low Katy barely heard them. "That was painted by Maria Had-field-Cosway. It is worth a fortune now, for she completed only a few miniatures. But when she saw your mother at a reception given by the Prince of Wales, she begged Katherine to sit for her."

A fit of coughing overcame the duke, alarming Katy. She placed the picture on the table while she attended him. "You do not look well."

The duke seemed for a moment to be watching someone far off, then his eyes refocused. "I am well enough. However, it is not my health which we are here to discuss, but your progress in society. My people inform me that you have several suitors already."

"Oh, Father, I have the most wonderful news for you. You need not concern yourself with acquiring a husband for me. I have found one by myself," Katy said proudly.

Hammerfield picked up a sheet of paper from the table beside his chair and handed it to her. "Is his name on this list?"

Katy held the paper to the light. "No," she replied, but with eyes shining, she settled herself on the floor at the duke's feet, and placed her hands on his knees. "I am certain it is just an oversight, for he is the most kind and considerate of men—and I love him with all my heart." In animated tones she told him of Nathaniel Penbrooke.

As she was speaking, the duke reached out his hand as if to place it on her head, but withdrew it before touching her. He scowled. "Enough, daughter! You cannot seriously believe I would accept as my son-in-law a penniless apprentice to an art dealer? A mere grandson of a knight? Do not waste my time with such nonsense."

Katy gasped. "But Father—"

Another rasping cough wracked the duke's body effectively halting her protest. From out of nowhere, the butler appeared and after pouring a glass of dark liquid from a decanter on a sideboard, carried it quickly to his master.

Fright and concern written across her face, Katy leaped to her feet. "What is the matter?"

Hammerfield drank the brew and laid his head back against the cushions of the chair. "Sharp," he rasped.

"Yes, Your Grace?"

"Tell Miss Abbot I want to see her."

Broonie had no sooner left with the butler than Willie decided to follow. Not only was the room creepy with shadows, but she'd decided that she was not going to be left out of whatever was going on. She wanted to see Katy's happiness and hear the duke give Broonie the praise she so rightly deserved for doing such a splendid job of raising his daughter.

And how was her *Grace* to know in what high esteem the little orphan girl held him if she did not tell him herself? With that purpose in mind, she crept along the musty-smelling corridor with little fear of being seen in the darkness. As soon as Sharp came back into the hallway and headed off in another direction, she flattened herself against the wall outside the room Broonie had entered.

The sounds coming from inside were far different than Willie expected. A pottage of gruff male commands, Katy's weeping, and Broonie's pungent brogue. Puzzled Willie leaned closer and peeked through the narrow opening between the thick double doors.

Light from the flames in the huge fireplace illuminated three figures. A man sat hunched in the high-backed chair in front of the hearth. It was he who was shouting. Broonie, as unbending as a Scottish pine, stood facing him.

Seated on the floor between them, her face in her hands, Katy pleaded, "But if you would only receive

Mr. Penbrooke, you would see that he is a splendid young man."

Willie saw the duke put his seal on a packet. "Miss Abbot, you will give my sister her orders. These are the names I have judged to be acceptable. I am not the blockhead my sister thinks and have done my own investigating. She thought to trick me by sending a list of unacceptable men. Tell her I rejected all of her names—all except one." He handed the packet to Broonie. "Only those men I have listed are to be sent to this house. Let it be understood by all, that I, and I alone, will choose my daughter's husband."

Katy's sobs echoed in the cavernous room.

Willie shuddered. This could not be her *Grace,* her prince. Unwilling to believe he could be so unfeeling, she stood stricken until a hand clamped down upon her shoulder. Startled, she tumbled forward. The momentum propelling both her and her attacker through the double doors.

Hammerfield's head snapped up. "What is the meaning of this, Sharp? Who is that person?"

The butler's strong grip did not lessen. Willie felt herself half lifted, half shoved across the hardwood floors, until she stood before the duke.

Broonie's big, warm arm reassuringly encircled Willie's shoulders. "This be the maid that waits upon Lady Katherine."

The duke was on his feet in an instant, enraged. "I gave my sister orders that only you and my daughter were to come here today."

Willie's mouth fell open. This was not the young man she remembered. His face showed no life but rather looked like a withered thorn bush in winter. She strained to look up at him. How tall he was, his hair silky in the flickering firelight. For a second, Willie glimpsed a shadow of the proud young nobleman who'd visited the foundling home. He had looked unhappy then, and he looked unhappy now. Pity replaced her fear. Yes, indeed, a word of praise, not censure, was needed here. She smiled as brightly as she could and said, *"My Grace,* I have always wanted to thank you for what you did for me."

Blue eyes glared down at her, much like they had that day in the orphanage. "How dare you address me in such a way? Stark, remove her. Miss Abbot, you are dismissed also."

Willie didn't know what she had said to distress him. Confused, she followed Broonie out of the room.

Katy scrambled to her feet, but her father stopped her. "I have something to say to you, daughter, before you leave."

Half an hour later, Willie and Broonie were joined by a Katy they hardly recognized. The fairy child was gone.

Sharp called a footman to escort them to their rooms on the next floor. An hour later, a serving girl carried supper to them. The duke didn't appear again, and the next morning after breaking fast, they were on their way back to London. Not that Willie was in the cheeriest of moods herself, but there was nothing she or Broonie could do to break Katy out of her dismals. Neither could Willie get her to reveal what her father had said to her.

When they approached Dalison Hall at four in the afternoon, the faded cobalt blue door looked like a haven to Willie. It was only as they stepped down from the coach that she noticed a familiar, stylish phaeton standing across the street. Willie's heart sang. Lord Wakeford was here.

Duncan had stayed on at the estate a few days longer to finish up his affairs. His mother surprised him when she announced her desire to visit their house in Kent. He suspected she had some sort of ulterior motive, but he had long ago given up trying to puzzle out her reasons. In time she would tell him what she was about if she wished him to know. He saw her off cheerfully, then set out for London. He had thought hard and long about taking a wife, and once his decision was made, he lost no time. As soon as he arrived in Town, he called at Lady Jacomena's, only to find Lady Katherine had gone to see her father.

Perhaps it was for the best, he thought, since he'd have to approach Lady Jacomena first anyway to help him gain an audience with the Duke of Hammerfield. To his satisfaction, she agreed to do so.

"Indeed," she said, waving her cane in the air, "I am pleased to give you my blessing."

Successfully dodging the stick, Duncan suppressed a grin. He'd noticed she was not using her cane as frequently as a means of support, but more as a weapon to make a point. "I am glad to see you enjoying improved health, Lady Jacomena."

"The visit to your mother did much to restore me," she replied. "Must have been the country air. But do stay and take tea with me—or something stronger, if you have a mind to it. I know I do." And with that, she took a decanter of brandy out of a cupboard and poured two drinks.

And so it happened that she was just seeing the earl out of the green salon a half hour later when Katy and Willie entered the house.

Broonie followed them and handed a packet to Lady Jacomena. "His Grace said I was to give you this," she said unceremoniously.

Her ladyship tore open the seal and glanced quickly down the page. "The scoundrel! Thinks he can best me, does he?" she said, then smiled. "Demmed if he didn't put you on his list also, Wakeford."

Duncan's attention was riveted on the two young women conversing in low murmurs at the other end of the hall. From the stoic look on both their faces, he knew something was amiss. But he didn't have time to think about it, for Lady Jacomena demanded his attention.

She held up the paper. "My brother says you are welcome to call on him. However, he is inviting several other gentlemen as well. I suggest you go as soon as possible, before these other men receive their letters."

Although Willie couldn't hear what they were saying, she watched Lady Jacomena address the earl. Wrapping an encouraging arm around Katy, Willie urged her forward. His lordship's tall, commanding figure made her think of what he had said to her in the library. *I want to help you. If at any time you would like someone to talk to* . . . Well, help was what they needed now. She would ask him to speak to the duke on behalf of Katy and Nathaniel. "Be brave, dear," she whispered. "Lord Wakeford is very influential and I am certain if you approach him, he will do what he can."

Katy blinked to keep from weeping. "The earl has always been most kind, but I am a little fearful of him. Do you really think he would help us?"

Willie spoke emphatically, "You want to marry Mr. Penbrooke, don't you?"

"Oh, you know I do," Katy said, her eyes brimming over.

Duncan heard a cry behind him and turned to see Lady Katherine break into tears. He took her hand, intending to let her know that whatever her dilemma, she had his support, but before he knew it, she was in his arms, sobbing her heart out on his shoulder. Dear

God, the meeting with her father had to have been a very emotional one for her to be in such a state. He talked to her as he would to a child, soothed her fears and wiped her cheeks with his handkerchief. From the way she clung to him, she obviously did not have an aversion to his touch. That was good. He didn't want a wife who came reluctantly to the marriage bed.

Then his gaze fell upon the little magpie. He thought he had succeeded in putting her out of his mind, but only one look into those deep, violet eyes and Duncan felt as though a knife had been plunged into his stomach. Trying to ignore the unexplicable pain, he turned his attention back to Lady Katherine.

Lady Jacomena raised her eyebrows and coughed. As much as she wished to encourage Wakeford, she could not approve this sudden display of affection.

Duncan had nearly forgotten he held the baroness in his arms and immediately released her. "A thousand pardons for my unseemly behavior, my lady."

Duncan thought Lady Katherine was about to say something to him, but the Scotswoman stepped forward and pulled her away, then hurried her toward the stairs.

Duncan spoke with concern. "I hope that my lapse in manners will not exclude me from being welcome here in the future, my lady."

Lady Jacomena, trying to hide her expression of secret pleasure, pointed her cane at Duncan, missing his nose by a mere inch. "I believe my niece has been overstimulated by her reunion with her father, my lord. Mayhaps, it would be best if you returned to see her at a later date."

Duncan had always prided himself on his agility in the boxing ring at Jackson's, and sidestepped quickly to save himself from permanent injury.

Lady Jacomena chattered on, showing no awareness of nearly causing a disaster. "Oh, by the by, Mrs. Vesey is giving a musicale on Saturday. She has asked that Katherine sing. I would like you to be our escort, if you are not otherwise engaged, of course."

Duncan sensed Lady Jacomena was trying to flirt with him. He hid his amusement the best he could and said sincerely, "It would be my pleasure, your ladyship."

Abovestairs, when they were alone in their room, Katy turned to Willie. "I have made such a jumble of things. Do you still think Lord Wakeford will help us?"

Willie swallowed hard. She was only a serving maid and an orphan at that, but the truth could not be denied. She was jealous. The earl was in love with Katy. Putting her own heartache aside, she patted Kathy's hand. "I do not think he was put off by your tears, dear. In fact, I surmise the earl thinks it's a woman's nature to be unable to keep her emotions under control as well as a man. But try not to let Lady Jacomena know that all did not go well with your father. As we were climbing the stairs, I heard her say you are to attend a musicale with her on Saturday, and his lordship agreed to escort you. Surely sometime during the evening you will be able to speak to him alone. I suggest you approach him after you have sung." Willie knew no man could refuse Katy anything after being charmed by her enchanting voice.

Katy nodded submissively as she always did, but she was thinking otherwise. She had always believed that her loved ones would see to her happiness. Now her father had shaken that trust. How could she be certain that Lord Wakeford would rise to her cause any more than her father had? Katy decided to take matters into her own hands and sat down at her escritoire to compose a letter.

> *Dear Mr. Penbrooke,*
> *My father has bought a house in the country outside London, where he will receive the gentlemen who he thinks will be good husbands for me.*
> *When I visited him I spoke of you, but I do not believe he understood the deep feelings we already have developed for each other, or the high esteem in which I hold you. Were he to meet you in person and see your noble character, I am certain he would be persuaded to accept your suit.*
> *I hope for my sake, you will call on him.*
> *I shall include a letter of introduction for you to present at the door.*

Katy followed with directions to Odin's Woods, certain that once her father met her dear Nathaniel, he would see how wise a choice she had made. It was foolish for her to have a husband with a lot of money when she had so much herself. There was no other man in her estimation, who could compose such beautiful, thoughtful poetry, or use watercolors with such freshness. He was a magician who had only to look into her eyes to know what she was thinking.

The next morning, Katy sought out Johnny and asked him to take her missive to the gallery of Jacob Tellerman on Oxford Street. Feeling quite proud of herself, she hurried back up to her apartment.

When Duncan returned to his townhouse late Wednesday afternoon, he found a message from the Duke of Hammerfield giving the direction to Odin's Woods and listing his specifications for a son-in-law.

Duncan realized that the other men on the duke's list must have received similar letters, and if he wished to wed Lady Katherine, it behooved him to make haste.

The question was, did he really wish to wed her? Unbidden, an image of Willie came to mind, and he swore fluently at the way the girl seemed to possess his thoughts. She was only a serving maid . . . and he had a duty to his family to marry well, to preserve the name. If he married Lady Katherine, the little abigail would always be nearby. How would he be able to stand it? Unless—

Marry for love, his mother had told him. Never before had Duncan let the thought enter his mind of taking a mistress, once he was wed. His parents' happy union had always been his ideal. Determined to put such jaded thoughts aside, Duncan retired early. Lady Katherine waited. He would call on His Grace in the morning—before the other gentlemen had the opportunity. Sleep, however, eluded him, and he spent a restless night.

Early Thursday morning, before the fog rolled up its carpet from off the muddy streets, Duncan mounted his chestnut gelding and headed out of town.

Duncan rode into the park two hours later. He presented his card at the door and showed the summons from the duke. Only after the butler thoroughly scrutinized both the card, the letter, and the earl, was he permitted to enter. Sharp took Duncan's cape and hat and showed him into a dismal anteroom. A maid was removing the last of the dust covers from the furniture, while another rubbed sweet smelling beeswax into the top of a walnut table. The duke was obviously expecting callers, but it surprised Duncan that no one had bothered to open the curtains. An oversight, brought on by his early arrival, no doubt. But Duncan had no sooner settled into a chair, preparing for a long wait, when the butler returned.

"If you will follow me, my lord, his grace will receive you now."

The first thing Duncan noticed when he was ushered into the smoke-filled room was the huge fireplace, second, the variety of gaming tables. The heads of an African ibex and a rather mangy-looking male lion, eyed him from one wall. There were also some shadowy mounted creatures set about on shelves, but he had no time to study them. Lady Jacomena had mentioned that her brother had just purchased the old estate. Duncan thought the predilection for sport must have been habits of the former owner, for the man sitting stiffly in the chair near the hearth did not look the sort to welcome the hardships of veldt or jungle. He looked rather frail, but startled Duncan with the strength of his command.

"Come closer where I can see you, Wakeford."

The click of Duncan's boots resounded across the stone floor. He knew immediately that the Duke of Hammerfield was going to be difficult man to like. A hard crust of cynicism surrounded him.

Duncan inclined his head, politely. "Your Grace."

The duke glanced down at a long piece of foolscap he held, then fixed the earl with an undecipherable look. "I probably know more about your affairs than you do, Wakeford. But a piece of paper doesn't tell me the mettle of the man." It took Hammerfield another half hour to outline in a direct and forceful way what he had in mind for his future son-in-law and the husband of his daughter.

Duncan listened, amazed. His expression did not change, but he surmised the document in the duke's hand chronicled everything about him from birth to the present day. "And what has Lady Katherine to say about all this?"

Hammerfield gave him a look of surprise. "Why, nothing. She will do as I tell her and marry whom I choose."

Duncan took another step forward and spoke forcefully. "I acknowledge the honor you do me, but I will not coerce Lady Katherine into marriage. The final decision must be hers."

The duke's eyes narrowed for a brief second, but at the mention of the baroness, Duncan saw a sudden shift in the older man's concentration. He began to speak of his wife instead of his daughter. The deep baritone lost some of its anger, and his eyes were not as focused. Duncan began to wonder if His Grace had mixed the two ladies in his mind. The duke picked up a small miniature portrait which he cradled in his hand.

Then the harsh voice returned with all its command. "That will be all, Wakeford. You have my permission to address my daughter."

When Duncan stepped outside the room, he referred to his watch and was surprised to see that nearly an hour had passed. Sharp awaited with his coat and hat. As Duncan passed the anteroom, he heard male voices from within. The jackals were converging already. Descending the steps, he met the Marquis of Wainscotte and Sir Phillip Norton on their way up. Sir Phillip was only a knight, but he was from an old, distinguished family and one of the wealthiest men in England. Wealthier than himself, Duncan admitted, but a sour man who gained much of his fortune from the labor of children in the coal mines. On passing, each man did no more than nod to the others.

Duncan quickly mounted his horse which was being held by a groom. He saw that the other men had come in coaches, probably thinking it more impressive. Thank God, he'd gotten his bid in before any of the others. He only hoped his outburst had not diminished his chances, but Duncan refused to put himself in any man's pocket.

The letter Nathaniel Penbrooke had received that morning threw him into such a quandary that he felt paralyzed. Lady Katherine loved him. Hope, fear, disaster, bravado, crushing defeat, ran through him like quicksilver. Finally, by the end of the day, the young man had worked himself up to such a fever that he knew he would risk going to the gallows to win his baroness. There was a matter of transportation to consider, of course. He had none at his disposal, except his feet, and no blunt to pay for a horse or coach. He had not as yet sent his monthly stipend home to his father, but did not feel at ease using that money. The more he thought on it, the more he realized he really had no choice in the matter.

Friday morning, Mr. Penbrooke, with the money from the teapot in the pocket of his brown coat, made his way to the post office and purchased a ticket on the next mail coach. With the many stops to deliver and pick up the mail, the journey took several hours. It was late in the afternoon when the driver let him off on the road nearest Odin's Woods. Nathaniel set out to walk the rest of the way. Two fine coaches and a racing curricle with a highhanded whip at the ribbons passed him, but none offered him a ride. By the time he reached the park entrance, he was quite badly covered with dust.

Had Sharp been at his usual post, Nathaniel Penbrooke would never have been admitted. But the butler was occupied in ushering other callers to and from the anteroom, and David, the young footman who replaced him didn't know how to read, and was too flustered to realize Nathaniel's name was not on the list of accepted callers. So it was that Mr. Penbrooke found himself in a dark, vast room, along with three other gentlemen.

Nathaniel waited for permission to be seated, but none came. His companions acted as if he were not visible, so he retreated to a corner and stood well hidden in the shadows. At intervals, a dark clad servant announced one of the gentlemen's name, then led him to see the duke. Finally, Nathaniel found himself alone.

Realizing that his name was not on the coveted list, and that no one seemed aware of his existence, Nathaniel gathered his courage and stepped to the door. Silence lay like a blanket over the dark hall. Then he saw the butler emerging from a set of double doors further down the dimly lit hall.

"Is that the lot, Sharp?" a voice bellowed from behind the doors.

"Yes, Your Grace," the butler replied, turning slightly back towards the room. "Lord Winthrop was the last name on the list."

A low murmur ensued. Nathaniel couldn't make out the words, but he knew this would be his only chance to see the duke. As the tall servant hurried toward another part of the house, courage poured into the young man. Keeping the image of Lady Katherine fixed firmly in his mind, Nathaniel squared his shoulders and marched bravely toward the double doors.

Chapter Twelve

Saturday morning Old Tom found a letter addressed to Lady Katherine Dalison on the front doorstep. Pansy carried it upstairs with the tray of hot chocolate, scones and jam.

Katy sat on the edge of the bed and eagerly tore open the seal.

My dear Lady Katherine,

It is with heavy heart that I write this. Threatening me with great reprisals, His Grace has forbidden me to ever see you again.

At first he said that he was affronted that I should even dare to be so bold as to approach him, but I asked him to hear me out. I declared my deep admiration for you and promised to do everything in my power to make you happy. I told him of my prospects at Tellerman's and that someday I hoped to open my own gallery. This did not suffice, of course. Thinking to show him my abilities in distinguishing artistic merit, I remarked on the beautiful miniature painting I saw beside him on the table. I recognized it immediately as a rare piece by Richard Cosway's wife, Maria. He said that it was a

*portrait of the late Duchess of Hammerfield and
for a moment his eyes seemed to soften.*

*To keep the conversation in what I thought to be
a pleasant vein, I asked to see it, and hoping to
prove my great affection for you, I said that I
thought you even more beautiful than your mother.
Instead of agreeing with me, he grabbed it from my
hand. He then began to order me out when a fit of
coughing rendered him helpless. The butler arrived
and escorted him from the room. I quickly withdrew and returned to London before I could be
accused of causing him bodily harm.*

*Our dream is hopeless, my beloved. I knew when
I first saw you I could never hope to reach so high.
Know that I shall remain your servant forever.*

When Katy burst out crying, Willie hurried to her
side. "Whatever is the matter, dear?"

Katy handed her the letter. By the time Willie finished reading it, Katy had dried her tears and was
pacing the floor, a frightened look on her face. "I must
go and speak to Father."

Willie looked up in surprise. "You know your aunt
would not let you do that."

Katy put a finger to her lips and whispered, "She
shan't find out. We shall say that we are going for a
ride in the park."

"Alone? You are not thinking, dear. You cannot go
alone, and you cannot ask one of your gentlemen
friends to drive you. If you ask Old Tom, he will report
you to Lady Jacomena."

Katy furrowed her brow in deep concentration, then
brightened. "We will sneak out of the house and hire
a hack," she said, smiling at her brilliant idea.

Willie shook her head. "Mrs. Butterworth or your
aunt never miss a trick. They would see us. Besides,

you are to attend the gathering at Mrs. Vesey's to-night."

Katy's voice became more determined. "They will not see us if we sneak down the servant's stairway and go out the back entrance. Daisy and Pansy are cleaning in the front of the house at this hour, and if I wear one of your hooded capes over my dress, we shall look like household maids. We can go straightaway to my father's house and be back before dinner."

Willie looked at Katy in surprise. "But Broonie will know."

Subterfuge was not a talent Katy had ever shown before. Her newfound determination had her cheeks blooming pinker than the roses of Gilfallen, and Willie watched fascinated as the usually reticent baroness began to count the coins in her reticule.

"Go tell her that I wish to sleep all day, so that my voice will be rested for the musicale tonight," Katy said gaily, throwing off her robe. "Oh, do hurry, Willie. I shall dress myself."

The excitement of a new adventure proved too irresistible for Willie to pass up and she rushed off to find the old nurse.

If the driver of the dray thought it strange that he was being commandeered to carry two young maids so far from town, he said nothing when he saw the amount of coins he would earn if he got them to Odin's Woods in record time.

David, the footman, could not hide his astonishment when he opened the door of the Duke of Hammerfield's house to see a rather disheveled baroness of Gilfallen and her maid standing on the doorstep.

Katy didn't wait for him to address her before she sailed past him and headed toward the room at the end of the corridor. It was all Willie could do to keep up.

The two girls hurried into the large gameroom. One look told them the duke was not there, when Sharp appeared.

"I have come to see my father," Katy said. "Where is he?"

Disapproval shown in the butler's eyes, but he answered civilly. "His Grace has not arisen as yet. He had a harrowing confrontation yesterday which set off one of his fits. The doctor had to be called."

Katy jumped forward. "Oh, I must see him."

Sharp hesitated as if he were thinking the matter over. "If my lady will be so kind as to wait here, I shall inform His Grace of your arrival."

Willie put her arm around Katy and led her to a chair.

Katy wrung her hands. "It is all my fault. I insisted Nathaniel come. 'Twas his visit which set him off. I know it was. He said in his letter that Father went into a frightful rage when he asked permission to marry me."

Willie made a sweep of the room with her arms. "Nonsense. See all the empty glasses and bottles sitting about on the tables. His Grace must have done a great bit of entertaining with the gentlemen who came to ask for your hand. I am certain your father has only your best interests at heart and is only tired from the great responsibility he has taken upon him to find you a suitable husband." Willie hoped she was right, but after her disappointing encounter with the duke on their previous visit, puzzling questions remained.

Katy glanced about hopefully. "Do you really think that is it?"

Willie doubted His Grace had developed an understanding heart overnight, but she nodded encouragingly.

Katy's attention was drawn to the tiny painting of her mother on the table beside her. She picked it up and ran her finger around the dainty frame. "I never really knew her," she said.

Several minutes later, Sharp returned. Ignoring the baroness' abigail, he said he had orders to escort Lady Katherine to her father's apartment. Willie followed at a discrete distance and watched Katy enter the dark, cave-like bedchamber. When the butler withdrew, Willie tiptoed to the door and peeked in. Although it was quite warm in the house, there was a fire blazing in the fireplace. The drapes were pulled shut, and the duke lay in a large, canopied bed, propped up against several pillows. The coverlet was drawn up to his chin and his face appeared quite flushed in the light of the flames.

Katy stood beside him, her voice pleading. "Oh, Father, please reconsider."

For someone professing to be so sick, the duke's angry words were not difficult for Willie to hear. "I told you once and tell you now, I will choose your husband. Whatever possessed Miss Abbot to bring you out here, anyway?"

Willie edged closer to hear Katy's reply.

"Broonie doesn't know I am here."

Oh, dear, Willie thought, they were in trouble now. Although Katy was showing a decidedly new strong side to her personality, she could not yet prevaricate.

"You mean to say that you came all this way without a chaperone? You will be so scandalized no one will want you," the duke roared.

"Willie accompanied me."

The duke's reply was so low that Willie leaned further into the room to enable her to hear better.

"That little urchin? She talked you into this scheme, didn't she? For once my sister was right. I should have selected a maid of good breeding and morals—if there is such a woman alive on the face of the earth." Suddenly Hammerfield's voice grew louder. "I see you in the doorway, miss. Come here!"

Caught in the act, Willie came forward. She should not have agreed to this act of folly, for His Grace was more outraged than ever. He would never be persuaded to let Katy marry Mr. Penbrooke now.

The duke's face turned redder as he stared at Willie. "Is this how you repay me for taking you out of that foundling home? I should have known my act of charity would come back to haunt me. You lead my daughter into your own wanton ways. Blood always tells."

Willie heard Katy gasp and felt an arm go around her shoulders. "Father, you cannot mean that. Willie is my best friend. She would never do anything to hurt me."

The duke doubled over coughing, then taking a deep breath, he collapsed back onto his pillows. "Water," he gasped, pointing to a glass on the sidetable.

Katy's hand trembled as she held the glass to her father's lips.

Hammerfield drank greedily, then abruptly pushed the glass away, spilling a great deal of it on the floor. "Your mother was an angel. The Lord punished me by taking her away. Now I have a disobedient daughter who will surely hasten my death."

Katy cried, "Oh, Father, forgive me! I do not want you to suffer on my account. Don't blame Willie for my sins. I will do anything you say."

For a moment, Willie feared that she had been wrong about his illness and a terrible guilt washed over her.

"Enough, daughter!" Hammerfield sat up so

quickly that his foot knocked something from under the coverlet.

A brick fell and sizzled as it hit the wet spot on the planked floor. A footwarmer. Katy, rivulets of perspiration running down her cheeks, looked at Willie and her eyes grew large.

As Willie's fingers went to her own wet face, both girls met each other's gaze with understanding.

Katy whirled on the duke. "Father, you are bamming me. I do not believe you are as sick as you protest to be. And I am going to tell you now, that if I can't choose whom I want to marry, I won't marry at all! If I have to be as unhappy as you, then you can give all your money to whomever you wish. I'm going back to Gilfallen with Willie and Broonie. Gilfallen is mine. And I'm going to ask Nathaniel to marry me, if he'll have me."

Willie's mouth fell open. She could not believe this was her timid Katy speaking.

The duke sat straight up in bed and reached for the bellpull. "Enough of this foolishness. I shall finish this drama here and now. You will obey me and marry whomever *I* choose. Do you hear?"

For someone who professed to be so near death's door a moment ago, Willie thought his grace had made an amazing recovery.

"My sister has turned you against me on purpose," he barked.

Katy rushed from the room, crying, her short pretense at bravery, exhausted.

The duke yanked the bell rope. "Sharp!"

The servant appeared almost instantly. "Yes, Your Grace."

Before Willie could follow Katy, she found herself trapped between a large chair and the butler. Trying to be inconspicuous, she slipped around the piece of furniture and along the wall toward the door.

The duke acted as though she had ceased to exist.

"See that David accompanies my daughter back to Lady Jacomena's. A twenty-four hour watch is to be put on Dalison Hall. Lady Katherine is to remain confined there until I say otherwise. All persons coming or going from the residence are to be logged and followed. I do not trust Lady Katherine to obey me, and in her defiant mood she may take it into her brain to run off to Gretna Green and marry that impudent Mr. Penbrooke."

Willie finally gained the door and scurried down the corridor, only to have the sounds of the duke's voice still followed her. "Bring me some writing materials, I want you to send messages to—"

She didn't catch the last of his sentence.

Back at Dalison Hall, the two girls were called into Lady Jacomena's chambers, where she waved a piece of paper at them.

"I am shocked by your breach of etiquette, young lady, sneaking out like that. Now see what you have done. Your father says you cannot go out of the house."

Although the words were spoken severely, Willie thought she caught a spark of admiration in her ladyship's eyes as she looked at her niece.

Willie received no such approval. The darkest censure was reserved for her part in the escapade, and though her ladyship didn't say it outright, Willie feared that if she made one more mistake, she could expect to find herself cast out on the street.

* * *

The next morning, two letters were delivered early to Duncan's London townhouse. Charles placed them on the silver salver when he brought his master the Morning Post.

The sun shone in the mullioned windows and spread good humor throughout the breakfast room. Sitting forward in his chair, Duncan took in the rich aroma of the creamed eggs, ham and hot-buttered scones heaped on his plate. "Thank you, Charles. I'll ring if I need anything."

Duncan, immediately recognizing the seal of the Duke of Hammerfield, opened that missive first and ran down its contents.

"Damn!" he swore through clenched teeth.

The jackanape had sent a notice to several London papers announcing the engagement of his daughter Lady Katherine to Duncan Fairchild, Earl of Wakeford.

Thrusting aside the other small note, Duncan tore open the newspaper and flipped the pages. Thank God, the announcement was not yet published, but that did not mean it wouldn't be in the afternoon editions. He'd told his grace that he wouldn't have Lady Katherine forced into marriage with him.

He slapped the paper down on the table, knocking two scones off onto the floor. While removing the edge of a page from his cup of coffee, another article caught his attention. A police report of a theft at Odin's Woods of a very valuable miniature portrait. Good lord! Hammerfield's residence. That surely was not going to add any honey to the duke's crusty nature.

Momentarily distracted, Duncan read it through. The police magistrate said they were investigating and hoped to apprehend the runagates shortly.

Duncan, his appetite gone, was about to rise, when he spied the little note. It was probably a reminder from one of his tailors that he had an appointment for a fitting, and he was about to leave it for Charles to tend to when he thought of his busy schedule and opened it.

> *Dear Lord Wakeford,*
>   *You told me that you wanted to be my friend and that if I ever needed your advice to feel free to call you. I am doing so now.*
>   *There is a personal matter which Lady Katherine cannot discuss with her aunt. Therefore, I assured her that you have proven by your propitious manners to be an honorable man, your word trustworthy. She is now convinced that you would not divulge her secret, and I was able to persuade her to speak to you about helping her find a solution to her dilemma.*
>   *Come as quickly as possible, please.*
>   *Your friend,*
>   *Willie Winkie*

Duncan chuckled when he saw the signature. He could not believe Lady Katherine was in great danger of any kind. She was not one to have racked up a gambling debt. No, probably she had overspent her allowance on some nonsensical amusement, or paid too much for a bonnet and was too embarrassed to approach Lady Jacomena. But Duncan knew that a trivial indiscretion could appear quite large in the eyes of a young girl.

Knowing Lady Jacomena's strong opinions on the waste of money spent on frivolities, he could understand the baroness' reluctance to face the stern reprimand of her aunt. The more Duncan thought about the matter, the more agreeable he was to helping the baroness out of her scrape, however inconsequential it was. Covering an expense for some little foolishness would only raise him in Lady Katherine's esteem, he thought, and therefore, make her more amiable to his address. After all, he did plan to marry her.

A ray of hope shot through Duncan, and the day suddenly looked brighter. He would pay a call on Lady Katherine this afternoon, before the engagement was announced in the papers. Perhaps the little magpie had done him more of a service than she could have imagined.

Duncan pulled the bell rope. "Charles, I want a note delivered immediately to Dalison Hall."

That afternoon, Katy and Willie sat in the green salon awaiting the arrival of Lord Wakeford. Broonie had been told by Lady Jacomena that she could stay in her room and rest if she wished, since his lordship said his visit would be brief.

"He answered your summons quickly," Katy said, looking at Willie with admiration. "Do you think he can help persuade Father to accept Mr. Penbrooke?"

"Now don't you worry. I'm sure the earl will give you some good advice on the matter of how to bring your father around to your way of thinking." Willie said. "Being one himself, he certainly is much more adept at knowing how to handle men than either you or I."

Katy nodded in agreement. "But how am I going to get rid of Aunt Jacomena so that I can talk to Lord Wakeford? Perhaps it would have been best if we had claimed we were going for a ride in the park and by chance met him there."

This new direction of Katy's toward mischief was surprising Willie more and more. "I'm certain you will think of something, dear. Don't fret so."

Willie had seen no reason to tell Katy that the house

was being watched. She had decided it would only add to her anxiety.

Katy pulled out her handkerchief and cradled it in her hands. "Oh, I don't see why you cannot stay in the room with us."

Indeed, His Grace's disagreeable actions had brought about this problem, Willie thought, but she couldn't bring herself to think that he did it with any malevolence. After all, he had not had much experience at being a father these last fourteen years, and she was certain he thought he was doing what was best for his daughter. He was bound to make mistakes. Someone just had to point him in the right direction. She hoped the earl would have some good suggestions as to how to go about it.

Katy turned to Willie with anxious eyes. "Are you quite certain Lord Wakeford will be able to persuade Father to accept Nathaniel?"

"Are you quite certain it is Mr. Penbrooke you wish to marry?" Willie countered.

"Oh, yes!"

"Even if you break Lord Wakeford's heart?"

Katy looked at her in amazement, then shook her head. "I do not believe the earl holds any special feelings for me. He has been more than kind, but he shows none of the fervor that other young men have shown. No, I believe it is only because of his mother's special friendship with my aunt that has precipitated his attentions here in London and our invitation to his country party."

Oh, Willie hoped so. She knew that Lord Wakeford would someday marry, but if he chose another lady other than Katy, she would not have to suffer the pain of seeing him every day. "Perhaps you are right," she said.

The sound of voices outside in the hallway brought

a halt to their conversation. Willie turned to Katy and said anxiously, "I hear Lady Jacomena coming, I will have to go now."

Katy's hand shot out to catch Willie and she dropped her handkerchief. It fell to the floor and unfolded. There nestled in the linen and lace lay the face of a redhaired girl, smiling up at them from a glittering silver frame.

"Your mother's portrait," gasped Willie.

"I didn't steal it," Katy cried, reaching for the picture. "It belongs to me."

At that moment, another voice, deep and masculine, was added to that of Lady Jacomena's.

"Lord Wakeford!" they said simultaneously.

Willie scooped up the miniature before Katy could. *Whatever was she to do?* "I shall take care of it," she said breathlessly. "They cannot find you with it."

The door began to open, and looking about for some place to hide the tiny painting, Willie quickly placed it at the base of the potted fern by the door.

Lady Jacomena walked in, a very pleased look on her face. Her ladyship seldom used her wheeled chair anymore, Willie noted.

"Katherine, Lord Wakeford is here to call."

The earl, right behind her, entered. He was dressed resplendently, Willie thought, in a coat she'd never seen before, of a brighter blue than usual, light gray trousers and a dark blue waistcoat. It was the first time she'd seen him carry a cane. It gave him a dignified air. His cravat was impeccably tied, and his dark brown hair was combed in a fuller, freer fashion. Willie felt herself grow warm, just looking at him, and her feet refused to move.

She thought she saw a look of apprehension cross his lordship's face momentarily. Then he stepped round her to greet Lady Katherine. Holding one hand over his watch pocket, he extended the other to Lady Katherine and bowed.

With an air of importance, Jacomena announced, "His lordship says he is here to see you on a very personal matter, Katherine, and has asked permission speak to you in private. After we have chatted awhile, I shall leave you alone with him for a few moments only."

Katy blushed prettily and curtsied.

Lady Jacomena watched the proceedings with a look of great satisfaction, then turned to Willie, who had now gathered some of her wits. "Remain outside in the hallway, Wilhemina, in case I want you to run an errand for me. I told Mrs. Butterworth to keep Pansy and Daisy in the kitchen, for his lordship said he will not be here long enough for tea."

Willie shot Katy a reassuring look, then bobbed a curtsy and left the room. The door closed behind her.

Katy was on her own.

Chapter Thirteen

It wasn't long before Lady Jacomena stepped into the hallway. To Willie's surprise, her ladyship didn't frown when she saw her. In fact, when she sat down on a cushioned bench, which nestled against the wall between a fern and a statue of Aphrodite, she had a pleasantly distracted expression upon her face.

On the other hand, Willie was in a state of fidgets wanting to know what was happening in the green salon. She walked along staring blindly at the paintings, and when she was far enough away so that Lady Jacomena could not see her, she flung her arms around in big circles to get rid of the tension in her shoulders. Eternity, she felt, could not be longer.

Without a warning, Lady Jacomena rose and scratched on the door of the salon, then entered.

Although Willie heard their voices, they were not loud enough for her to understand what was being said. Frustrated, she leaned as far forward as she dared without falling into the room, but to no avail. She had to wait until Katy came into the hallway, a few minutes later, smiling.

Willie grabbed her arm. "Well, what did he say?"

Before Katy could answer, Lady Jacomena, head held high, her mouth stretched across her face in a rigid line, appeared. The earl followed, his expression unreadable, though Willie was certain she saw a puzzled look in his eyes. He bowed to both ladies before proceeding down the entry hall to the front door, where Old Tom waited to show him out.

"Katherine, help me to my room," Lady Jacomena said crossly.

"Yes, Auntie," Katy raised her eyebrows and threw a worried look back toward the salon.

Willie shooed her on, indicating with a nod that she would take care of matters. As soon as she saw Katy escort Lady Jacomena through her chamber door, Willie rushed into the salon and thrust her hand underneath the fern. She had no sooner pulled out the miniature portrait than a large hand reached over her shoulder and magically whisked it out of sight. Eyes wide, she turned and stared upward.

"Lord Wakeford," she squeaked.

Duncan leaned over her, glaring. The little silver frame dangled from his fingers.

"I have made excuses for you too many times," he growled. "No more. You have gone beyond petty thievery." The look of fright in her eyes nearly undid him. She looked like she was about to cry, and he wanted to hold her and tell her things would be all right. Instead, he told himself, *Be rational, Don't let this strange feeling you have for this little thief cloud your judgement.*

She still hadn't spoken. Duncan placed the tiny picture in his coat pocket and walked over to pick up the cane he had forgotten.

"The painting will remain with me until I decide what steps need to be taken. Tomorrow, I shall advise you of your fate." Duncan had no idea what he was going to do, but he hoped he sounded ominous enough to strike some sense into the cunning piece of baggage.

Willie did no more than nod, woodenly.

He left her there and stalked out of the room. Duncan had not quite reached the front door when Lady Katherine came running toward him.

"Lord Wakeford," she called, "wait, please."

Forcing himself to hide his frustration, Duncan turned. If he was to get to the newspaper in time to stop the engagement announcement, he would have to hurry. It seemed that ever since he'd made the decision to marry, his life had been nothing but a series of disasters. "Yes, my lady?"

Lady Katherine placed her hand on his arm, smiling graciously.

Lady Jacomena stuck her head out of her room and called after her. "Katherine! What in the world has possessed you, gel? Have you lost all sense of propriety?"

"Of course not, Auntie. I forgot to express my gratitude to Lord Wakeford for calling."

Katy turned to Duncan and whispered, "I am so glad to find you have not yet left. I am afraid I did not thank you properly for your kind understanding, but it was impossible, you know, to say anything once Aunt Jacomena came back into the room."

The baroness giggled so charmingly that Duncan felt the anger flow out of him. *Oh, if only all women were so charming and uncomplicated as this one,* he thought. "It is my pleasure, my lady," he said, bending over her hand once more before he departed Dalison Hall.

It wasn't until later that evening and they were preparing for bed that the girls had a chance to be alone.

Willie tried hard to disguise her own anxiety behind a mask of curiosity.

"Now tell me all that happened this afternoon. By the look on Lady Jacomena's face, I take it she was not as happy as you with what transpired."

Katy giggled. "Auntie was rather put out at dinner," she said. "I do believe she thought that Lord Wakeford had come to propose marriage to me. Isn't that ridiculous? And poor Broonie. She didn't know what to make of it all. She appeared quite disconcerted when she could get no response from Aunt Jacomena during the entire meal."

Willie bit her lip to keep it from quivering. "And Lord Wakeford? Was he willing to help you with your problem?"

Katy nodded, her expression thoughtful. "His lordship appeared quite shocked when I first told him how much Mr. Penbrooke and I cared for each other—which proves how clever Nathaniel and I have been not to let on—but, it was as you said, he was very understanding and agreed to see what he could do."

Willie forced herself to smile. "See, I told you he is an honorable man."

Suddenly Katy looked Willie straight in the eyes. "You are not fooling me, Willie, and I will not pretend any longer. I was coming out of Aunt Jacomena's chambers when I overheard Lord Wakeford blame you for what I did. I will tell him I took the painting, even though it is rightfully mine."

"Oh, no, you won't!" Willie exclaimed. "Think of the scandal it would cause, dear. You would be ruined forever." She took Katy's hand. "I love you, and it is not as important for me as it is for you to keep a spotless reputation."

"But, I love you just as much, Willie, and it is not fair for you to take the blame for what I did."

Willie took Katy's hands in hers. "Now, look me in the eyes and swear to me that you will not tell Lord Wakeford that you took the portrait."

"All right, I promise I will not tell Lord Wakeford that I took the portrait."

Willie sighed with relief, then putting more conviction into her voice than she felt, said, "Come, dear, let us get a good night's sleep. His lordship will return the miniature to your father. Everything will work out. You wait and see."

As soon as Duncan had left Dalison Hall that afternoon, he hurried to the offices of the Morning Post, but found he was too late to remove the announcement of his engagement from the next day's edition.

He returned to his townhouse and entered the library, telling Charles he didn't want to be disturbed. He shrugged out of his coat, and after pouring himself a glass of Madeira, sat down to assess the rigmarole facing him. By morning, the entire fashionable world would read of the coming nuptials of the Earl of Wakefield and the Baroness of Gilfallen—the lady who had just confessed to him her undying love for another man.

Aside from the humiliation of finding himself being compared to a simple apprentice in an art gallery and found wanting, he was angered at the unscrupulous shenanigans of the duke. Just to set the duke in his place, Duncan decided he would champion Lady Katherine's cause. He would persuade her to pretend to go through with the engagement, then at a later date, she could cry off.

Duncan poured himself another glass of wine and sat staring into the pale liquid. In the meantime, he contemplated, he would have to think of some way to return the painting undetected. It was small. It could easily have fallen on the floor and been swept under a piece of furniture—the same way as his watch had gone undetected for several weeks under his bed. Yes, that was a good solution.

He rose and went to fetch his coat. His little magpie had failed him. That thought for some reason galled him more than all the other events of the day. This time she'd gone beyond reason and stolen a priceless work of art. Still, Duncan could not bear the thought of Willie going to prison. He reached into his coat pocket to retrieve the tiny painting. It was not there. Then he laughed, for it occurred to him that he was holding his coat backwards. He dug into the other pocket and fished around, when suddenly the ugly truth dawned upon him.

"Bloody hell!" he swore. "She did it again!"

After midnight, when all in the Dalison household were sleeping, Katy rose quietly from her bed and dressed in the dark. She covered her gown with one of Willie's black capes and sneaked out the back door into the alley. A light rain had begun to fall, and Katy drew the hood forward to cover her face. Willie had made her promise not to tell Lord Wakefield what she had done, and Katy meant to stay true to her word.

But she knew they would take her mother's portrait away from her if they found she had it. To Katy's way of reasoning, her mother had left her the castle in Scotland and all that went with it. That meant the little portrait, the only likeness of her mother that she had, was hers too.

There was only one person left whom she could trust to help her. Nathaniel. Just thinking about him sent loving thoughts flowing through her.

Out on the street, she hailed a hack which had only minutes before unloaded a fare at a neighboring residence. Keeping her face well hidden, she gave him her direction.

Katy had no idea what sort of place she would see, only that when Nathaniel told her his address, he said he lived very simply in a very modest room in a modest part of town.

The streets became narrower, and darker, when finally the hack stopped.

She asked the driver to wait for her. There were no lights on the street, and it took close inspection of three doors before she found Number Eighteen. Upon her knock, it was not Nathaniel who answered, but a very disgruntled, sleepy-eyed old woman in nightcap and wrapper.

"Is Mr. Penbrooke in?" Katy asked, sweetly, as if she were making a morning call.

The woman looked surprised. "I runs a respectable house."

"Oh, I'm very certain you do," Katy said, not quite knowing what the woman meant. But Katy found she was learning every day that what people said and what they meant were two very different things. She reached into her reticule and pulled out a coin. It was too dark to see what it was, but, regardless, as soon as she pressed it into the woman's hand, it got results.

"Third door on the right, dearie," she said, muttering to herself as she disappeared back into her own room. "Mr. Penbrooke. Faith, who woulda believed it?"

Nathaniel, shirt unbuttoned at the neck, book in hand, answered the door. At the sight of Katy, his first expression was one of disbelief, then ecstasy, and finally alarm on realizing she was alone.

Before he could speak, she threw herself into his

arms, knocking his book onto the floor. "Oh, Nathaniel, you must help me. I have done a terrible thing."

He drew Katy into the room and closed the door. After seeing her seated in his one chair, he handed her his handkerchief. "Now, now, my sweet. You could never do anything so disastrous as to have brought on such a shower of tears." All the while he was saying words to console her, shivers of apprehension were running up and down Nathaniel's spine. As soon as she quieted, he asked, "Now tell me what has you in such a dither?"

Katy withdrew the little miniature painting from her pocket and handed it to Nathaniel.

He gasped. "This is just like the one your father has."

"It is the one Father had. But 'tis mine," Katy said defiantly, taking it back and crushing it to her chest. "Lord Wakefield thinks Willie stole it, and I am afraid he means to tell the police. Will you hide it for me? If they don't find it they can't accuse her. Can they?"

Finally, when he could think of no other solution, Nathaniel agreed to do as Katy asked, and accepted the little painting into his keeping.

"I shall place it inside the little teapot my mother gave me," he said.

Then, to make certain no harm came to her, he insisted on accompanying her back to Dalison House, and didn't leave until he saw her in through the back door.

The next morning, Duncan waited until the *Morning Post* arrived before entertaining thoughts of taking any drastic steps. His darkest fears were answered. The duke's announcement of their engagement was there for all the world to see. *The bastard!* Duncan had promised Lady Katherine he would help her win the man she loved, and now she would think he'd lied to her and was forcing her into a marriage she didn't want.

Time would be against them, so before he dressed, Duncan sent off a message to Lady Jacomena to expect him to call before noon.

Duncan didn't want to insult Lady Jacomena by accusing her brother of being a scoundrel, so, in his note he blamed himself for not having come to an understanding with Lady Katherine yesterday afternoon. He asked Lady Jacomena's forgiveness, saying the sooner they took care of the matter, the less likely there was chance of scandal.

In the meantime, while he was there, he'd corner the little minion and force her to give up the portrait. Duncan nodded in disbelief. What a fast top she was. Her fingers were as quick as her tongue. Did she think she was playing some sort of game with him?

When Duncan arrived at Dalison Hall at five minutes before noon, he thought he had mistakenly taken himself to Bedlam. The door was answered by neither Old Tom or Mrs. Butterworth, but by a man from the police magistrate's office. Duncan identified himself and was admitted. Starting down the hallway, he heard Lady Jacomena's voice roar from the back of the house. "The bastard! How dare the scoundrel have one of my servants arrested?"

So much for her ladyship's sensitivities, Duncan thought.

Next he saw Mrs. Butterworth hurry out of the room wringing her hands. A bewildered-looking young man in uniform was trying to fend off an attack by Miss Abbot, two serving maids were crying into their aprons, and a distinguished-looking gentleman, came out of the green salon with an ashen-faced Lady

Katherine. Duncan recognized him immediately as Sir Broderick Nevelspoon, the police magistrate of London.

The moment the baroness saw Duncan, she ran and threw herself into his arms, sobbing. "Lord Wakeford, they arrested Nathaniel. Now they have taken Willie away, and I don't know what to do—because I promised her . . ."

Duncan held the hysterical girl in his arms, soothing her, but his thoughts were on another. *Willie in prison?* He had warned her, but she had not heeded him. He should have tried harder to convince her of the dangerous path she'd chosen.

Failure was a hard pill for Duncan to swallow, and angered by his inability to relieve the terror his little magpie must be feeling at being dragged off to gaol, he spoke much louder than he meant. "Enough! All this noise is not doing anyone any good. Miss Abbot," he ordered, "take Lady Katherine to her room." Duncan then turned to the housekeeper. "Tell Lady Jacomena that as soon as I find out from the magistrate what is going on here, I request permission to speak to her. And the rest of you," he said, looking sternly at the servants, "go to the kitchen."

With a look of relief Sir Broderick wiped the perspiration from his brow, and said, "Thank you, my lord."

Indicating for the man to follow him, Duncan walked into the library, and as soon as they were alone, demanded, "Now, sir, will you tell me what this upheaval means? I take it the baroness was making reference to Mr. Nathaniel Penbrooke—and what is this about arresting the lady's maid?"

"The Duke of Hammerfield has had this house under surveillance round the clock, my lord. His daughter, Lady Katherine, was not to be allowed to leave, and all visitors were to be checked. Anyone suspicious was to be followed."

Damn the man. Duncan didn't like the thought that his own movements had been equally logged and filed in someone's notebook. He nodded for Sir Broderick to continue.

"We'd been notified by the parish constable of the investigation going on into the theft of a painting from the earl's residence outside London. His Grace gave him the name of a young man who had called on him late in the afternoon of the previous day and admired the miniature portrait of his late wife, the Duchess of Hammerfield. A ploy, we believe, to throw his grace off guard. That was the last the duke remembered seeing the painting. The young man was Mr. Nathaniel Penbrooke. Well, my lord, last night, after midnight, a serving girl in a dark cape, sneaked out of this house and was followed to a rooming house on the east side of London. Half hour later, she came out with a man. They entered a hack. One of the investigators stayed to search the premises, and found the duke's miniature painting. When Mr. Nathaniel Penbrooke returned, he was arrested."

"And the maid?" Duncan said, coolly.

"We obtained papers to make a search this morning and found a wet black cape hung over the back of a chair in Lady Katherine's sitting room. It belonged to her abigail. She was promptly arrested. We surmise, my lord, that the two were accomplices, the woman doing the stealing, and the cove receiving. We just caught them in the act, this time, before they fenced their loot."

Duncan groaned inwardly but remained silent. He knew that Willie's wicked activities had started long before she met Mr. Penbrooke, and he feared it was she who had implicated him in this caper—if he was guilty at all. He couldn't imagine the mild mannered Mr. Penbrooke as a seasoned receiver of stolen goods. Perhaps she had beguiled him as she had John Teagardner.

Lady Katherine loved Mr. Penbrooke, that was obvious. Could she have been fooled into thinking Mr. Penbrooke loved her? Curiosity now filled Duncan with the necessity of questioning the young man further.

Fifteen minutes later, Duncan was admitted to Lady Jacomena's chambers. She sat in her wheeled chair, looking suddenly old, but if it hadn't been for the occasional blinking of her eyes, Duncan would have thought her as composed as ever.

Her ladyship was holding the *Morning Post,* and when asked if she had seen the announcement, launched into a diatribe of her brother's most undesirable attributes. "The whole household was discussing it, just before the police came," she said.

Duncan stopped her with a curt nod of his head. There was no time to spare, he told her, and unfolded his plans to carry through on the engagement.

Jacomena was, of course, quite shocked to hear that her niece carried a tendre for the young art apprentice, but she agreed that they should allow the earl's and Katherine's engagement to stand for the time being.

"It is Katherine's future which is at stake," she said, giving a yank on the bell pull. "I think once you explain our position, she will be sensible."

Pansy appeared and was sent to fetch the baroness.

Lady Jacomena turned to the earl and spoke knowingly. "Now I can understand why Katherine went into such a state when the magistrate told her this morning that they had arrested Mr. Penbrooke. I cannot imagine him to be involved in any intrigue. Such a gentle man—quite unsuitable a match for the daughter of a duke, of course. Katherine was quite devastated by the betrayal of her abigail, also."

Jacomena hated to admit it, but she'd begun to feel a certain attachment to Wilhemina. Common born as she was, the maid showed a great deal more bottom than most of the missish young chits who were presented to society. Obviously, she was too clever for her own good, though. "I should have seen the danger signs," she continued.

Duncan sat up at her remark. "Signs, your ladyship? What signs?"

"Small things disappearing. Fancy scissors—some laces gone from Mrs. Butterworth's sewing box—a silver candlesnuffer. Even an insignificant pearl pin, not worth a hill of beans, which I wore to keep my shawl from slipping. But I never dreamed it would escalate to the point of stealing *objets d'art* like my brother's miniature of the first Lady Katherine."

God! Duncan thought, this had been going on, while all the time, he'd thought he was reforming the little pickpocket. The poor baroness had been betrayed by the worst kind of disloyalty.

"Lady Jacomena, may I have your permission to speak to Lady Katherine privately? I think a delicate matter such as this should be done with as little embarrassment as possible."

Jacomena tapped her chin with her finger. She was beginning to think her plans were going to come to fruition sooner than she had hoped. Surely Katherine would get over her calf-love for Mr. Penbrooke, and Wakeford was in their pocket. "Of course, your lordship," Jacomena said, quite her old self again. "We must protect Katherine from hurt."

Just then, Katy appeared.

"His lordship has something of great import to say

to you, Katherine. You may go into the green salon for a few minutes with him."

After escorting her in, Duncan tried to put it to the baroness as gently as he could that her father had placed the announcement of their engagement in the paper. He was glad to see that she seemed to be giving him her full attention. He assured her his sensitivity for her feelings was genuine, but he and her aunt felt they should play along with her father's little game for now. After a reasonable time had passed, she could cry off their engagement.

He hoped it was trust which he saw in Lady Katherine's expression. Only yesterday, he'd promised her that he would do what he could to elevate Mr. Penbrooke in the eyes of her father, but with the evidence so strong against the young apprentice, even Duncan's position in society might prove worthless. It was a puzzle which needed his greatest concentration.

When he and Katherine returned to her ladyship's room, Jacomena's tongue loosened considerably, and she kept up a gay chatter until Duncan said he must leave.

"I wish to say something to his lordship, Katherine. You may go."

Wide-eyed, Katy looked back and forth between her aunt and the earl. Without speaking, she had nodded to everything they asked, and upon her aunt's command left without having said one word during the whole conversation.

"The day has been a disconcerting one for her," Lady Jacomena said solicitously. "Katherine is a sensitive young woman. I do not want her to become ill, so it may be best if you give her a day or so to compose herself."

Duncan nodded. The fragile Lady Katherine was obviously in a state of shock, and he didn't want to

upset her anymore. "As you wish, my lady," he said.
"In the meantime, if there is anything you want me to
look into, don't hesitate to call."

Abovestairs, a dry-eyed Katy put her arms protec-
tively around her old nurse and said soothingly,
"Now, now, Broonie, don't you cry."

"My wee darlin' Willie—she wouldna hurt a fly.
Now she's rottin' in one of these Englisher's dirty
gaols."

Katy sat upright. She had a lot to think about. It
had never occurred to her that dear old Broonie
needed nurturing, for she had always cared for others.
"It's all my fault. If I hadn't been so selfish, none of
this would have happened. I shall tell the authorities
the truth."

Broonie's moment of weakness dissipated as suddenly as fog on the moors. "No! You will tell the
authorities naught. Promise me noo."

"Well, all right," Katy said reluctantly. "I promise
not to tell the authorities."

Broonie stood up, threw out her chest, which was
formidable indeed, and after straightening her rumpled skirt, looked quite her fierce old self again. "I
think Broonie will go doon and find oot what her
ladyship is doin' to get my Willie oot of this pickle."

Katy stood up. "I shall go with you."

"No!" Broonie said emphatically. "I doon want to
be worryin' about your swooning behind me back."

Katy stuck out her lower lip. "I never swoon, Broonie. You know that."

"Aye, that is a fact, you never do, but be a good
duck noo and obey Broonie."

As Katy watched the old woman march out of the
room, she made a quick study of her problem. Reflec-

tion took only a moment. Everyone was always telling her what to do, as if she had no brain at all. Well, she'd sworn to Willie she wouldn't tell Lord Wakefield her part in this escapade, and she had just promised Broonie not to tell the authorities, but no one had told her not to go to her father. She would take it upon herself to get this whole situation cleared up in no time.

Katy put on her dark green riding skirt, then slipped into one of Willie's plain black dresses. They were the same size around, but Katy was, of course, much taller and needed the longer skirt. She pinned her blonde curls up under Willie's plainest black bonnet, and made certain she had enough coins in her reticule before stepping into the hallway. She was getting quite good at this, she thought. All the servants were in the kitchen and Broonie had gone to confer with Aunt Jacomena.

As Katy passed her aunt's chambers, she heard a heated discussion. Although she could not hear their precise words, the confrontation sounded like two old warriors at battle.

Excitement ran through Katy. She hurried toward the library, where she clambered over the sill of the casement window and dropped into the small side garden. This time she did not go into the alley where she now knew her father's agents watched, but squeezed through the hedges and over the walls of the neighboring gardens and made her way to the street.

Chapter Fourteen

Willie sat on a pile of straw in the corner of the shadowy pit at Newgate Prison, her ankles encased in heavy irons. She heard sniffling and moans about her, but could not see the people making the sounds. She scooted away from the cold stone wall and pulled her skirt tighter around her legs. Thank goodness she'd wrung a promise from Katy not to confess her indiscretions, for Willie shuddered when she realized that it could have been Katy surrounded by this filth.

Smudges of dirt covered Willie's hands and most likely her face as well. It couldn't be helped. Everything she touched seemed layered with grime. She sneezed. Remnants of rancid food and offal permeated the air with a terrible stench. The straw, she could tell, hadn't been freshened for heaven knows how long. It was plain to see that good housekeeping was not a priority at Newgate.

Willie thought sadly of Lord Wakeford. Oh, yes, she could tell he had been quite disappointed in her when he found her holding the little portrait of Katy's mother, but she was glad she had kept Katy from telling anyone her part in the matter. Thank goodness, Willie sighed, her dearest friend was safe and sound at Dalison Hall with Broonie and Lady Jacomena.

But Willie's thoughts were not all doom and gloom, because she knew *he* would come to her rescue. Lord Wakeford had said he would always be her friend, and she knew that no matter how disappointed he was with her, he was a very high-principled man—a regular pattern-saint—and would honor his word.

She heard squeaking in the straw at her feet and kicked out at the unknown intruder. The dim light from the tiny window in the door was fading. Willie was contemplating the coming night when her solitude was broken by the sound of keys racketing back and forth along the bars in the small opening of the cell door.

Hope ran through her, only to be replaced by apprehension, as the odious, toothless face of the jail keeper leered in upon her.

The old iron hinges screeched and the ill-fitting heavy oak door scraped along the stone floor. When the door opened, and a large, familiar figure was silhouetted against the light. *He had come.* The earl ducked his head and stepped through the low archway, filling it.

She heard his quick intake of breath, then he turned and was gone.

So much for a romantic rescue, Willie thought, trying to fight her disappointment. Lord Wakeford must think the very worst, for he gave her no word, no greeting, no scold. She could not blame him, of course, for not wanting to stay longer. This wasn't exactly his mother's drawing room at Wakeford Manor. After all, he was one of the Quality, but it would have been nice if he had at least said, hello.

Willie hugged her knees closer to her body. Her stomach rumbled and she realized she hadn't eaten since morning.

The door thrust open once more. A large wooden

trencher with foul-smelling victuals slid across the stone floor, losing half its contents over the sides. "Here's yer slush, ladies," a raspy voice croaked.

Willie's cellmates shuffled out of their corners to put their hands into the mash. Willie backed off.

The man leered at her. "Stand to, wench. As soon as I throw out the rest of the slops, I'll be back to get ye."

The caustic words sent shivers down Willy's spine.

"Seems ye has a benefactor. The fancy bloke what the gaoler says is to be leg-shackled to some baroness. He ordered yer to be moved to a more fittin' cell."

Willie clasped her hands. "Bless Lord Wakeford," she said in a whisper. Even if all was hopeless for her and Mr. Penbrooke, at least her dear Katy would be saved.

As soon as Duncan had heard that Willie had been confined in one of the filthiest rat holes in Newgate prison, he had gone immediately to investigate.

When he saw his little magpie huddled in the corner like a wounded bird, it was more than he could stand, and he couldn't trust himself to speak. No human should have to suffer such indignities. He went directly to the gaoler and paid to have her moved into a better section.

Duncan wanted to talk to Mr. Penbrooke first to hear his side of the story before he spoke to Willie.

Nathaniel swore to the earl that it was he, and he alone, who stole the portrait. Yet his story did not ring true, and the more Duncan questioned him on the details, the more mixed up the young man became. The only tale he stuck to was to insist that *Miss Willie* had not come to his boardinghouse. If it was not Lady Katherine's maid, then who was it? Mr. Penbrooke refused to say.

No matter how Duncan's mind mulled over the facts, the finger of guilt kept pointing at Willie. Yet, in his gut, he knew something was wrong. God, he hoped his instincts were right. This attraction he felt for the little minion was beyond his comprehension. He could not stand to see her suffer and would have to think of a way to get her out of this predicament.

Duncan shook his head. He was going to get no more information from the apprentice, so after seeing that Nathaniel was removed to a better cell, also, Duncan returned to his townhouse where he stayed up most of the night in his library trying to come up with a plausible alibi for Willie to give the authorities. What was this compulsion he had to want to get her out of trouble, to keep her safe?

Finally, Duncan had to admit, he cared for her.

Early the next morning, Duncan was shown into the women's section at Newgate.

"Willie," he said, "why in God's name have they put you in this box?"

Willie bobbed a curtsy. "They did not exactly ask for my preferences, your lordship."

He extended his hand to her. "Perhaps they didn't. But I told them mine."

She glanced around the small room. Light filtered through the window in the upper part. The strong stone wall was lined with planks, studded with broad-headed nails. It was plain, but at least, she had a barrack bedstead and a crock of water.

"Sit down," he said, pointing to the bed.

What she really wished to do was throw herself into his arms and thank him for having her removed from a true hell-hole. But she hopped up on the cot, her feet dangling several inches above the floor.

He hovered over her for a moment, then started pacing the small area. "I talked to Mr. Penbrooke. I cannot help you if you don't cooperate with me."

"I'm sorry, my lord. The blame is all mine."

"That is exactly what he said. That he worked alone."

"Well, he is just being nice."

"Putting his neck in a noose is not just being *nice.*"

Willie's eyes widened immeasurably. "In a noose, my lord?"

"Archaic as they are, there are still laws which state that the only penalties for such offenses are death or transportation," Duncan said. "The accused goes before a judge. The government has a lawyer to present their case, but the accused cannot be represented. Until those laws can be changed, I'm afraid you will languish in gaol for the rest of your life or be transported to New South Wales."

Willie gasped.

He seated himself beside her and took her hands in his. "Ah, Willie. If we had only been born in a different time, in a different place—if only we were not who we are—"

"I have an excuse for not knowing who I am, my lord, but what excuse can you give for not knowing who you are?"

It was then he took her in his arms and kissed her. Obsession . . . desire . . . compassion. Duncan was through analyzing his addiction. It boiled down to one thing—he couldn't stand to see her suffer. When he released her she looked at him, wide-eyed. His practicality took over.

"Willie," he said, "I have come up with a story which will get you out of here. I am ready to swear to the authorities that you were with me at my townhouse all that night. Charles will back me up."

Willie stared at him. "I would not sleep with a man who is not my husband."

He looked at her proud little chin tilted upward. "I am offering you my protection from now on, you little minx."

"You believe in honor, do you not, my lord?"

"An honorable man is as high in my esteem as a faithful woman."

Willie shook her head. "Lies will not make matters better."

Duncan ran a finger over her cheek. "Then tell me the truth."

"I will not betray someone I love."

A knife cut into Duncan's gut. "You love another?"

Willie buried her face in his shirt. "Please do not ask any more questions."

Duncan recalled a remark Lady Katherine had made at the Bellrumple Ball. It had not made sense to him then, it did now. *It isn't fair, is it? It isn't Willie's fault that she has no family.*

Now the little minion was turning down his offer of protection, because only the sanctity of marriage for her would suffice, and that option was impossible.

What had he offered? Food, clothing, shelter—and yes, his bed. In exchange for what? To do his bidding, to please him when he chose. Many women in her position would jump at the chance. But she had turned him down. Who was the noble one here?

No! Marriage was unthinkable. He must make a good match. He had to think of his late father, and more importantly, his mother.

He remembered her words once more. *I want you to be happy. What your father and I had is beyond price. To live in a loveless marriage would have been intolerable for me. Find someone to love.*

That was Willie. Intelligent, witty, generous, honest

and loyal. He looked at her—and very, very beautiful. All the attributes he admired in his own mother.

Willie cocked her head to one side. "What are you thinking, my lord?"

Duncan realized Lady Wakeford would not give a whit what society thought. He threw back his head and laughed.

Willie looked at him as if he had sparrows flying out of his ears.

Duncan caught her up in his arms and whirled her around. "Willie," he said, "marry me."

Willie grabbed him around the neck and hung on for dear life. "What did you say, my lord?"

He set her back down, still holding her close. "I said, marry me." He then kissed her soundly, giving her no time to answer.

When Willie got her breath back, she said, "You are not thinking clearly, my lord. I have read the law, you see, and you cannot have two wives in England. You are engaged to Lady Katherine."

"That is but a hoax, my dear. As soon as a little time has passed, Lady Katherine is going to cry off. In the meantime, you will have to stay awhile in Newgate, but I shall have you removed to another prison, one much more comfortable. It may take months before your trial comes up. By that time, Lady Katherine will have ended the engagement. You may have to admit that you were with me that night. The scandal will pass over, for *on dits* have a way of popping up like weeds during the Season, fading away by Autumn."

"But if you marry a lady's maid, my lord, you will be shunned by society."

"Perhaps that is best," he said, with a bit of humor. "I won't be inundated with countless invitations to boring social functions. I cannot lose my seat in Parliament over the matter. Of course, the members of the gentlemen's clubs will most likely make lively sport of the whole thing for awhile, but men judge such matters in a different light than women."

Then Duncan's thought turned to his mother. He hoped he was right in his assumptions about her. After all, he was following her advice. *Find someone to love.*

"It is you I love," he said. "All the wealth and titles in the world are not worth having if I cannot have you. I have several estates besides Wakeford Manor and we can travel to other lands. Would that please you, my little magpie? You will have everything that money can buy. You will never again have to steal."

Willie turned her face away from him. She did not want Duncan to see how her cheeks burned.

Gently, Duncan's hands raised her face to his. "Look me in the eyes and tell me you don't love me?"

Her expression told him everything he wanted to know. "Will you marry me?"

His eyes were kissing her, and Willie didn't understand the thrill which swept through her entire body, but she knew that she felt for Lord Wakeford something she had never experienced before. Exaltation, yearning, physical agony.

"Oh, yes, your lordship, I will."

Several miles away, the Duke of Hammerfield watched his daughter, Katherine, enter his den. He held the little portrait of her mother in his hand. As she marched across to face him, his eyes narrowed. He didn't know why he wasn't surprised to see her.

She came right to the point. "Father, Mr. Penbrooke has been falsely accused of stealing the miniature."

The duke half rose from his chair. "Do not speak of

that money-chaser to me. He is where I want him, and that is where he will stay."

"He didn't steal it. I did."

His steel blue eyes fixed on her. "Don't lie to me."

" 'Tis true. I took it the second time I came to see you. You were upstairs in bed."

Hammerfield turned his face from her. "I will not listen, and I forbid you to repeat that to anyone. Do you hear me?"

"You cannot mean that, Father."

"I mean every bit of what I say. You have been a most disobedient daughter."

"Only because you are being so unfair. Willie has been arrested, too."

He swung around to face her again. "Hah! That little termagant? 'Tis just as well. I knew she was a bad influence on you from the moment she walked into this room."

Katy snapped back. "Don't you dare say anything against Willie. She is my best friend. She's like a sister to me. If you don't withdraw your accusations, I will go to the authorities as soon as I leave here. You cannot lock me away forever."

"Do not tell me what I can and cannot do. I forbid you to cause a scandal that would bring shame down around the Dalison name." The duke's expression suddenly changed, and he smiled charmingly. "I will let you have the choice of whether or not your friends will be pardoned."

"Oh, thank you, Father." Relief flooded through Katy. She was glad to see he was finally coming around to her way of thinking.

"I will strike a bargain with you."

"Anything, Father."

"I shall drop the charges if you promise you will never tell the authorities what you did—"

"Oh, I see," she interrupted. "You will say that it was all a very unfortunate mistake."

He sat forward in his chair. "I did not finish. *And* you will marry Duncan Fairchild, the Earl of Wakeford."

Katy's hand flew to her throat. "Father! I love Nathaniel."

"If you wish your Mr. Penbrooke to be a free man, you will do as I say."

"And Willie?"

"I shall see that the gel is placed in a suitable position. They are looking for well-trained domestics in Australia."

Katy gasped.

The duke looked cunningly sympathetic. "The prisons are hard enough on men, my dear, but for women they can be a living hell. Sometimes they languish in gaol for months before they get a trial."

Katy refused to cry. "You are a very wicked man, Father, and I don't think I like you very much."

The duke slumped back in his chair. "I should've known it would be a mistake sending you to that rackety, blue-nosed sister of mine."

"Aunt Jacomena is a bluestocking, not a bluenose."

"Each time I see you, you sound more and more like her. Stubborn. Stubborn to the core. She put you up to this, didn't she? She probably had a list of possible husbands entirely different than the one she gave me."

"Tell me, Father, would you have felt differently about Mama if she had had no money?" Holding her head high, Katy turned and walked out of the room.

The duke, ashen-faced, picked up the little portrait of his wife and gently touched her lips with his fingertip. "Someday, my darling, our daughter will understand that I did what was best for her. The family name must be preserved."

* * *

When Katy returned to Dalison Hall, she found her aunt and Broonie once again in Jacomena's chambers, their voices overlapping.

Katy entered the room and faced the two women.

"Where have you been, gel? I thought you were resting, until Miss Abbot reported she could not find you," Jacomena barked.

"I went to see my father."

"You did what?" Lady Jacomena shouted. "That is unconscionable behavior, young lady."

Katy held her head high. "I promised him that I would marry Lord Wakeford."

Jacomena sat back, looking pleased. "Well, then I can forgive you. For once I must say Harcourt has done something right. Whatever made you come to your senses that an alliance with an impoverished art assistant could ever compare to a *non pareil* like the earl?"

Katy looked helplessly at Broonie.

The old nurse's words of congratulations stopped halfway up her throat. "Somethin's no right here," she said to Katy.

Broonie didn't have time to pursue the subject further, for the Earl of Wakeford chose that moment to call at the Dalison household. The sudden revelation of his love for Willie had Duncan feeling tip top, and he wanted to tell Lady Katherine of his latest plans to get Willie and Mr. Penbrooke out of prison.

However, he found Lady Jacomena bursting with her own earth-shaking announcement. "Jolly news, Wakeford! My niece has come to her senses and accepts your proposal."

Duncan thought it strange that the young lady whose heart he was supposed to have captured, stood by saying nothing, her gaze fixed upon some object on the carpet. But perhaps it was just as well, for he was having enough trouble keeping his equanimity as the disconcerting revelation hit him. *Good God, what a coil! I have not one, but two fiancées.* His only thought was to get into the city to seek out information on the consequences of such a complicated matter. Therefore, after a short visit in which Lady Jacomena did all the talking, Duncan managed to say his goodbyes, still pondering Lady Katherine's silence.

Instead of going straight back to his townhouse, he headed for Inns of Court, where he hoped to dig up something in the legal library to show him a way out of this coil. He didn't want to reveal even to a lawyer what he had done or planned to do. Especially when he wasn't quite sure himself.

Duncan consulted his watch. He would have to pass up his plan to eat at his club. Since he'd become involved with the Dalison household, he found himself meeting fewer and fewer of his deadlines.

As soon as the earl left, the Scotswoman turned to Katy. "Now, lass, tell ol' Broonie what ails you."

Katy began to cry. "I told Father that it was I who stole the portrait."

Lady Jacomena gasped. "Why did you tell him such a prodigious lie?"

Broonie frowned and shook her head, but Katy continued. "No, I did it. He said if I did not tell, and promised to marry Lord Wakefield, that he would see that the charges were dropped against Nathaniel and Willie."

"I don't believe a word of this," Jacomena spouted.

"Wait," Katy said, rising. "Wait here, and I will be right back." With that she ran from the room.

The two older women looked at one another, puzzled. Before either could speak, Katy was back with a drawer from her bedside table. She emptied the contents upon the floor. There was an array of objects; a glove, a crystal salt cellar, laces, an enameled snuff box, and a little pearl pin, which Jacomena recognized immediately.

"I take things," Katy said, looking wistfully at the pile. "I don't know why, but I take things which don't belong to me."

"Oh, my little widgeon," Broonie crooned. "You canna help it."

"But it is wrong," Katy said. "And now my friends are being punished for something I did."

Jacomena looked, unbelieving, at the pile of items. "Well, I agree with my brother. You cannot tell anyone this. It would be a scandal that we would never live down. No, leave things the way they are. Mr. Penbrooke and Wilhemina will be released from prison." Actually, Jacomena felt relieved to hear the little maid was innocent. The house had been missing a certain gaiety since she had been taken away, and Jacomena had enjoyed the company of the apprentice, too. He was a talented, intelligent young man, but most unsuitable. "You will marry Wakeford as your father ordered," she said to Katy. "You will get over your tendre for Mr. Penbrooke."

"How can you look at my angel and say that? Fie on you!" spat Broonie. "You and your brother are two peas in a pod." Then like a mother hen sheltering her chick under her wing, the big Scotswoman gathered the weeping girl in her arms. "The Abbots never feared fightin' for what they believed in. We may have lost the battles of Halidon Hill and Culloden, but we Scots never give up." With a withering glance at Lady Jacomena, the big woman marched out of the room, taking Katy with her.

"An art dealer's assistant? A most prodigiously unsuitable match," mumbled Jacomena, watching them go. "Why, 'twould set the fashionable world on its ear."

A short while later, Lady Wakeford arrived at Dalison Hall. "I seem to have missed Duncan twice today already," she announced cheerfully, pulling off her gloves, as she settled into a chair.

"Your son and my niece are engaged," Jacomena announced, stiffly.

"Why, that is wonderful!" the countess exclaimed.

"That is what I said," Jacomena said defensively.

Lady Wakeford knit her brows. "Then why so Friday-faced? Isn't that what we wanted?"

Jacomena's intense expression remained unchanged. "Today we have had two other young people connected with this house accused of theft unjustly, and they now languish in gaol."

"Oh, that is sad. Anyone I know?"

"One is a young art dealer's apprentice, Mr. Penbrooke. The other is Wilhemina. You remember Katherine's abigail."

Lady Wakeford clasped her hands to her chest. "Wee Willie Winkie?"

Jacomena gave a look of exasperation before responding, "They are to be freed."

"Thank heavens for that," Lady Wakeford said, too eager to impart her information to be offended by her friend's expression. "She is the reason I am here, you see. I am glad you are seated, Jaco, for my news will astound you. I have just come from the Dover coast where I uncovered the most amazing story . . ."

Chapter Fifteen

Jacomena leaned forward expectantly.

Lady Wakeford lowered her voice and whispered, "I believe that Willie is the daughter of my dear friend, Lady Patricia Grayson."

"How can that be?"

"When I first saw the little maid at Wakeford Manor, I was startled by the strong resemblance she bore to my good friend. Patricia was a tiny doll, like Willie. Exquisite. Dark curly hair, and eyes the color of violets. It was like looking back into my past. There could be no mistaking her identity. Then, turning up in the Dalison household? That was too coincidental, but I had to make certain. Immediately after the party, I went to our estate in Kent.

"It took some fine investigative work—for many of the people who would have remembered the incident were dead. My, I felt just like a Bow Street runner. It was quite exciting. Finally, I located an elderly widow, Mrs. Woolsey, who had worked as housekeeper-cook for a young noblewoman who had rented a cottage on the coast during the war years. She never gave her real name, Mrs. Woolsey said. The locals addressed her as 'my lady.'

"It was soon evident that the woman was with child.

During her months of confinement, her only visitor was a fine-looking, light-haired gentleman, whom she referred to as 'my lord.' He was there when the black-haired baby girl was born. The lady was delicate and did not have enough milk, so Mrs. Woolsey's daughter, who had just given birth to a stillborn child, was called in to wet-nurse the babe. The gentleman rode a white horse and came often during the next few weeks. He seemed quite solicitous of the lady's welfare, and was kind to her and the villagers, too, Mrs. Woolsey said."

Jacomena turned pale. "Good lord! Adrian! He had a white stallion."

"I thought as much," Lady Wakeford said. "I do believe that Willie is the natural daughter of your brother Adrian."

"Impossible!" Jacomena spouted.

"Not possible, Jaco? Listen to the rest of the story, for it becomes more interesting. The old woman said that about two months after the baby was born, the young lord called and was inside the cottage when a carriage came thundering up to the gate. An irate man in uniform called the nobleman outside. There was a terrible quarrel, and the young lady ran out and tired to separate them. A few moments later, Mrs. Woolsey said, she heard a gunshot. Men yelled. A woman screamed. The housekeeper peeked out the door in time to see the officer force the lady into his carriage and take off with her. Then Mrs. Woolsey ran into the yard, only to see another gentleman, a stranger, cradling the dying lord in his arms."

"Harcourt," Jacomena gasped.

"Yes. He told her he was Lord Harcourt Dalison. Of course, the authorities had to be called, but before they were, he asked to see the baby. He then told Mrs. Woolsey that her daughter was to tell the constable

that the child was hers. After the bodies of Patricia and
John had washed up on the shore, the gentleman returned and said that if Mrs. Woolsey would raise the
child, she would be sent a stipend every month for the
rest of her life.

"We all knew that it was the present duke who
found Adrian. No one was ever told there was a child,
you see," Lady Wakeford said. "Patricia's husband,
John, was at sea for a year prior to the birth, and
Adrian visited her regularly and saw to her confinement. He was killed by Sir John in a jealous rage. That
is why I believe Willie is the daughter of Lady Patricia
Grayson and your brother Adrian. It was just unfortunate that Harcourt arrived too late. So you have been
blaming him all these years for something he could not
help. And he did see to the welfare of the child, you
must admit."

"But Harcourt took Wilhemina from an orphanage
in Yorkshire," Jacomena said.

"I am coming to that," Lady Wakeford said. "It
seems the daughter's beau turned up one day and
persuaded her to go with him, promising to marry her.
There was plenty of work in the mill towns, he said.
The baby was still nursing, and she took her with
them. The boy deserted her daughter again, and she
returned home briefly a year later without the child.
She said when the baby'd started to walk, she'd been
too much to care for, and she left her at a foundling
home. The only thing Mrs. Woolsey remembered
about the place was that her daughter mentioned she'd
tied her to a big iron gate that had an oak-leaf and
acorn icon on it. Soon after that the daughter left
again. Mrs. Woolsey thought what the nobleman
didn't know couldn't hurt him, and since she had no
other means of support, she used the money he sent.
But one day several years later, his lordship turned up

and became furious when he found the child was no longer with her. She gave him the same information about the iron gate with the icon, and when he realized she could tell him no more, he left."

"Just like Harcourt—always too little, too late. But—" Jacomena paused a moment, then shook her head. "Perhaps he did his best. I hate to think that all these years I have misjudged my little brother. What else did you find out?"

"Even though Patricia had had another man's child, I could not believe that she would not have registered the birth somewhere. Mrs. Woolsey told me that during her confinement, the *lady* went every day to the village church to pray. I discovered the old vicar had been dead for several years, and the little chapel used only occasionally now for weddings and holiday services. The record books stored away in the vestry were in bad repair. Watermarks and mildew have eaten away whole pages. I asked permission to have them sent to a friend, Dr. Tillsbury, at King's College in Cambridge, to see what he could cipher from them."

Jacomena sat staring into space for a moment. "Then there is no proof that your conjecture is true."

"Well, I did not have time to investigate further, dear, because I wanted to catch you up on my news. I'm afraid we shall have to wait to see if your Willie was christened, or if she is that child." Lady Wakeford sighed, then smiled, her expression animated once more. "Now, I will leave. Tell Lady Katherine that I am sorry she could not receive me, but I am anxious to see my son and congratulate him on his coming nuptials."

After Lady Wakeford left, Jacomena sat trying to digest what she had been told. Adrian a father? Har-

court a savior? Something didn't ring true. She tapped
her forehead with her finger as if to get the wheels
turning. After her coze with Alice at Wakeford
Manor, Jacomena had hunted up her old diaries. Now
she rose and perused the bookshelves until she found
a particular little volume. She leafed through the pages
until she came to the dates she wanted, then scanned
the pages.

"You blackguard! You worsted-stocking knave!"
Not taking the time to exhaust her vocabulary of ex-
cessive adjectives, Jacomena pulled the bell rope.
"Butterworth," she yelled.

That woman appeared almost instantly. "Yes, my
lady?"

"Tell Ol' Tom to have the Dalison carriage brought
round immediately with its fastest horses. I am going
to see my brother."

"His grace?" the housekeeper asked, in amazement.

"Unfortunately, he's the only brother I have.
More's the pity."

Three hours later, Lady Jacomena confronted the
bewildered Duke of Hammerfield in his large den at
Odin's Woods, her cane in one hand, the book in the
other.

"Damn you, Harky! Wilhemina is *your* daughter,
and don't you deny it."

The duke's eyes narrowed. "You've got bats in your
belfry, Jacomena. Always knew it. Who the hell is
Wilhemina?"

"She's your daughter's abigail."

He went pale. "You can't prove it," he said, trying
to dodge a sweep of her cane before it decapitated him.

Jacomena waved the small book in his face. "This is
my diary. I wrote everything down. Adrian cannot

possibly be her father. He wasn't even in the country when the child was conceived. You were the one escorting Lady Patricia Grayson everywhere."

The duke seemed to shrink in size with each word she spoke. "I didn't know she was with child until after I became engaged to Katherine. It would have spoiled everything. Adrian told me he would take care of the matter."

"Adrian always took care of everything for you, didn't he? And it got him murdered."

Hammerfield buried his face in his hands. "Don't you think I haven't thought about that every day for the past eighteen years?"

The picture of a four-year-old boy, crying, came to Jacomena's mind. She'd refused to let Harcourt accompany Adrian and her to the country fair many years ago. She hadn't wanted to bother. For a second, she felt pity for him, but she couldn't get herself to admit it. "Don't you go into the mopes on me, Harky."

"You never cared for me."

"You always were spoilt. Spoiled to the core. Mama gave you your way too much."

"Don't you ring a peal over me, you shriveled up old prune," he spat.

Jacomena winced.

The duke glanced over at the little portrait on the table beside him. "You always have to rub up old sores, don't you? What would my daughter have thought if she had known I had a child by another woman than her mother?"

"I don't think Katherine would begrudge Willie one thing." Jacomena threw up her hands, "Oh, that ridiculous name. Now I am saying it. How could you face your natural daughter and hear her called Wee Willie Winkie? Katherine has more charity and more forgiveness in her little finger than we ever had for each other. Those gels love each other like the sisters they are. Adrian, for all his rakehellion ways, was worth more than you and me together." Jacomena's voice softened. "We're not very nice people."

The duke glowered at her. "It isn't my fault."

"Yes, it is, and 'tis time you turned things round. I think of that poor child, my niece, languishing at Newgate Prison." *Knew there was something about the gel,* Jacomena thought, with a chuckle. *She showed quite a bit of the Dalison lip, if I do say so myself.*

"I already sent word to the authorities to release her—and Mr. Penbrooke, too," Hammerfield said. "But Katherine *will* marry the earl."

"What's wrong with Mr. Penbrooke?" Jacomena said stubbornly, surprising even herself for taking on the apprentice's defense. But habit was too strong and she couldn't help countermanding her brother.

"You have no say in the matter. I am her father, and I am ordering her to marry Wakeford."

Jacomena pointed her cane at his nose. "You do and I shall shout to the world that you deliberately delayed warning Adrian. You could be accused of acquiring your title and wealth fraudulently. Now tell that man of yours who has been lurking outside in the corridor to make you presentable. You are accompanying me back to London to make restitution for your sins."

Late the next afternoon, when Lady Wakeford returned to her son's residence, she found two messages awaiting her. One was from Duncan saying he'd received a grave summons for the both of them to come as soon as possible to Dalison Hall. A crisis had arisen. He wrote that because of the urgency of the note, he felt he should leave at once and told his mother to follow when she returned.

Lady Wakeford rang and asked that the coach be brought back immediately, that she would be going to Lady Jacomena's. Taking the other packet with her, she waited until she was seated in the carriage before she opened it. It proved to be a missive from her professor friend at Cambridge. Her gaze ran quickly over the pages, but it wasn't until the last that she let out a little cry and clasped the letter to her chest. "Oh, thank God!" she exclaimed. Tears came to her eyes, but she wiped them quickly. Now was not the time for sentimentality. Now was the time for action. That poor child—her dearest friend's child—in that hideous prison.

When Duncan arrived at Dalison Hall, he was ushered at once into the green salon where he was confronted by an unusual group of people. Lady Jacomena sat ramrod stiff in her wheeled chair. Duncan had a feeling it was not because of her infirmity, but because it looked more like a throne than any chair in the room. The Duke of Hammerfield, looking a reluctant participant in the party, sat in a chair as far away from her as possible and still be in the same room. On Lady Jacomena's left sat Mr. Penbrooke, looking quite uncomfortable, and on her right was Lady Katherine, her hands clutched trembling in her lap. Next to her, Miss Abbot, arms crossed over her bosom, fearing no one, he was sure. And on her other side—Duncan's heart stopped—on her other side sat his little magpie. She was no longer a black and white bird, for she was dressed in the charming orchid dress she'd worn in the herb garden. A purple ribbon was entwined in her black curls and tied in a bow at her neckline. He didn't know whether to be angry or elated. He had spent the last two days at the Inns of Court trying to find a way to get her out of that filthy prison, worrying about her, feeling her pain. And here she was, looking like a lovely princess.

Mr. Penbrooke jumped up immediately and bowed. Willie followed and curtsied, blushing in the process.

"Wilhemina, be seated," Lady Jacomena ordered, motioning to Duncan to come nearer.

As he stepped forward, Willie wriggled back up on her chair.

"I have called everyone together, because there are some grave family matters which must be discussed. Is your mother not with you?"

"She had not yet arrived home, my lady," Duncan replied, turning to acknowledge the other three women. "The urgency of your note compelled me to come ahead. I left word for her to follow as soon as she could."

"Then sit down and we will wait."

Duncan nodded to the duke, then walked over to the fireplace and braced his arm against the mantel. "I have been sitting most of the day, my lady. If you do not mind, I will stand."

"As you wish," Jacomena said dismissively.

Besides from that vantage point, Duncan felt he had a much better view of the entire company. From their blank expressions he gathered none of them knew why they were there either, except of course, their hostess, and perhaps the duke, who looked as if he were mumbling something unfit for ladies' ears.

Silence followed for the next half hour, until Old Tom showed Lady Wakeford into the room. She looked around quickly.

The men rose, and Duncan held a chair for his

mother to be seated, but she would have none of it and hurried over to Jacomena.

"Has something terrible happened?"

"It depends on how one looks at it," Jacomena said, waiting for Old Tom to close the doors. She then turned and looked sharply at the duke. "I believe my brother has something to say."

Everyone's attention centered on Hammerfield, who looked as though he wanted to bolt the room.

Lady Wakeford waved the packet. "Oh, but I have some exciting news, too."

The duke stood up suddenly. "I will speak first, if you do not mind, Lady Wakeford."

Duncan was ready to take offense at his tone, but his ever-gracious mother seemed to take none. So he held back his comment.

Lady Wakeford smiled, although she did look disappointed. "Why, of course you may, Your Grace. But do hurry, I do not know if I can keep back for long what I have to say."

The duke took one step away from his chair, his blue eyes turned toward Willie.

Willie once more saw in her mind the tall young man who had come to the orphanage, and her heart stopped. The last two days had been most confusing, and she wondered now if she might be dreaming.

Some men had taken her out of the gaol and put her in the waiting Dalison coach. There was a tearful reunion with Katy and Broonie, and even Lady Jacomena had seemed happy to see her again. She had known that the Duke of Hammerfield was in residence, but he hadn't come out of his rooms until this afternoon when they were all told to assemble in the green salon. Daisy came to tell her she wasn't to wear her black dress, but put on something prettier. That was no problem, because she only had one dress that wasn't black, the lovely sarcenet that Katy had given her. She hadn't known until an hour ago that Mr. Penbrooke had been freed also.

Jacomena cleared her throat.

Hammerfield squared his shoulders. "Lady Katherine has my permission to accept the suit of the man she loves."

Katy, her face glowing, jumped off her chair and ran to her father. "Oh, do you really mean it?"

The duke smiled, briefly. *The eyes,* he thought. *Her eyes have the same expression in them that her mother's had.*

"That is wonderful! Is it not, Duncan?" Lady Wakeford said, forgetting for a moment the papers she held in her hand. "But of course, you are already engaged."

The duke spoke so low, his words were barely heard. "And my other daughter is acknowledged by me to be my natural child, and will no longer wear the clothes of a maid."

Jacomena smiled, smugly. Lady Wakeford just blinked. Confusion showed in Duncan's eyes. Nathaniel didn't move from his seat. Broonie frowned and Willie sat staring. Only Katy caught the meaning of what her father had said.

"Willie?" she cried, looking at the duke. "Willie is your daughter? Oh, Father, why did you not tell us?"

For the first time he spoke with feeling. "I'm sorry, Katherine. It happened a long time ago, before I met your mother. I was not married to the woman. I know I have not been an attentive parent, but I did want to save you this hurt."

"Hurt? But if Willie is your daughter, that means she is my sister." Turning, she ran to Willie and pulled her off her chair. "Oh, Willie, that means I won't have to adopt you after all. We are already family."

"But wait, everyone," Lady Wakeford said, fully recovered from her brief lack of words. "I have more news."

No one paid any attention to her, as they watched Katy turn to Duncan. "I am sorry, my lord, but I am going to have to cry off of our engagement." With that she ran across the room to Mr. Penbrooke. Nathaniel shyly looked at his beloved who with much less reluctance threw her arms around his neck and kissed him.

Duncan, when he saw which way the wind blew, gave a triumphant cry and wrapped Willie in his embrace. "You are mine, you little magpie. But I shall have to stop calling you that, won't I? Now that you won't be wearing black anymore."

Lady Wakeford looked wide-eyed back and forth between the two couples, while Jacomena threw a triumphant glance at her brother, who really looked as if he wasn't that unhappy over the outcome.

"Oh, dear, will no one listen to me?" Lady Wakeford said, plaintively.

Broonie stepped forward, her words encompassing the room like rolling thunder. "Never heard such blether in all me born days, Do na you English have any manners? The countess has sumthin' to tell us."

"Oh, I wish I had a voice like that," Lady Wakeford said, with admiration, as all those present grew silent. "Thank you, Miss Abbot. Now," she said, unfolding the paper in her hand. "My friend, Dr. Tillsbury from Cambridge, has sent me this copy of the registry of Willie's birth. Only her name isn't Willie." Now that she had everybody's attention, Lady Wakeford made the most of it. "Her mother was my best friend, Lady Patricia Grayson. But that is a long story, my dear," she said, turning to Willie, "which I shall tell you in detail later. Your birth date was recorded in a little parish church near St. Margaret's-at-Cliffe. You were born on August 20, 1801, and were registered as the daughter of Sir John Grayson, Knight, and Patricia, his wife. Your name is Alice."

"Why, that is your name, Mother," Duncan said.

Lady Wakeford held out her arms to Willie. "You are my namesake, dear. I hope you don't mind. I always thought it quite a plain name."

"There is nothing plain about you, Mother," Duncan said, looking at his parent fondly.

"Why, thank you, son. I hope that is a compliment, for from what I am observing, you now will be responsible for two Alices."

Duncan threw up his hands in mock horror. "I shall have to take what fate gives me," he said, kissing her on the cheek.

Willie ran to the countess and hugged her. "Oh, I think it is lovely." She then moved back to Duncan. "I have a real name, now—*Alice,*" she said softly, looking up at him.

Keeping her locked against his side, Duncan decided it was time for serious talk. He turned to the others, his expression alone commanding their attention. "What has been revealed here this afternoon will go no farther," he said. "The old scandal took place eighteen years ago and will be remembered by only a few. We will say that Sir John Grayson's lost daughter has been discovered. It will make quite a romantic story if told in the right way. No one need know the details or that the Duke of Hammerfield is her natural father. In the eyes of the law and the church, she is the daughter of Sir John Grayson and his wife, Patricia."

Then with a hint of humor in his voice, he said, "I believe my mother has been dying for me to get caught in the parson's trap and now there are two weddings to plan."

"One," Katy said, stepping forward, her eyes aglow. "May Willie and I have a double wedding?"

"I've told you before, Katherine, that is a ridiculous name," Lady Jacomena said, not quite able to keep the smile from her lips. "Her name is Alice."

"I always thought I wanted to be named *Grace.*" Willie laughed, looking at the duke. "I never did get to thank you for taking me out of that orphanage and carrying me to Gilfallen. I had a lovely childhood growing up with Katy."

Hammerfield, his face turning an astonishing shade of red, scowled and waved his hand, dismissively.

The new Alice looked at Lady Wakefield. "I am proud to know that my mother named me for her best friend—and when we have our first daughter—" she said, looking at Duncan, "I shall name her Katherine after my dearest friend—and sister."

Epilogue

The lovely double wedding was held in the family chapel at Wakeford Manor three weeks later. Only the closest of friends were invited to attend. The duke told Katherine he was having a large oil painting copied from her mother's miniature for her to hang in the castle at Gilfallen. To his daughter, Alice, he gave a lovely strand of pearls, which he said had belonged to his mother, her grandmother. He also ordered a complete new wardrobe to be made before she left on her honeymoon trip to the Mediterranean Sea. After hearing her Aunt Jacomena's tales of those mysterious lands, Willie—that is—Alice Fairchild, the new Countess of Wakeford, wanted to ride a camel in Egypt.

Hammerfield walked his two daughters, the lovely blonde Baroness of Gilfallen, and the dark-haired pixie, Miss Alice Grayson, down the aisle of the little church to meet with their prospective bridegrooms. Miss Grayson, he told acquaintances, had been a member of his household for fourteen years, and since her father, Sir John, was no longer with them, he was acting as his substitute. Both girls kissed their father on the cheek before he left them to return to his seat beside his sister. He and Lady Jacomena left a sizable gap between them, and did not look at each other during the whole of the ceremony, but at least they were sitting together.

Early the next morning, the two married couples said their goodbyes to go their opposite ways. Katy and Nathaniel to Scotland, Duncan and Alice to Portsmouth, where they were to set sail on the evening tide for Lisbon. The earl pulled out his watch to check the time, for they had a tight schedule.

The new Countess of Wakeford chided her husband, "Really, my lord, must you always consult your watch?"

"Punctuality, my dear. Discipline is needed for an orderly life. Much of the world's problems can be laid to lack of punctuality." Duncan had planned on being in the coach fifteen minutes ago, but there were so many people to thank.

"Well, I hope you are not going to consult your watch for everything we do on our honeymoon."

"Not everything," he said with a grin.

"I shall miss you, Alice," Katy said, hugging her sister. "And you, too," she said, giving Duncan a squeeze and a kiss on the cheek.

Nathaniel shook hands with the earl and shyly hugged his new sister-in-law.

Charles had gone ahead with the coach loaded with the trunks of clothes, accompanied by Anna, whom the dowager countess had insisted that her new daughter-in-law take along as her lady's maid. Duncan's mother had not missed the shine in the valet's eyes when he saw the pretty miss climb into the coach ahead of him.

The journey was swift to the southern port and they boarded the yacht that Duncan had leased. They set sail in time to enjoy the lovely sunset before they returned to their staterooms to prepare for dinner. Their accommodations were large and luxurious and Charles took great pains to dress his master properly for dinner with Captain Daniels.

When he was ready, Duncan scratched on the door connecting their suites and peeked in to see his wife standing alone before the wardrobe in her petticoat. "We will be late, my dear, if you do not make up your mind on what to wear."

"It was so much easier when I only had one color to choose from."

"Let Anna decide for you."

"She got sick the minute the ship left the harbor, and I told her to go lie down."

Duncan laughed. "So that was the reason Charles was so eager to get away."

"Possibly," she said, turning to look at him. "You know, Duncan, you cannot expect to be the center of his life forever."

Duncan swallowed hard. She was a beguiling wench standing there in practically nothing and he found it difficult to keep his mind focused on their appointment. "What did you say?"

She came to stand near him—too near. "Really, Duncan, is it so important to be early to everything?"

At that moment, Duncan was thinking several things he'd rather be doing than going to dinner with the captain. One in particular came to mind and he reached out to touch her bare shoulders, but again, propriety prodded Duncan and he turned to go back to his own room.

"Come, my dear," the earl said, reaching for his watch. "We don't want do be late, do we?" He sucked in his breath, as he pulled out an empty chain from his pocket.

Tiny arms encircled his waist from behind. "I cannot imagine anything more shocking than being late for a meal. Can you, husband?" she chided softly, burrowing her nose into his back.

A grin spread across Duncan's face. "Now that you bring it up, my little thief," he said, whirling around and catching her up in his arms, "Perhaps I can, and to show you how frightening it can be, I may have to imprison you for life."

"Duncan," she asked, "Did you really set out to reform me?"

He kissed her. "Don't change the subject. Now where is it?" He dangled the chain in front of her face.

Alice stared, then giggled. "Your watch? It's gone?"

Duncan kissed her again. This time, harder, longer. "Now, confess."

Her head was buzzing. Breathlessly, she clung to him. "Really—I don't know where it is. Without your watch, you'll undoubtedly be lost." Her jest changed to a squeal when she found herself lifted into his arms and carried to the bed.

"I am beginning to think you may have the right of it, wife," he said, dropping her onto the middle of the counterpane. "I do believe—" Duncan unloosened his neckcloth. "—for the first time in my life—" His coat came off. "—I am going to be late for dinner."

Alice watched in amazement. With each statement, her husband methodically divested himself of an article of his clothing, dropping each one unceremoniously on the floor, until all that remained were his trousers.

"You know, wife, I never thought you to be such a slowtop," he said, sitting down in a chair where he removed his boots.

Alice sat bolt upright and turned her back to him. "Slowtop, am I? I'll show you who is the slowtop," she said, pulling her petticoat over her head.

Duncan pinned Alice down on the bed and teasingly

kissed her neck. "Now—I promise I wouldn't consult it unless absolutely necessary, but I want my watch back."

Alice stopped her playing. "But Duncan, I swear I don't know where it is."

Duncan held her away from him, one eyebrow arched. "Oh, my God!" he said. "Katy kissed me goodbye."

Laughing, Alice pulled him down to her.

"Well, we shall just have to pay a visit to Gilfallen Castle first thing when we return from our honeymoon. Won't we, my dear?" he said, kissing his wife on the tip of her nose.

"There's no hurry, Duncan. I want to see the whole world with you."

Duncan sighed deeply. "Without my watch, my dear, I am afraid we will be late to everything."

"Do you think the captain will be worried when we do not turn up for dinner?"

"Not really. The captain is a married man."

Alice wriggled out from under him and sat upright, blushing. "Oh, then he will know what we are doing."

"Most likely," Duncan said, pulling her back down again. "But I assure you, you will like it."

About the Author

Paula Tanner Girard lives with her family in Maitland, Florida. LORD WAKEFORD'S GOLD WATCH is her first regency romance. Paula is currently working on her next regency romance, which Zebra Books will be publishing in March 1996. Paula loves hearing from her readers and you may write to her c/o Zebra Books. Please include a self-addressed, stamped envelope if you wish a response.

ZEBRA'S REGENCY ROMANCES
DAZZLE AND DELIGHT

A BEGUILING INTRIGUE   (4441, $3.99)
by Olivia Sumner

Pretty as a picture Justine Riggs cared nothing for propriety. She dressed as a boy, sat on her horse like a jockey, and pondered the stars like a scientist. But when she tried to best the handsome Quenton Fletcher, Marquess of Devon, by proving that she was the better equestrian, he would try to prove Justine's antics were pure folly. The game he had in mind was seduction—never imagining that he might lose his heart in the process!

AN INCONVENIENT ENGAGEMENT   (4442, $3.99)
by Joy Reed

Rebecca Wentworth was furious when she saw her betrothed waltzing with another. So she decides to make him jealous by flirting with the handsomest man at the ball, John Collinwood, Earl of Stanford. The "wicked" nobleman knew exactly what the enticing miss was up to—and he was only too happy to play along. But as Rebecca gazed into his magnificent eyes, her errant fiancé was soon utterly forgotten!

SCANDAL'S LADY   (4472, $3.99)
by Mary Kingsley

Cassandra was shocked to learn that the new Earl of Lynton was her childhood friend, Nicholas St. John. After years at sea and mixed feelings Nicholas had come home to take the family title. And although Cassandra knew her place as a governess, she could not help the thrill that went through her each time he was near. Nicholas was pleased to find that his old friend Cassandra was his new next door neighbor, but after being near her, he wondered if mere friendship would be enough . . .

HIS LORDSHIP'S REWARD   (4473, $3.99)
by Carola Dunn

As the daughter of a seasoned soldier, Fanny Ingram was accustomed to the vagaries of military life and cared not a whit about matters of rank and social standing. So she certainly never foresaw her *tendre* for handsome Viscount Roworth of Kent with whom she was forced to share lodgings, while he carried out his clandestine activities on behalf of the British Army. And though good sense told Roworth to keep his distance, he couldn't stop from taking Fanny in his arms for a kiss that made all hearts equal!

Available wherever paperbacks are sold, or order direct from the Publisher. Send cover price plus 50¢ per copy for mailing and handling to Penguin USA, P.O. Box 999, c/o Dept. 17109, Bergenfield, NJ 07621. Residents of New York and Tennessee must include sales tax. DO NOT SEND CASH.